HIS TRUE WIFE

The Marwood Family Saga Book Five

Amy Licence

SAPERE
BOOKS

HIS TRUE WIFE

Published by Sapere Books.

24 Trafalgar Road, Ilkley, LS29 8HH

saperebooks.com

ISBN: 978-0-85495-821-4

To Rufus and Robin

By you, Fair Glance, Love's officer,
They are arraigned, our poor hearts,
Oft when surrounded by sweet arts,
   Yet, oft, of their foes a prisoner.

   Before the court, that tries a lover,
   Its justices, and their counterparts,
   By you, Fair Glance, Love's officer,
   They are arraigned, our poor hearts.

   And swiftly you bind them over,
   So they may further feel your darts;
   As subjects, servants, for their part,
   Endure many a strange manoeuvre;
   By you, Fair Glance, Love's officer,
   They are arraigned, our poor hearts.

— Charles d'Orléans

ONE

May, 1529

Thomasin Marwood held up the looking glass and gazed into it. Outside, the daylight was fading, but the candle flame danced and flickered, making the room alternately bright and dark. She turned her face right and left, then back again. She could make out a pair of warm, dark eyes, the soft curve of cheeks and chin and two generous red lips, pursed together. The eyes followed her as she moved, fixing her in their stare.

"It's so strange to see your own face looking back at yourself, like a stranger," she marvelled, lifting her little chin. "To think this must be how others see you, every day, from the outside."

The hand-held mirror had been a gift from her mistress, Queen Catherine of Aragon, as a reward for Thomasin's discreet and loyal service in her household. The royal Spaniard had proved generous to those who understood her private griefs and helped her present her best face to the world. The mirror was set in silver, in the Spanish style, with knotted vines and love hearts, entwined with flowers and the queen's own device of the pomegranate, spilling its seeds from within. Thomasin traced her finger over the handle, where the fruit was ripest. At nineteen, she had been serving the queen for almost two years, watching sadly as the royal marriage disintegrated.

"My eyes are not plain brown at all," she said, peering closer. "They have a ring of green, and flecks of amber. And has my nose always been that long, or is it just today?"

Across the room, her cousin Ellen did not try to suppress her laugh. They were in the back bedchamber at Monk's Place, home to Thomasin's uncle, Sir Matthew Russell, situated on London's Thames Street. Queen Catherine had granted them a few days' absence from her side in order to visit family, who were assembling below, ahead of the dinner hour. Thomasin had not confided in the queen about her special reason for requesting the time, as if she did not wish to tempt fate, barely able to imagine her plans might come to pass.

"Come now, put that down." Ellen rose, the rich crimson of her silk skirts rustling as she crossed the room to take the looking glass from Thomasin's hand. "You look well enough. You do not need to fret about your nose or your eyes. They are the epitome of perfect beauty, not least in the eyes of someone we both know."

Thomasin blushed. She knew who Ellen was referring to. The past few months had been a challenging time, full of adventures and hard lessons. The court was like the sun, drawing all into its orbit, desperate for its warmth. It offered glamour, fortune and fame, and she herself had danced in golden slippers and received visits from ambassadors from all round the world. But she had also learned how the glittering surface of the royal world concealed envy and malice, and how those who smiled in public might deliver fatal words in private. On the other side, she now knew that friends might be found in the most unlikely of places. It had been a harsh lesson for the little country girl from Suffolk, steeped in the scent of hayfields and apple blossom, to learn the realities of court politics. But it had also been a voyage of self-discovery, and now, upon this May evening, with the fading light skimming the river outside and the sweet scents of the garden stealing in through the chamber window, she could look herself in the eye

— in the queen's mirror — and say that she truly knew who she was.

Thomasin Marwood of Eastwell Hall: too vain, too impulsive, too rash, too quickly drawn to a handsome face or a dazzling gown. She had learned how fast passion could grow within her, and how hard she had to battle to keep it in check. How quickly ideas could take root in her head and spread through her like fire. Yet she was also kind, warm, devoted, too keen to feel the pain of her loved ones, unable to turn away from even her enemies in their suffering. She had a desire to learn, to seize ideas and forge her own path. And yet, she still loved to dance, to twirl about in her wide skirts and feel the pulse of the music race through her, bringing her to life. And to plunge out into the cool of the garden, where birds sang and flowers bloomed, and the warmth of the sun beat down upon her back. She felt what a pleasure it was to sleep amid soft, scented sheets and wake to clean water with rose petals, and to join the others in the dining hall, where dishes with spices and cream were placed before her. Never before had she felt so fortunate, so blessed, as she did that May evening. And surely, Thomasin thought, things were about to improve, a thousand times over.

"Have you seen him arrive yet?" she asked Ellen.

"Of course not. You know I would have told you the second his boat arrived."

Thomasin went to stand by the window. The diamond-shaped panes overlooked the garden at Monk's Place, with its criss-crossed paths, colourful rose beds and long walk that stretched down to the river. The Thames gleamed silver in the evening light, but there was not yet any sign of the little craft she was impatient to see. Excitement and frustration mingled inside her.

"Do you think this dress will do?" she asked, looking down at the ash-coloured silk that fell in folds about her feet. "You do not think it too plain? After all, this is a special occasion."

"Have we not spoken of this a dozen times already?" Ellen said with a roll of her eyes. "You know it becomes you very well and it is one of the queen's own favourite colours. But if you don't like it, then let's quickly swap it for the cream, or the green, then perhaps you will stop asking."

"No, no, the cream is too pale and the green is the wrong shade of green. Are you sure this suits me well enough?"

Ellen forced her usually smiling eyes into a frown. "Now, cousin, stop. You are working yourself into a state. It is unlike you to fret so much about such matters; it becomes you ill."

Thomasin let out a deep sigh. "I know, I know. But I am not like myself tonight. It is pure nerves, dear Ellen, putting me on edge. I can think of nothing else but what may transpire. My entire future depends upon it. What if … what if…"

Ellen's expression softened. "I know your fears, dear cousin, but at this moment there is no remedy for them but patience. There is no dress, no looking glass that can calm you as well as your own faith and trust in your loved ones. Unless… Here, take some wine; that might steady you a little."

She poured out a glass from the jug on the table. With a shaking hand, Thomasin sipped the rich liquid, tasting its overtones of citrus and nutmeg.

"He will come, won't he?"

"I would stake my life upon it."

"He won't … he won't change his mind, because of his situation…?"

"I am certain he will not. I never saw a man so devoted these past few months."

Thomasin sighed. She felt the truth of her cousin's words, but only wished she could share that happiness with her a little. Ellen had recently known the sting of a broken heart, but the inheritance that followed soon after had brought her the freedom to make her own choices.

"Wait, look!"

Thomasin pointed through the window. The two women held their breath. In the far distance, a small vessel was drawing up against the quay adjoining Monk's Place, bobbing on the tide. As they watched, a tall, dark figure climbed ashore and began to make his way towards the house. Both knew at once that it was him.

Thomasin's heart leapt into her mouth. She turned and hurried down the wooden staircase, through the hallway where lamps gleamed on the walls, and out through the back door.

It was a gentle evening in late spring, ripe with the promise of summer. The air was cool and scented, the colours dimming as the sun sank behind the trees, its last rays flaring through the leaves. Above, the stars were beginning to show their faces through a rich mantle of blue, and a half-moon hung shyly among them, as if waiting its turn.

Yet Thomasin saw nothing of this, felt nothing of its charm. Usually, the beauty of such an evening would affect her deeply, but today she noticed none of it as she picked up her skirts and hurried down the path. At the far end, beyond the sundial, the dark figure hastened towards her with the same eagerness.

Rafe Danvers was dressed in his habitual black. It was one of the things that had first struck Thomasin about him when her eyes had first met his at court, the autumn before last. It was partly through circumstances, partly through preference, that he wore his dark velvet doublet and the midnight cloak that seemed to blend with the sky. As a member of the household of the mighty Boleyn family, he was always conscious of his position, following in the shadow of Sir Thomas, dining at his table, curbing the dictates of his heart. Yet no one knew better than Thomasin what passions raged within. Theirs had not been a smooth path to romance. She had fought against the desire she felt for him, while he had struggled with his temper and jealousy, until both had realised that the emotions they felt for each other were sincere. And that spring, amid the emerging blossoms at Windsor and Greenwich, they had learned to trust each other.

On the other side of the sundial, he paused. Thomasin's feet failed her as she drew to a halt with the stone plinth between them. Across the space, she could feel Rafe's deep chestnut eyes burning into her, eyes she had once barely dared to meet for fear of the passions stirring within. He brushed back a lock of his blue-black hair.

"Stop! Stop just there." His rich tones enveloped her. "I want to remember this moment forever, to fix the image of how beautiful you look tonight."

But patience was still a virtue that challenged Thomasin. She sprang forward and threw herself into Rafe's open arms.

"How much better to see me closer, to feel me in your arms."

He buried his face in her hair, inhaling its scent of lavender. "Ah, Thomasin."

"I started to fear you would never come."

"I had to make my excuses. Explain myself to Sir Thomas."

"And he does not mind? You mean, you explained everything?"

Rafe drew back and looked deep into her eyes. "Yes, everything. He knows about us. He gives us his blessing."

"Really?" It was hard to believe their match had the approval of the head of the Boleyn household, given Thomasin's checkered relationship with that family. "Let us hope all such blessings are as easily given tonight!"

"What is the mood within?"

"Mother is merry enough, as she has a new diamond to set into a brooch, and Father is as content as Father ever is, despite not being in the countryside."

"Then all the signs are good, and the stars are auspicious."

"Are they?"

"They are indeed. The moon is in Taurus, the sign of plenty, and Orion's belt is bright, right above us."

"You may as well be speaking in Turkish to me, but if you say so, I will believe it."

"Are they assembled? Shall we go in?"

Thomasin cast a glance up to the first-floor chamber she had just left, where Ellen had drawn the heavy curtain across the window.

"Yes, that is the sign. Dinner is about to begin."

"And they expect me, but know nothing?"

"Nothing yet, although I cannot vouch for what my mother suspects."

"Of course. You think she favours me?"

"Who could not?"

He bent swiftly and pressed his lips to hers. The kiss was warm and firm, lingering longer that it should.

Rafe finally broke off. "Shall I wait for your sign, at the right moment, before I speak?"

"Yes, let me be the judge of my father's mood, then it shall be done."

"Come, then." He took her hand in his. "Let us go into dinner, my soon-to-be betrothed."

Thomasin's stomach fluttered as they turned towards the brightly lit house.

TWO

The family were already assembled in the dining room as Thomasin crept through the door with Rafe behind her. Although it was almost summer, a low fire was burning in the grate, set within the large, carved fireplace. Due to his advancing age, her uncle, Sir Matthew Russell, often felt the cold in his bones at night, in this old monastic-style house with its thick stone walls. He was leaning against the mantel, his short hair and beard almost completely white now, but the jolly look he used to wear was gone. Since the death of his son, Barnaby, he had aged more quickly. Having his daughter-in-law, Ellen, in the house was something of a consolation.

Beside Sir Matthew, on the other side of the hearth, stood Thomasin's father. Sir Richard Marwood was tall and lean, but as with Sir Matthew, recent cares had etched lines about his grey eyes. He had elected to spend most of his life in the country, returning only occasionally to court, happiest when he was riding through Suffolk with his dogs yapping at his heels. To his right, in a carved chair, sat Lady Elizabeth Marwood, whose pale beauty seemed more exaggerated with every passing year. Her fair hair, once the colour of butter, was streaked through with white but her water-blue eyes missed very little. For many years, there had been distance between Thomasin and her mother; she had always favoured her elder daughter, Cecilia, who had inherited her ice-blonde looks, but recent troubles had brought them closer.

"Here they are," said Ellen, appearing from the corner. "Now we can be seated."

"Ah, Mr Danvers," said Sir Richard, looking up in recognition, "I am pleased that you were able to join us this evening. I trust it was not too difficult for you to obtain leave?"

"Not at all, thank you," Rafe replied. "My master was most accommodating. It is a great pleasure to accept your kind invitation."

"You are looking most handsome tonight, Mr Danvers," said Lady Elizabeth, rising slowly to her feet. Her old heart trouble still left her weakened on occasion. She had had plenty of rest since the Marwood parents' arrival in London three days before, and though her movements were slow, her glance, and her tongue, were as sharp as anything. "Come, sit by me."

Thomasin took the seat on the other side of Rafe, with Ellen opposite, along with the two older men.

"How fares the king?" asked Sir Richard. "Is he hale and hearty? You are the most recent of us to have seen him."

"Hale and hearty, I believe, as he always is," Rafe replied cautiously, "but he loves not this situation, and is consumed with the arguments he must present to the court."

Servants entered, bringing dishes of steaming meat dressed in herbs, wine and thick cream sauces. A pie with a golden crust, decorated with the Russell coat of arms was placed before Thomasin, while Rafe was presented with a platter of stuffed larks in honey.

Sir Richard waited until the door was closed again. They all knew that Rafe was speaking of the impending Papal Court, which was to open at the end of the month, to investigate the validity of the king's marriage. "I do not doubt it. It is an unenviable situation for any man to find himself in, let alone a king. Is he prepared?"

"I believe so, my lord — as prepared as he can ever be for such a battle. He has a team of lawyers at his disposal, as well as the university rulings from across Europe, the bishops and some of the leading authorities in the land."

"And the queen?" asked Lady Elizabeth, recalling the woman she used to serve in her younger days. "Who will be speaking for her?"

"She will not go undefended," Rafe assured her. "You need have no fear on that account. She has a strong team led by Bishop Fisher, although the two lawyers that were to have come from Flanders never arrived, as the emperor advised them it was not safe."

"Her own nephew advised that?"

"Her own nephew, yes, but he is also Henry's fellow king. The queen will speak for herself too, won't she, Thomasin?"

Beside Rafe, Thomasin nodded. Over the past weeks, she and Ellen had observed her mistress preparing herself for the coming ordeal by reading scripture, meeting her councillors and burying her head in prayer. Queen of England for the past twenty years, Catherine had no doubt that she had right on her side, but she was wise enough to know how men could twist even the word of God in order to suit their purposes. It was to be the fight of their lives, and no one was sure how things would look afterwards.

Yet although Thomasin would be standing by Catherine's side soon enough, tonight she wished they could move off this sombre topic.

"She will speak from her heart and soul. She has a clear conscience in this matter. What will be will be."

"Pray God deliver her the true verdict, amen!" added her mother, crossing herself elaborately with a jewelled hand.

"I have been summoned by Lord Cromwell to attend," said Sir Richard, his face betraying his dislike of the situation. "No matter how many times I have tried to evade him, or offered my doubts, he is not a man to be refused."

"So will you speak for the king's defence?" asked Rafe.

"Not if I can help it. Once I have sworn my oath to speak the truth, I will do nothing but that, no matter how much Cromwell dislikes it."

Thomasin recalled the unpleasant, porcine man she had encountered several times at court. He was in attendance upon Cardinal Wolsey, but his ruthlessness was entirely his own. He had been a constant figure in the background, trying to convince her father to use his considerable legal experience to the king's advantage, even though the Marwoods had long been devoted friends to the queen, having served her in former days.

"If only it could be concluded swiftly," added Ellen. "Whatever the outcome, this matter has dragged on long enough, and taken a toll on the poor queen's health."

"Let's drink to that," agreed Sir Matthew, raising his glass. "Good health and happiness to Her Majesty. May she find peace again."

"May she find peace," Thomasin added, wondering if this was the right time for Rafe to speak up. As they lowered their glasses, she turned towards him, but he was reaching for the dish to his right.

"My Lady Marwood, might I offer you some of this fine venison?"

"Oh, you are kindness itself," Thomasin's mother replied, beaming. "Just a little then, as you ask so nicely."

Ellen caught Thomasin's eye. It was gratifying to see Rafe making an effort, and the warm response it elicited. And sitting there, at table with her family, with night falling outside and the fire crackling in the grate, Thomasin could picture it all. A few years down the line, she and Rafe could be happily married, an infant or two asleep upstairs. After waiting so long, the vision seemed so real that she could almost reach out and touch it.

Suddenly, there came a tremendous banging upon the outer door. Lady Elizabeth cried out in alarm.

"Who can that be, at this hour?" said Sir Matthew, frowning. "I know of no other expected guests."

"Nor do I," added Sir Richard quickly. "Hardly anyone knows of our arrival here. Who can it be?"

Rafe's eyes turned gently to Thomasin, as if he could feel the fluttering sensation in her chest. Some presentiment seemed to darken the room, as if she knew the intrusion would disrupt her dreams.

The knocking came again, and they heard one of the servants hastening down the hallway, followed by the creak of the bolt being drawn. Locked in the back of the building, Sir Matthew's two dogs began to bark.

"Just as we sit down to dinner," said Lady Elizabeth. "Is there no peace to be found?"

Now heavy footsteps were approaching. The door was flung open, with the nervous servant consigned to the shadows, unable to intervene. Into the room stepped a tall, hooded figure, dressed for travelling, in a long cloak, boots and gloves, with the night air still clinging to him. Drawing back his hood, the intruder revealed a head of copper-coloured hair and a pair of matching eyes, afire with indignation. Thomasin recognised him at once, but she had never previously seen her mild brother-in-law looking so angry.

"My lords, ladies, please forgive this sudden rude intrusion." Sir Hugh Truegood turned to Sir Richard. "Sir, I would speak a word with you on some urgent matter."

Thomasin's father looked troubled. "Goodness, Sir Hugh, what can be the meaning of this? As you can see, we are in the process of dining."

"Sir, I have just ridden up straight from Sussex on the most pressing business. May I speak with you?"

"This is family business?" Sir Matthew enquired.

"Indeed, sir."

"Is all well?" asked Lady Elizabeth. "Is something the matter with Cecilia?"

Sir Hugh's marriage to Thomasin's elder sister Cecilia had been arranged the previous autumn, and they now resided down at the magnificent Raycroft Hall, which sat in extensive grounds on the border of Sussex and Kent.

"The matter indeed! Sir, I must speak with you in private."

"If this is a family matter, you will observe that we are all family gathered here today."

Sir Hugh shot a brief look at Rafe, who was trying to go unnoticed.

"For the last time, sir, I urge you to hear me in private, or else I must speak aloud that which you may not wish to hear."

But the manner of Sir Hugh's entrance had irritated Sir Richard to the point that he would make no concession. He did not rise from his chair. Thomasin twitched awkwardly, wishing he would depart, given the warning that it was not good news.

"You have interrupted everyone's dinner, sir, so you may tell everyone the reason for it."

Sir Hugh's eyes blazed. "Very well, since you request it. I have returned from the Netherlands to discover that your daughter is with child, sir! With child!"

"Oh, that is good news, is it not?" asked Lady Elizabeth feebly, a blush rising to her pale cheeks. Thomasin wondered at once whether she already knew something of this, from one of the many letters she exchanged with her elder daughter.

"Not when the child is not mine, madam." Sir Hugh turned to her. "A child which has quickened in the womb already, and can only have been conceived when I was in Antwerp, with the North Sea between us! A firstborn child which will bear my good name, raised as a cuckoo in the nest to inherit Raycroft and everything in it! This is anything but good news."

A stunned silence descended upon the room. Thomasin dared not meet the eyes of her parents or uncle, knowing full well that Cecilia had been discovered in bed with her lover five months earlier, at Christmas time. They had packed her off home to Sussex and not spoken a word about it since. It was misfortune indeed that she had conceived after one interrupted encounter. Unless, of course, there had been other occasions?

It was at that moment that Ellen quietly rose to her feet and slipped out of the room. Thomasin could not blame her. There had been a time, before Hugh's marriage to Cecilia, that Ellen had believed him to be in love with her, and on the verge of proposing. Deeply in love with him, she had pictured herself as the mistress of Raycroft, bound to Hugh forever by ties of affection. It had broken her heart when he'd submitted to court pressure to accept Cecilia as his wife.

"Are you sure?" asked Lady Elizabeth after a while. "There can be no question of mistiming? These things can occur with a first child."

"No question at all, madam. My wife is carrying another man's bastard. What do you propose that I do about it?"

Lady Elizabeth sank into her chair and put her head in her hands.

Hugh readdressed himself to the aghast-looking Sir Richard. "I come here to ask you, sir, whether you have any inkling of whom the father might be, so that I may demand satisfaction?"

"Oh no," said Thomasin, unable to stop herself. "You must not do that. It is not worth risking your own life over."

But Rafe put a warning hand upon her arm.

"It is what I must do. My honour demands it. Will you give me a name? Whose bastard is she carrying?"

Lady Elizabeth began to weep, turning her face away. This proved too much for her brother, urging him into action.

"Sir, you have caused enough distress for one day," Sir Matthew said angrily. "You have forced entry into my home, disturbed my dinner and upset my guests. I ask you now to leave us in peace."

"Peace? What peace will I have with that whore under my roof?"

Sir Richard and Sir Matthew both rose to their feet.

"To the outside world," said Sir Richard slowly, "there is nothing amiss in a married woman carrying a child. This matter may never be known beyond these walls."

"Am I to have a bastard inherit my estates, while your daughter laughs at me and carries on with God knows who? You do me a dishonour, sir, and you know it. I will have his name."

"Where is Cecilia?" asked Lady Elizabeth through her sobs.

"In Sussex. I could not bear the sight of her."

"Please be kind to her."

"The kindest thing I can think of is to send her to a nunnery."

Lady Elizabeth collapsed in sobs again.

"That's it!" Sir Matthew pointed to the door. "Out!"

After the front door closed, Sir Matthew secured the bolt and returned to the dining chamber. The plates sat waiting, the food half eaten, the wine glasses still full.

"Well," he said, looking at the faces of his family, "that was an unexpected interruption. Once again, that young woman has brought shame upon us."

"I can only apologise profusely for her actions," said Sir Richard.

"Well, we all saw it happen," replied Sir Matthew. "We all knew there was a chance this could be the result."

"Did you know, Mother?" Thomasin asked.

Lady Elizabeth shook her head, but there was something about her eyes that caused her daughter to doubt her assertion.

"I should go and fetch Ellen back," Thomasin said, remembering her cousin's departure.

"No need," came a voice from the hallway, as Ellen entered. "I heard him leave." She resumed her place at the table.

"How do you fare?" asked Thomasin, leaning towards her.

Ellen's face was composed, with no signs of tears. "Later," she mouthed, and Thomasin was forced to be content.

"Well, let us not waste this good fare," said Sir Richard, "if any of you has a stomach for it."

For a moment, there was silence as they tried to eat again, but Thomasin had little appetite now. She picked at a piece of pie crust, wondering what would happen next.

"Mr Danvers," said Sir Richard, suddenly remembering that Rafe was in the room, "you must accept my sincerest apologies. As our daughter's guest, we had intended to entertain you with a feast, but instead you have been subjected to the most unpleasant nature of our private family business."

"Not at all, my good lord," said Rafe, wiping his mouth on a napkin. "Do not forget that I serve the Boleyns and have seen all manner of behaviour under their roof. On the contrary, I continue to be impressed by the dignity of your family and offer my services if there is any way I may be of assistance."

Thomasin glowed at his words.

"Good man," said Sir Matthew. "You could not have spoken better. You will always be welcome at this table."

"A baby," Lady Elizabeth interrupted softly. "Cecilia is having a baby. I will be a grandmother."

"Alas, it seems that way," replied her husband.

"Not alas, Richard, it is a baby! A baby! But what can we do?"

"Nothing. It is between them to sort out, and the baby is coming whether Sir Hugh likes it or not. He will have to square it with his conscience, and learn to stay home with his wife more."

"That is hardly the point," said Sir Matthew. "For all his outburst just now, Sir Hugh is not at fault. We all saw what happened at Greenwich. I speak plainly, but the girl is unruly. She has brought nothing but disgrace upon your heads, for all the good kindnesses you have done her as parents. I think it the fairest outcome if she is sent to a nunnery, as Hugh suggests. Goodness knows what she will do next."

There was a frosty silence.

"Well," said Sir Richard, "as you said earlier, there is nothing to be done tonight, so let's not allow this good dinner to spoil."

Thomasin caught Rafe's eye. This was not the time for their announcement, nor to request her parents' blessing. The moment had slipped away. She ate as much as she could in that sombre room, where the heads of her family were filled with questions and fears. She should have known, should have guessed, that it all felt too good to be true.

After the meal, they walked out into the garden. Night had fully fallen and the air was fresh and clean, bringing the tang of the river across the lawn.

As they walked, Rafe reached over and took Thomasin's hand. "You're quiet."

Thomasin sighed. "I'm shocked, I think. I didn't expect it."

"Tonight didn't go to plan, but there will be other opportunities."

"I know." She paused on the path, turning to him with disappointed eyes. "It's just that this was going to be our night. Everything was perfect. The timing, the evening, everything. It could have so easily happened, and we would be engaged now, with Father's blessing."

"Never fear. Things happen for a reason. We will wait for this to calm down, then the right moment will present itself, I promise."

He leaned forward and kissed her lightly, skimming her lips before pulling back. How different the kiss was from the one he had given her earlier.

"But do things happen for a reason?" Thomasin asked. "Earlier you said the stars were in our favour. Is there a grand plan? Was the night supposed to be ours? Or was the reason simply my sister's bad behaviour, yet again?"

Rafe sighed. "Do not think too long about it. Think ahead instead, of the happiness that we will enjoy, and how proud your parents will be of you, Thomasin. Do not let this spoil things."

"I won't."

"And there is the queen to think of too. When are you back at court?"

"The day after tomorrow."

"I will be there, with Sir Thomas."

"And Anne?" Thomasin asked after a moment. "Where will she be?"

It was King Henry's driving passion for the dark-haired Anne Boleyn that had determined Queen Catherine's fate. Ever since the young woman had caught Henry's eye, an uncomfortable triangle had existed at court, while Henry sought ways to put Catherine aside in order to remarry and father a son. Thomasin had seen both sides of Anne: her jollity and spirit, as well as her jealous temper. Only last Christmas, she had unleashed the full force of it against Cecilia, with disastrous results.

"Anne is to remain at Durham House, well out of the way once the court convenes."

"I hope she does remain there. It will be hard enough for Catherine, without having to bare her soul before her rival."

They walked down to the quay, where the boatman was waiting.

"Two days, then," said Rafe, his dark eyes opaque in the shadows.

"Yes, until then."

"And remember what I said. Do not dwell upon this. Look to the future."

He pulled her close again, and kissed her more warmly. "The future is ours, Thomasin, never forget."

Thomasin watched his boat pull upstream across the dark mass of the Thames and turned back to the house. A light gleamed in the upstairs chamber that she shared with Ellen. Poor Ellen — she'd had to witness Hugh's outburst, knowing that she would have been a true, loving wife to him. Thomasin wondered if the thought ever crossed Hugh's mind, too.

Thomasin found her cousin in her nightgown, sitting on the edge of the bed. Her long brown hair was loose about her shoulders, and she was staring into the looking glass.

"I am not as beautiful as her, I know. I cannot hope to match her looks, but I am not unpleasant to gaze upon, I don't think."

"Ellen?" Thomasin closed the door behind her. "What is the meaning of this?"

"I know why he chose Cecilia. I can't blame him. She is more beautiful than almost any other woman at court, with her icy blonde looks." She put down the glass. "But I loved him, Thomasin. I truly loved him, and I would never have given him a moment's doubt or unkindness. I would have thought it an honour to bear his children."

"Oh, Ellen." Thomasin put her arms about her cousin. "Do not torture yourself so. He is not worth your tears."

"Oh, I know it. He shall not have them. I am quite resigned to it, because he made his choice. And now he must face the consequences."

"That is right, exactly right. He might have had a true wife in you, but he allowed others to influence him, and this is his reward."

"I just felt a little wistful, considering what might have been, but I will be well again. And merry again, at some point, I am sure."

"And you will fall in love again."

Ellen laughed. "I'm not sure about that. No, I have my inheritance. I don't need a husband."

Thomasin smiled. "I know your heart, Ellen Russell. We shall see."

"And Cecilia? What will become of her?"

Thomasin kicked off her shoes. "Now, that I cannot say, but she has brought it upon herself."

"And her child? We cannot overlook the child, who is innocent in all this. Your niece or nephew, Thomasin."

"Let us think about it in the morning. I have had quite enough for one night."

She started to undress, unlacing her bodice. Ellen got up to help remove her heavy outer garments and lay them carefully in a trunk, as they were accustomed to doing for the queen.

"I'm sorry your special night was spoiled."

"Rafe says there will be another chance."

"Of course there will. You will be Mrs Thomasin Danvers. It has a nice ring to it."

Thomasin smiled. "Thomasin Danvers. How strange it sounds."

"Well, you had better get used to it. When will you ask the queen for permission to marry?"

"After the court is over. I cannot speak to her of marriage whilst hers is under trial."

"Of course, quite right. That is thoughtful of you, Thomasin. Now, let us close our eyes upon this strange night. Tomorrow is another day."

As Thomasin blew out the candle, a fox screeched in the garden, sounding like a woman's strangled cry. Then all fell silent.

THREE

Queen Catherine sent her carriage to collect Thomasin and Ellen from Sir Matthew's house in Thames Street. It was an elegant, dark grey coach trimmed with gold, bearing the queen's coat of arms. Two bay mares waited patiently before it, draped in red velvet to match the cushioned interior.

"I shall see you in a day or so, once the Papal Court opens," said Sir Richard, placing a gentle kiss upon his daughter's forehead. "Try not to think about that other business. Keep your focus on the queen."

There had been no further appearance from Sir Hugh, and Thomasin hoped he had thought better of his wild threats and returned to Sussex. After all, he could not fight a duel with a man whose name he did not know. And none of the Marwoods were about to tell him that Sir William Hatton was the father of Cecilia's baby.

"Is Mother coming down?" asked Thomasin, unwilling to depart without having seen Lady Elizabeth.

"Yes, yes, she said she would. Let me go inside and see what is keeping her."

Thomasin turned to Ellen, who waited at her side, dressed in a new summer cloak of forest green with a silver trim. She had always loved clothes, picking out coloured ribbons and engraved buttons, but now her wealth allowed her to wear good-quality fabrics, sewn by the court dressmakers. Her dark eyes were bright this morning, lighting up her face. Ellen always appeared lovely, thought Thomasin, because the goodness of her heart shone through.

"You are looking well this morning, cousin."

Ellen smiled, her cheeks dimpling. "I made the decision to forget what happened here the other night. It is none of my business. I shall think no more of it."

Thomasin squeezed her arm. "That is a bold and brave decision. It suits you well, and soon we shall be too busy to think of anything else."

"I do hope we find the queen in good spirits."

"We can only serve her the best we can, and try to ease her pains."

Sir Matthew's two dogs came rushing out of the house, giving small, excited yelps at the sight of the women waiting before the carriage.

"Ceasar! Brutus!" Sir Matthew came striding out after them, calling the pair back to his side. He looked up at Thomasin and Ellen. "So, you're off?"

"Thank you again," said Thomasin, "for being such a generous uncle, even when circumstances make it difficult."

Sir Matthew gave them a small smile. "We are family. We share our troubles. My home is always open to you both. Just make sure you behave yourselves at court!"

"We always do," said Ellen, smiling.

"I know," he replied. "We can count on you two, at least."

Sir Richard appeared in the doorway with Lady Elizabeth on his arm. This morning, she was dressed in her favourite combination of blue and silver, with pearls at her throat and across the band of her headdress. The morning light made her look very pale.

"I am glad I did not miss you. Come, let me kiss you."

Surprised, Thomasin went towards her mother's outstretched arms. Lady Elizabeth clasped her tight and kissed her cheek, while Thomasin inhaled her mother's scent: lavender and cedarwood.

"I am very proud of you," Lady Elizabeth whispered unexpectedly in her daughter's ear before she let her go.

Thomasin felt the colour rush to her cheeks. She could not recall her mother saying such a thing to her before, in what had always been a slightly combative relationship. Now it seemed that Cecilia's disgrace had opened her eyes to Thomasin's true value.

"Right, into the carriage," urged Sir Richard. "You cannot keep the queen waiting."

Ellen climbed in first and Thomasin followed, rearranging the folds of her own silk skirt so they would not be creased.

Sir Richard closed the carriage door and stepped up to the window. "I wish I had some words of wisdom for you, girls," he said, with a sombre expression. "I know you will do all you can to lift the queen's spirits, but I fear the coming weeks will be tough. But listen, pay no heed to rumours you may hear about the court, to stories about the past or accusations the king's counsel might make. They will try all means possible to discredit Her Majesty, but you must see them for what they are: the weapons of war."

Thomasin nodded.

Sir Richard lowered his voice. "And give no ear to those who might approach you, asking for private details of the queen's habits and functions, such as when she had her last courses. They will try to flatter or coax you, or even bribe you for details. Speak to no one."

Ellen's eyes opened wide in wonder.

"No," said Thomasin, "we will keep our counsel and share none of the queen's secrets."

"Not even to those who profess their friendship."

"Not even to them."

"Then God speed, and I will see you again soon. We shall dine together at Bridewell before long."

He nodded to the coachman and the wheels started to turn on the cobbles. Thomasin turned to wave back at the three figures in the doorway of Monk's Place, wondering when they would all be together again.

It was a short ride, along the length of Thames Street, to the house of the Blackfriars, across the river Fleet, through the city wall and into Bridewell Palace. Thomasin and Ellen might have walked, but it was the way of the court to shield its ladies in carriages, rather than have them rub shoulders with those in the street. Thomasin appreciated the protection it offered as they trundled past busy shop fronts, pedlars crying wares, wary-looking sailors, foreigners, stray sheep, dogs and children running amok. Soon they pulled into the outer courtyard and came to a halt.

Climbing down, the pair passed through the first yard, where red brick walls rose on each side, catching the May sunshine, and through the archway into the main court. Ahead lay the grand staircase which would conduct them up to the royal apartments, but before they could reach it, a pair of feet came hurrying down. Thomasin and Ellen caught a ripple of blue skirts, full white sleeves and an embroidered bodice, before Mary, Countess of Essex appeared, panting in her haste.

"Finally, ladies, you are back."

Thomasin looked at Ellen in surprise. "What is the hurry? This is the time arranged for our return."

"Oh, I know it, but try telling the queen."

Mary hurried them to one side. "She has got herself worked up. She will hear no words of comfort and spends all her time upon her knees in prayer. It is this place, this wretched place, with all its whispering corridors."

"As your father advised us," whispered Ellen.

"She has heard all manner of reports," Mary continued, her grey eyes filled with concern, "that she is to be sent away, or removed at night, to some distant place or a nunnery. There is even talk about her being carried down to the coast at night and put on a ship bound for Spain! You can imagine how she has taken it. She can scarcely sleep at night. But this morning, there was a new report. Apparently, there is an Italian plot to slip poison into her food, so we are dining exclusively in her chamber on food made only in her kitchens, and we have to taste every dish before she will take any form of nourishment." Mary paused for breath.

"Goodness," said Thomasin, "things have become much worse since we left."

"Indeed. I am heartily glad to see you both back again, as Maria and I are almost at our wits' end."

"Come, let us go to her."

"Oh, she is at prayer again. She has some of her Spanish ladies with her, and they speak only in foreign tongues between themselves."

"Still, we should join her, to show that we have returned."

"Very well," said Mary, with resignation. "Follow me. She will not go into St Bride's, but prays in her closet, for fear of strangers."

Thomasin and Ellen headed up the wide stone staircase, along to the entrance to the queen's chambers. The guards stepped aside to allow them into her outer room, a pleasant, panelled space with wide windows, where young women sat sewing or reading. From there, they proceeded through small, dark antechambers into the main room, where the table was being cleared after a recent meal and embers glowed in the grate. Little Catherine Willougby, the daughter of the queen's oldest friend, came bounding up to greet them.

"You are back! I am so glad!" She twirled around them, fanning out her kirtle. "Do you like my new clothes? Mother had them made up from one of her old dresses, but I am still not allowed to dine in public."

"They look very well indeed," Thomasin said, smiling. "Tell me, have you seen Princess Mary these past few days?"

"Oh, just a little. She is always with her tutor. She never has time to play anymore, and she said my poppet was for babies." Catherine held up the offending doll with a frown.

"I am sure she will come back and play soon."

Her mother, dark-eyed Maria Willoughby, appeared from the further door and called the girl to her. "Are you coming in to see our lady?" she asked Thomasin and Ellen.

"If we may," said Thomasin.

"She is finishing her prayers and will be out shortly. Come in and wait."

They followed her into the queen's bedchamber, which was hung with green and silver cloth. An embroidered coverlet lay heavy across the deep featherbed. The scent of Castile soap with its olive oil lingered in the air. Heavy drapes partially obscured the windows, and a line of candles on the mantel struggled to light what was rather a gloomy space.

Presently, the curtain in the corner was pulled aside. Queen Catherine appeared, dressed sombrely in black and white, a heavy gold cross hanging from a chain about her neck and a veil masking her face.

Thomasin and Ellen knelt at her approach.

"You may rise," said Catherine in a thin, careworn voice.

She slowly walked past them towards her chair, which was placed by the fireside. Maria hurried to arrange the cushions before the queen sank into them, as if exhausted.

"My veil," she whispered. "My shoes. Another log on the fire."

Ellen knelt to remove the tight leather shoes that pinched the queen's feet and replace them with soft slippers. Thomasin gently lifted back the dark veil and arranged it across the queen's shoulders. Drawing back, she was dismayed to see how tired Catherine was looking, her eyes red from weeping, her cheeks sunken. A surge of anger against the king rose within her, for making his wife endure such suffering, but she knew better than to voice it. It was treason to criticise Henry's actions.

Catherine cast her pale eyes upon the newcomers and spoke with an effort. "All is well?"

"Yes, my lady," Thomasin replied.

"Your parents, Mistress Marwood?"

"Both in good health, thank you."

Catherine nodded, as if she was processing a new thought. "I will rest here for a while. Maria, read to me from the Scriptures. Bring wine, bread. Someone send a message to Bishop Fisher, to dine with me later." She closed her eyes.

Feet scurried in all directions, obeying her commands.

Thomasin and Ellen took their places on the window seat, where the sewing basket sat, while Maria's gentle tones filled the room. As she threaded her needle, Thomasin felt that the Papal Court could not open soon enough, in order to lift this mood of gloom and pain. Clouds passed over the sun outside, and the room was plunged into shadow.

FOUR

At the dinner hour, servants arrived in Catherine's apartments, bringing plates of food from her private kitchens below.

"Now leave us." The queen dismissed them with a wave, even those who were supposed to serve her, waiting until the door closed.

Thomasin watched as Maria and Mary came forward, each with a spoon or knife, to carefully taste each dish. A slice of meat or pie, a sip of sauce, a mouthful of pastry. The women chewed slowly, with caution in their eyes. Catherine watched them intently for any signs of illness that might rapidly take hold. This was serious, Thomasin realised. The queen really was afraid of losing her life to poison.

And then another thought dawned upon her. Would she, Thomasin, also be expected to take a turn in this macabre new ritual? Perhaps the next morning, she may be called upon to taste the bread or cheese, or the potted marmalade from Seville with which Catherine liked to break her fast. There may be no foundation whatsoever for her fears, but if she was cautious enough to test each dish in this manner, she believed a plot possible. Maria and Mary might, at any moment, be thrown into convulsions, or seized by racking pains. Devoted she might be, but was Thomasin prepared to risk her own life in the queen's service?

Thomasin looked up at Ellen, who was standing demurely on the other side of the table. But her cousin gave no indication that the same idea had occurred to her, appearing lost in her own thoughts.

Finally, the queen nodded. Then she slowly rose from her chair and came to take her seat at the table, where Mary and Maria spooned the safe food onto her plate. Thomasin joined the others warily, watching as they began to eat from the plain, simple fare that the queen favoured, wondering how mealtimes had changed so dramatically in her few days of absence.

Presently, Bishop John Fisher was admitted to the chamber. Thomasin rose, along with the other waiting women, out of respect for the senior clergyman. Thomasin had also met Fisher on several occasions at court before, and found him to be wise, intelligent and sharp of wit, which was belied by his austere appearance. Tonight, his face looked more careworn than ever as he approached the table. Almost sixty, he wore a simple black robe and hat, without the kind of jewelled adornment that other clergymen like Cardinal Wolsey wore.

"My dear Bishop, do join us." Catherine gestured for him to take a seat close by her.

"You are most kind, my good lady."

Fisher eased himself slowly into a chair.

"Will you eat?"

"Perhaps a little. My appetite is not what it once was."

Catherine nodded. "This matter is enough to turn any man's stomach."

"How do you fare, madam?"

"Passing well. I seek God's guidance daily and remind myself that this is a trial sent from him, in order that I may prove my devotion."

A cloud darkened Fisher's brow. "I think there can be no doubt about the depths of your devotion, my lady."

"Well, as it may be. How fares the king?"

"He was out riding this morning, but since his return, he has been closeted away in his chambers."

"Taking advice, no doubt?"

"I believe so, madam."

"Would that he would turn to the Lord for advice, for there is no better guide for us humble mortals."

"Indeed so." Fisher drank from his wine cup. "I must add, though, most respectfully, that there are reports reaching the king's ears which cannot help your cause."

The queen sat up. "What reports are these?"

"His advisors are calling it extreme behaviour: your refusal to leave your chamber, dining in secret, having all your food tasted. I understand your reasons, and the importance of protecting your person, but I think it better to present yourself as if all were well. Be seen about the palace. Dine in public."

"What are they saying about me?"

"They claim it implies a little... What is the word ... eccentricity? Which is not desirable in a queen."

Catherine's face hardened. "I find it most desirable in the preservation of my own life."

"Do you really have grounds to believe that there will be an attempt made upon you?"

"Can you assure me, Bishop, that there will not?"

He sighed. "I suppose not, but do not give them cause to cite paranoia or reclusiveness. Otherwise they can argue that you are best fitted for the cloister, not the court. If you are already living like a nun, you might as well do that elsewhere."

Catherine fell silent, thinking. "And who, might I ask, is the architect of these arguments?" she demanded at last. "No, let me guess. It has the reek of Master Cromwell, does it not?"

"I never said so, my lady," Fisher replied tactfully, bowing his head.

"That man would have me shipped out to a nunnery first thing in the morning, if he were able. I am sure he would get between the shafts and pull my carriage himself!"

Fisher cleared his throat. "It is but two days to wait, my lady, before the court opens. Are you well advised? Do you wish us to meet tomorrow to discuss the matter further?"

"You have given me your excellent counsel, good Bishop, and I trust in the Lord. I shall leave my chamber tomorrow and pay a visit to Archbishop Campeggio, for his final thoughts. That will also have the effect of making me visible about the court, as you advise."

"I think it for the best, my lady. And another thing I might mention: there is a rumour circulating that the Pope has died."

Catherine dropped her knife with a clatter. "The Pope? Dead?"

"Indeed. The king heard it this morning and was greatly cheered by it, believing that another man might judge his case more favourably, but, my lady, I personally set no store by it. His Holiness has been suffering from ill health, but none of my sources confirm his death. My correspondent in Rome spoke with him recently and mentioned nothing."

"You think there is no danger?"

"I think we should give no credence to any rumours we might hear. And under no circumstances should we accept the king using this to question the validity of the Papal Court."

"I thank you for warning me about this. I shall certainly not respond should the matter reach my ears."

"It may serve to distract the king and give him false confidence in his case."

"I shall speak to Campeggio. Surely he will know the truth of it."

"Has Mendoza left yet?"

The old Spanish ambassador, Bishop Mendoza, had been Catherine's advisor and friend since his appointment to England three years earlier. He had suffered the indignity of imprisonment by the French on his journey to her side, then had been placed by Henry under house arrest while Spanish relations deteriorated. Finally released to carry out his business, he suffered from the most terrible gout, racking his legs with pain, so he had requested leave to return home to his family.

"He will depart shortly and comes hither to take his leave as soon as all his affairs are resolved."

"I shall pray for an equally sympathetic replacement."

The meal continued, and talk passed on to the Princess Mary, Catherine's only daughter, and how she progressed in her education under the formidable Lady Salisbury.

Thomasin judged that the moment was right. She turned to Ellen. "I am going to slip out for a moment — not too long. If I am missed, say that I was dizzy and needed some air."

"Rafe?" Ellen had guessed her motive at once.

"I must see him after that awful business last night, just to check that he has not changed his mind."

"Of course he has not changed his mind!"

"But what man would wish to be united with such a family, where scenes like that take place?"

"A man who loves you deeply and who understands human nature. Besides, it is only one of your family members who causes all the problems."

"Indeed, but Cecilia is quite enough for us all. I shall not be long, I promise. Cover for me."

"Of course, go!"

Thomasin needed no further encouragement. She slipped through the doors, along the corridor, where the lamps flickered, and down the staircase. There was no guarantee that

Rafe was even at court. The Boleyns might be here, dining with the king, but equally they might be at Durham Place, keeping out of the way, given the impending court. It would not do for Thomasin to hang about the king's chambers, but she might place herself in the path of those coming and going, who might be able to answer her questions.

She crossed the dark court, her skirts catching on the little hedgerows of sweet-scented box that marked out the flowerbeds. The central fountain still flowed, with the sound of water tinkling upon its surface. From an open window above, the strains of a lute crept through the night air.

In the doorway opposite, two men passed across Thomasin's line of vision, but neither was known to her. She dared creep a little closer, lurking near the bushes to see if she might overhear any conversation. Presently, a servant boy crossed the open space, arms full of wood for the king's chamber.

"Hey, boy!" Thomasin called.

He paused and looked at her with startled eyes.

"Don't be alarmed. I'm one of the queen's ladies. Tell me, do the Boleyns dine with the king tonight?"

She could see him hesitate, as if this was secret information.

"It's all right — it's not the queen asking; it's me wanting to know if a friend is here."

He shook his head. "None of the Boleyns, only Wolsey and Cromwell."

"You're sure?"

"Sure as eggs is eggs, madam."

Thomasin waved him on his way. It meant that Rafe was probably at Durham Court too, so there was no chance of her seeing him tonight. She would have to be patient and hope he would return to Bridewell in the morning.

"Mistress Marwood?"

The voice sounded slightly familiar, as if it was calling to her from the past. She turned and peered through the darkness. A man of her own height was standing there, with light brown hair and a merry face, his blue-green eyes fixed upon her. She took in his snug, well-structured form, flattered by its rust-coloured doublet. Yes, she knew that firm chin and square jaw, that smile that was spreading over his sensuous lips.

"Giles? Giles Waterson?"

He stepped forwards, beaming. "I thought it was you! I wasn't sure, as you're older, obviously, as we all are. It must be not quite two years since I saw you last."

When the Marwoods had first come to court, Lady Elizabeth had cherished hopes that Thomasin might marry her distant Waterson cousin. In fact, a great friendship had been established between them, based on their love of merry words and the finer aspects of the dining table, and Giles had felt able to confide in her about the loss of his first wife. Soon after Thomasin had entered the queen's household, Giles had left court on family business.

"I had heard you were in the north?"

"Yes, there was much to do to put my uncle's affairs straight. Some counterclaim upon his land, a dreary enough business, but it is now resolved. But you are well? You look well, Thomasin."

His compliment touched her. "I am well, still serving the queen through this difficult business."

"Indeed, I have been learning more of it since my arrival. A sorry state of affairs indeed, that must touch all hearts. That is what prompts my return. The king summoned me to act as his secretary."

"His secretary?"

"Yes, he has a sudden surfeit of secretaries. Our task is merely to read every book in existence on the matter and write summaries of evidence that might assist his case. It is dull work indeed and I did not ask for it."

"And may I congratulate you? There was talk of an engagement while you were away. Are you now a happily married man?"

"Me? No, that was my uncle who married. I have not been so fortunate. And yourself?"

It was on the tip of her tongue to tell him about Rafe, the postponed engagement and her hopes for the future, but Rafe was not there. And Giles still felt like a stranger. Instead, she blushed and shook her head.

"Well, there is time enough for all of that. I shall be in the court every day after it opens, and I trust I will see you at some point. Perhaps we might share a dish of pork and mustard, if you will let it out of your sight."

"You remembered my favourite dish."

"My favourite also. Let every table be graced with pork and mustard." He glanced up at the staircase. "But now I must depart; the king awaits me. How pleased I am to see you again, Thomasin."

She watched him disappear through the dark garden and up the stairs. A shiver ran through her that was not caused by the cold of the evening, but she shrugged it off and turned back towards the queen's chamber.

FIVE

Catherine paused in the walled garden and turned her face to the sun. Its warm rays lit her red velvet sleeves as she stretched her arms out wide, and the golden trim of her headdress sparkled.

"Here, let us linger a while to show ourselves to the court," she said defiantly up to the lines of windows that encircled them. Behind them, men and women of the court might gather, unseen, to watch those enclosed below.

Thomasin and Ellen stopped a little way behind her. The queen had roused them early, demanding to be dressed in her splendour to return to the church of St Bride, before heading to the lodgings of Cardinal Campeggio. Bishop Fisher's words the previous evening had struck home, and she would do anything not to appear weak or afraid in the eyes of the court. It was essential that she put on a display of strength, no matter how she felt inside, so the little stone church that stood just outside the palace was firmly back on the itinerary.

Last night it had been Thomasin's turn to sleep on one of the truckle beds in Catherine's room, along with her usual companion, Maria Willoughby. She had heard the queen's muffled sobs and her whispered prayers continue into the early hours before Catherine finally drifted into a deep sleep.

"Perhaps I should announce myself," Catherine said to the garden, almost playfully, although there was bitter sarcasm in her voice. "Here is the Queen of England, dressed in scarlet, still married, still alive!"

Thomasin and Ellen exchanged glances. This wasn't what Bishop Fisher had in mind.

More worshippers from the morning service were entering the garden now, returning to their chambers or their employment. Catherine made a point of greeting them all with a cheery good morning or nod of the head, depending upon their rank.

"Never let it be said that the Queen of England is one to hide away!" she muttered under her breath.

From a door on the east wall, the red-robed figure of Cardinal Thomas Wolsey appeared, solid and serious about his purpose. He paused upon seeing Catherine, then bowed and headed towards her as protocol dictated. A man whose career at court had advanced alongside Catherine's queenship, he would be the second of the two cardinals to preside over the Legatine Court, taking his place beside Campeggio.

"My lady," he said, bowing low.

"I believe we match this morning," said Catherine brightly. "Both of us in flaming red, Cardinal."

"You are looking very well, my lady. It is good to see you in health."

"I have sought spiritual guidance and am confident of my case," she replied. "God knows the truth, Cardinal: I was truly married in his eyes, and he will be my only judge in this matter."

Wolsey looked uncomfortable.

"We have been to St Bride's," the queen continued, "to thank him for his mercy. I trust the proceedings will soon be resolved to his satisfaction."

"To God's satisfaction, my lady?" Wolsey asked. "Or to that of the king?"

"Can there be a difference?" Catherine jumped in quickly. "Surely the king cannot wish for a different outcome from that which God desires? Or does he place himself above our Lord now?"

Wolsey shifted from foot to foot.

"My lady," whispered Maria, who was closest, "that is not so wisely said, especially so loudly."

"You see, Wolsey, I have good counsel about me, who do not fear to speak the truth. I do hope the king has the same. Is Cromwell with him now?"

"My Lord Cromwell is working hard on the case."

Catherine laughed. "I expect he is. What a hardworking man he is. I do wonder where the king found him."

There was an awkward silence. Thomasin remembered that Wolsey, like Cromwell, also came from humble origins, so he would not have received the comment well.

Wolsey bowed his head. "I must beg your permission to depart, my lady. I must away to continue my work. There is much to be done."

"What, no words of advice or comfort for me? No reassurances, Thomas?"

The unexpected use of his first name brought Wolsey up sharp. "I am sure that all will pass as God wishes, my lady."

"Hmm." Catherine turned away from his lukewarm sentiments as he hastened away. "I have spent enough time in dalliance," she decided. "Now let us proceed to Campeggio's lodgings. He should have arrived from Richmond by now."

Dutifully, Thomasin and Ellen followed, although Catherine's forced jollity gave them cause for concern. The old cardinal had been housed on the palace's ground floor, as close to the Blackfriars site as possible, to allow for ease of access. Arrangements had been made for a litter to carry him across the Fleet bridge into the court room if the need arose.

However, at the door, Catherine paused. "I will take only Maria in with me. We need not all crowd in. The rest of you may go in to dinner."

"Are you sure, my lady?" asked Thomasin, trying to conceal her relief. "You do not need us with you?"

The queen patted Maria on the arm. "All will be well. Go."

The hour that the king liked to dine had not yet arrived. It was approaching ten, when the first meal of the day was served, but there was still a short while to fill, so Thomasin and Ellen resolved to take seats in the anteroom and wait for the doors to open. The place soon filled up, with various servants of the crown anticipating filling their rumbling bellies.

"Let us pray for a miracle with this court," said Ellen after a while. "I cannot see how the king will allow it to rule against him, no matter what God's intentions might be."

"We cannot influence the outcome," said Thomasin, realistically. "All we can do is be ready to support the queen, whatever is decided."

"Do you think they will send her to a nunnery?"

"I don't see how, against her will."

"It was done in France, I believe, and also in Spain, twice before! Lady Essex was telling me; there was Queen Joan, the first wife of Louis XII, and poor Blanche of Castile, although she was locked up by her family, just like the queen's sister Joanna is locked up."

Thomasin shot a look at her cousin. "You seem to know much on the matter."

"Like I said, Lady Essex told me, but we need to know these things, to be prepared. No doubt the court will use these examples."

"It's likely. Do you really think they might send her back to Spain?"

Ellen shrugged. "Who knows what Henry will do to get his way? He is growing impatient. I heard a rumour that he is determined to wed Anne this summer, after the court closes."

"Perhaps he will. It can hardly be a marriage Anne can feel confident in, then."

"I'm not sure she cares," said Ellen. "Once she bears a son, that will be the security she needs."

Thomasin stared at the stone flags on the floor, smooth with the passage of many feet. A feeling of helplessness on the queen's behalf came stealing over her.

"Would you leave with her?" she asked. "I mean, if she has to leave court. We are her ladies, so should our fate be bound to hers?"

Ellen sighed. "I do hope it does not come to that."

"But if she was to be sent into Spain, would you go with her?"

"I don't think I should like that strange country. I have heard they are savage there and the food is unpalatable. Yet, I could not abandon the queen. Perhaps I might accompany her there, and see her settled with Spanish ladies, then return to England."

"You might be swept off your feet by a Spanish gentleman."

Ellen gave a wry smile. "I doubt that very much."

"Or perhaps you will find a husband here at court."

"Like you have, you mean?"

"Yes, don't you want to marry?"

"Not particularly. Not at the moment."

"That obviously means you are going to fall in love with the next man you set eyes on."

At that moment, a figure came striding round the corner. Both women recognised the broad shoulders and long legs of Sir Hugh Truegood, dressed in his habitual chestnut shades which complimented his colouring.

"Oh, Lord!" breathed Ellen.

"Look away," said Thomasin. "He is heading over here."

"Ellen!" Hugh called towards them. "Ellen, I must speak with you."

"Sir Hugh," said Thomasin, neatly stepping between them, "did you not use up your quota of words the other night, when you interrupted my family's dinner?"

"My sincerest apologies for that," he replied, trying to pass her by. "Ellen?"

"Ellen is a servant of the queen, and she is about her business at the moment. What can you possibly have to say to her?"

Hugh looked around them, seeing that no one else was there, then frowned at Thomasin. "What business is it, when the two of you are sitting and talking? And my words are for Ellen's ears alone."

"And yet she may not wish to hear them, and then, sir, you will simply have to eat them."

"Is it the fashion now, Mistress Marwood, for young ladies to be so impertinent to their betters? What if the queen heard of your poor manners?"

"I should welcome the opportunity to explain to her how they arose."

He stared back at her, his tawny eyes flashing. She saw him make the decision to ignore her and repeat his advances. "Ellen? Ellen, for love of God…"

Ellen rose to her feet. "It's all right, cousin, let's hear him out."

"These are words for you alone."

But Ellen lifted her chin and looked at him evenly. "You have no right to request that. Whatever you wish to say may be spoken before my family, just like the other night."

Hugh frowned. "Very well. Ellen, I have made a terrible mistake. A dreadful, terrible mistake that haunts me day and night. When I think of what I had in your good self, what goodness, what simplicity, what trust and faith ... and I allowed myself to be influenced into throwing it away. And now I suffer for it, every day. My wife is a very devil, Ellen, and I cannot abide another day with her. She tortures me with every means at her disposal."

Thomasin turned away to conceal her smile. At least Cecilia could be thanked for that!

"Ellen," Hugh continued, "I wish to live simply, a retired life in the country with a woman who loves me, perhaps a family..."

"A woman who loves you?" interrupted Thomasin. "You would phrase it like that, instead of a woman whom you love?"

"Yes, yes, of course, a woman whom I love. That is you, Ellen. I have never stopped loving you. Please, give me some hope for the future. I will put Cecilia aside, through annulment or divorce, leaving us free to marry. You can be my wife, Ellen. We can be happy together. You could come with me, today, back to Raycroft and I will cast that woman out! What say you?"

Thomasin turned to hear her cousin's view, hoping that her resolve would not weaken.

Finally, Ellen spoke. "Sir Hugh, as a married man it is improper for you to speak to me in this manner. I will not be your wife, or your concubine, or whatever you wish. Nor would I be the cause of any woman being cast out of her legally married home, especially not my cousin. It is not my desire to be any man's second choice. Come, Thomasin."

Thomasin took the arm that Ellen held out to her and together they went into dinner. Yet Thomasin could feel her cousin's arm shaking through the material of her sleeve.

"That was excellent," she said. "I could not have spoken better myself."

"The cheek of him!" Ellen muttered through gritted teeth. "The absolute cheek! For me to be the instrument by which your sister is thrown out of her home! To replace her in his bed while it is still warm! I have more dignity and fellow feeling that he has in his little finger."

"To think we had him so wrong," Thomasin added.

"It is a lesson better learned now than later."

"Indeed, that is true. May all the men at court reveal their true selves to us in such a manner."

The dinner plates were being brought up from the kitchen as the two women found themselves seats near the fireplace. Thomasin's stomach growled as the scent of meat reached them. Ellen was watching the doorway, in case Sir Hugh had followed them in.

"Honestly, I hope he disappears back down to Sussex," Thomasin said. "He and Cecilia deserve each other."

"Let us not speak of him."

"Of course not. Let us put him out of our minds forever."

"I heard," said Ellen, "that in the early days of their marriage, the king and queen used to celebrate May Day by riding out into the woods in costume and staging pageants beneath the trees. There would be a feast, musicians playing and archery contests, as if they were legendary huntsmen, like Robin Hood."

Thomasin smiled. "The king as Robin Hood?"

"I think it sounds romantic. Do you think all happy loves must end up the same way?"

"I don't know," said Thomasin, caught off guard by the change in mood. "I suppose we will find out."

"Oh, look, there's your father!"

Sir Richard was making his way down the hall in his best court doublet. He hastened to join them, looking especially careworn as he took a seat opposite his daughter.

"Father, are you well?"

"I have not had the best of mornings. First I met with Lord Cromwell, and had to sit through his tiresome entreaties and threats, and then upon coming here I ran into Sir Hugh, who looked as if he had more to say to me, although I did not give him the chance."

"Oh dear. We saw him too. He had the gall to ask Ellen to run away with him to Raycroft, promising to cast Cecilia out of the house."

Sir Richard shook his head. "It is a bad business, a terrible business, but it is of their making."

"I assure you, sir," said Ellen, "that I gave his impertinent suggestions short shrift."

"I did not need to ask for your response, dear Ellen, for I know enough of the goodness of your heart already."

Thomasin pushed a dish of spring lamb with green sauce towards her father. "For that kind remark, you may take the first portion."

"Oh, and you know who else I have seen?" said Sir Richard as he helped himself. "Your distant relative. Sir Giles Waterson is back at court after all this time."

"Ah, Sir Giles," said Thomasin, nodding.

"Wasn't he the one that your mother had hopes that you might marry?" Sir Richard looked at his daughter pointedly.

It was on the tip of Thomasin's tongue to mention Rafe, to say that it was he who she desired as a husband. But she did not.

"Yes, indeed it was he," she confirmed, and took a large bite out of her bread, so that she could speak no more.

"Your mother will be pleased," said Sir Richard, beaming.

SIX

The last day of May dawned bright and fresh. When Thomasin woke to the usual sound of palace bustle, Catherine was standing by the window in her nightgown.

"My lady, are you well?"

Thomasin rubbed her eyes as the queen turned slowly towards her. Maria was still sleeping soundly, her blanket pulled up to cover her ears.

"Well enough," Catherine said wistfully, pulling a shawl about her shoulders. "The court convenes today. My fate is in its hands."

"Might I bring you anything? Do you wish to dress yet?"

"No, it is too early. I was waiting to hear the hour of Prime but I must have missed it, because the sun is quite up now." She traced a finger across the pane of glass before her. "I had hoped to spare my daughter this."

"Is Lady Mary now at Hatfield?"

"Yes, but I was thinking of moving her to Eltham, as it is a greater distance away. There she is less likely to hear…" The queen paused. "Reports."

"I am sure the Countess of Salisbury is vigilant in protecting her from idle gossip."

The princess's governess was a formidable woman, but Thomasin had every faith in her desire to protect her vulnerable young charge. The unravelling of her parents' marriage had opened Mary's eyes to suffering for the first time, and now, at the age of thirteen, she experienced low moods and severe toothache that Thomasin was sure were not helped by her sense of loss.

Catherine turned back to face Thomasin. "Your father is at court, is he not?"

"Yes, my lady. He was summoned by Cromwell, quite against his wishes."

"And what is his position on this matter?"

"He has always been a devoted friend to your good self, and will speak according to the dictates of his conscience."

"He was always beloved at my court." Catherine turned with a smile. "I remember him as a young man, with such energy and a warm smile. Did you know he used to play the lute and sing in my chambers? I did miss his smile when he retired to the country."

Thomasin wondered whether the queen knew the real reason for Sir Richard's withdrawal from court, all those years ago. She herself had only recently discovered the brief liaison that had occurred between her mother and the king. At one point she had even feared that Henry might be her own father, but the similarities between her and Sir Richard were too great to overlook.

"I can trust you, can't I, Thomasin?"

"Yes, my lady, with every fibre of my being."

Catherine smiled at her enthusiasm. "Yes, I believe so, despite the best efforts of others to convince me differently. Did you hear that Lady Norfolk has left court?"

"I had not, my lady." Thomasin recalled the Duke of Norfolk's quarrelsome wife, who had tried to turn the queen against Thomasin not so long ago.

"You will not miss her, I think."

"No, my lady."

"I need someone to attend the Papal Court for me, Thomasin. To sit at the back and listen, when I am not there. I will only attend at the time I am summoned, but I wish to know how proceedings fare. I think you would be a good choice, with your sharp wits and good memory, and your father is there too. Will you be my eyes and ears in that place?"

The immensity of this rushed over Thomasin in a wave. "Of course, my lady, if it will assist you."

"You do not need to speak. Just attend and report back at the end of the day."

"Is there anything in particular you wish to hear, or not hear?"

"You are most tactful, as ever. Your general impressions, I think: the mood of the court, and the law, evidence, precedents, but only when they are significant in determining my case. Also the main line of those called as witnesses. Do you think you can manage that?"

"I will do my very best for you, my lady."

"The court convenes shortly, so you must dress and break your fast quickly."

Thomasin started to fold her linen at once.

"Never mind that. Maria will do it." Catherine crossed the room and stood up on tiptoes to plant a kiss on Thomasin's forehead. "May God go with you, Thomasin Marwood."

The sun was climbing higher in the sky as Thomasin hurried across the Fleet Bridge and entered Blackfriars Priory. The building had the gloomy majesty of a religious site, but it was also used as a royal venue, and there were signs of the wealth and presence of the king everywhere. Scented braziers burned against the morning chill; rich tapestries and curtains hung against the stone walls. Crowds were milling about in the cloister, waiting to enter the Parliament chamber, where the hearing was to be held. Through the dark robes of dukes and earls, Thomasin glimpsed the flash of the cardinals' scarlet.

Her heart was beating faster as she approached. It was indeed a great honour to be asked to attend on behalf of the queen, but also a great responsibility. She did not look forward to the inevitable digging into the royal marriage, which she must bear witness to.

"Thomasin Marwood?"

She turned to see her good friend and scholar Thomas More, dressed in grey robes and wearing the most sombre of expressions. Over the past year, his intelligent conversation and kindness had saved her on many occasions, so he had come to represent something of an alternative father figure to her, especially when Sir Richard was absent. He had been speaking with Bishop Fisher, who was dressed in his black and white robes and tricorn hat, but now came over to greet her.

"Master More!"

"It does my heart good to see you, Thomasin. Are you quite well?"

"Well enough, I thank you."

"Why are you here, at the court? Surely you are not summoned already?"

"No, I am not summoned." She looked round to check they were not overheard, but lowered her voice anyway. "I am here on behalf of the queen, to be her eyes and ears while she is not present."

"Ah, I see." Concern flickered in his eyes. "And you are happy to do this?"

"Happy to serve my lady in any way I can."

"The queen is wise in her choices. In you, she has the best eyes and ears she might have, perhaps better than her own." He looked back at the crowd waiting to enter the chamber. "Do not be put off by all this. It will be mostly procedure today; there will not be much to interest you, I fear, and little to report before the important matter begins."

"It is of no matter. I think just having someone there to represent her will reassure the queen. I know she has you, and the Bishop, but I am to be an independent pair of eyes."

"Women's eyes," added More, "which see things differently to those of all the men here. We will find you a quiet spot, where you can follow the proceedings."

"May I not sit with you, or my father when he arrives?"

"There will be strict arrangements about who is to sit where. It will all be very formal." He turned to look at the doors to the chamber. "They should commence soon."

"And Margaret, is she well?" Thomasin had grown particularly close to More's daughter, Margaret Roper, with her combination of sharp wit and gentleness.

"Margaret is, yes, thanks be to God, but her little daughter has been unwell, so she is much occupied with her. It will turn out well, I think, but the child is delicate."

"Oh, I am sorry to hear that." Thomasin made a mental note to ask Catherine's permission to send the Ropers a gift of wine and fruit.

Then, the heavy doors behind them started to scrape open, and the attention of the crowd was turned in their direction. A figure stood in the doorway in bishop's robes, surveying those outside.

"That is John Longland, Bishop of Lincoln," explained More. "It is he who will open proceedings, as it was to him that the king first expressed his concerns."

Thomasin looked at the face of Henry's confessor, hoping to find some suggestion of empathy and mercy, but she could discern nothing behind his stony eyes.

"Make way!" called a voice from behind. They stepped aside to allow the two cardinals to enter, Campeggio drawing out every agonising step and clutching a cross in his hands, and Wolsey following behind, his chin lifted as if he might somehow rise above it all.

A train of bishops and archdeacons followed, with Fisher among them, after which came the other court officials. Thomasin saw Cromwell at the end, with her father walking reluctantly at his side. Sir Richard raised his brows in surprise as he saw his daughter waiting to enter, but there was no time for explanations. Another figure, tall, austere and hollow-cheeked came after him, not looking around, but keeping his eyes forward.

"That's Gardiner," whispered someone in the crowd. "He's come back to court to help Wolsey."

Once all the men had entered the chamber, Thomasin followed More and slipped into a seat at the back. The setting was dark and old, filled with heavy wood and a sense of history. She could imagine Parliament meeting here in times past, to discuss dangers and pass laws. Looking about, she saw that there were no other women present. Several of the officials looked at her askance, but she was known as one of the queen's women, so they must have guessed at her purpose. Thomasin sat up straight and looked ahead: she had every right to be there and would defend her presence if need be.

As silence fell, Bishop Longland stood at the front, surveying the assembly with the most solemn of airs. He began by presenting the papal commission issued to Campeggio and Wolsey, who sat on either side behind him, the two flashes of colour amid a sea of black and grey. The newcomer, Gardiner, had pride of place at his side, opening and arranging his folder of documents. Wolsey's clerk, a young Italian-looking man, read the instructions aloud to the court, with their complicated legal language, although even Thomasin could grasp their import. The validity of the marriage between the king and queen was to be tested, and as soon as possible, it was to be declared either as legitimate, or null and void. Both Henry and Catherine were summoned to attend, in person, on the eighteenth of June, in order to speak their minds.

Thomasin drew in her breath. Was the end of this terrible drama almost in sight?

The legal matters proceeded. First Wolsey, then Campeggio, shaky on his feet, rose to swear their oaths in Latin. Thomasin recalled the occasion when she had called for strong hands to help him to bed, as he had been suffering terribly from the gout. Where had that been, Greenwich, or Hampton Court? The remaining proceedings were more of the Pope's legal tangles, the validity of the court and role of the two cardinals. There was nothing else of use to Catherine yet.

Looking around, Thomasin noted that there were no Boleyns present in the chamber, not even Sir Thomas, or Anne's uncle Norfolk had attended on the first day. Probably, Thomasin thought, it was because they knew that the real proceedings would not get underway for a while yet. It also meant there was no Rafe.

She stifled a yawn and sat back in her seat as Bishop Longland resumed his speech.

The daylight was bright outside when the session concluded. In the end, they had been inside for little more than an hour, but the court had been convened and its wheels set in motion. Thomasin came out, blinking, feeling herself no wiser than when she had gone in, except now there was a formal date on which Catherine would be summoned to speak. She stood to the side of the door and watched as the others poured out, the cardinals and bishops having already led the way.

"Well," said More, dusting off his sleeves, "there was very little edifying in that. And more of it to come, I think."

"What happens next?" asked Thomasin.

"Again, very little." More pulled a face. "The court will examine the evidence and wait to hear from the king and queen."

"And both their views are well known."

"Indeed. I would not be a cardinal in England for anything at the moment."

Sir Richard had finally escaped the hall, and the clutches of Cromwell. "Ah, there you are. Sent by Catherine?"

"Yes, to watch and listen in her place."

"That is an honour, surely."

"A dubious honour, I fear," added More.

Sir Richard turned to his daughter. "I suppose you have not heard from your mother? She was set to write to you, but I think she has not yet."

"No, nothing."

"She has again taken to her bed over this Cecilia business and is bewailing her misfortune. I am to seek out some cloves for her, as it has all set off her toothache, but apparently there are none to be had anywhere in London!"

"I will send some. I am sure the queen has plenty and will not mind sparing a few."

"Ah, you see, now you have the queen's ear, or rather you are her ears, you might ask her for special favours."

"I do not really wish to be doing that, Father."

"No, I jest, but I have been plagued by your mother's complaints all night, so am grumpier than ever. All she speaks of is Cecilia and the baby, wanting her to come to London."

"Do you think Hugh will send her back to us?"

"He might; it is your mother's wish. I am to suggest that she could raise the child in Suffolk, while he divorces her quietly, without a scandal, if he is set on it, but then Cecilia is never one to do anything quietly. This is a terrible mess, is it not? I do wish we had no part in it."

"I will write to Mother with the cloves and try to comfort her."

"You are a good girl, Thomasin, thank the Lord. Now I will go at once to seek out Sir Hugh in his London lodgings, and I pray that I find him of a calm and sober mind."

"Good luck with that, Father. May God go with you."

"Family trouble?" asked More as they watched him walk away.

"My sister. Again."

More offered Thomasin his arm. "Shall we walk?"

"I must get back to the queen, who will be keen to hear everything, although she does not yet know there is so little to hear."

"Just across the bridge and through the gardens then, back to her lodgings," More said with a smile.

They passed over the Fleet, grey and fast as it collided with the Thames, and set foot on the further side. At once, the shaded paths and walkways inside the walled garden put Thomasin at ease.

"The thing about families," said More, "is that they are both our harbours and our storms. Sometimes both at the same time, and we can do little but try and keep our heads as we weather them."

Thomasin sighed. "I know that is true."

"But it is very difficult," he continued, "when the careful sailors are constantly working with another who knows or cares little for times and tides. It is a frustrating task to shoulder another's burdens, and we cannot avoid them becoming our own."

"You speak so kindly, so gently, but in truth, Cecilia is little more than a tempest. I fear what will become of her."

"All you can do is to gently guide her, and do not let her sink your ship. Your father's plan sounds like a solid one. She may do best retreating to the country, where she can at least reflect on her ways."

"And the child can enter the nursery, with my young sisters and brother. It will only be four or five years their junior."

"Will she consent to go?"

"That is quite another matter. As a married woman, she has certain rights now, although none so strong as her husband's. I fear it all depends upon Sir Hugh."

"I know the man only a little. Is he reasonable?"

"I used to think so; he once seemed one of the most reasonable and placid gentlemen. But we never know how we will react when a storm hits."

"Indeed. We are all angels until we are put to the test."

They had reached the staircase leading up to Catherine's apartments.

Thomasin turned to her companion, noticing the fine lines on his papery skin that the daylight revealed. "Will you walk up and see the queen?"

"Another time. She may not be in the mood for visitors, but please give her my kind regards. And this." He paused and removed a silver cross on a chain that he had worn about his neck. "Give her this with my deepest love. Dear Catherine."

Thomasin took the chain in her hand. If only every man at court was as good, kind and wise as Sir Thomas More.

SEVEN

Catherine was waiting for Thomasin in the window alcove of her antechamber. Her anxiety was plain as she wrung her small, jewelled hands together, rising to her feet as her gentlewoman approached.

Thomasin curtseyed low. "My lady, be not alarmed. There was little of import today beyond the swearing of oaths and laying out of procedures. Nothing was discussed touching your marriage, only the date that you would be summoned to the court, on the eighteenth of June. The clerks will visit you soon, to give you formal notification, but that was the sum of it."

Catherine held out a hand to her, and Thomasin took it.

"You are the most faithful and true of ladies, Thomasin Marwood. Take this as thanks for your pains." She held out a gold coin.

"Oh, I did not expect this. I truly did not; I did it in your service."

"But it is my pleasure to reward you. Put it aside for your wedding day."

Thomasin blushed and the queen smiled.

"Perhaps you already have someone in mind. You have visitors, Thomasin, in my main chamber. They came to pay their respects to me, but have lingered in their desire to see you, I believe."

"Me?"

"You are the only Thomasin in my household. They asked after you, quite boldly. Two young men; I could hardly decide which was more handsome. Go, go — they are still waiting."

"First I must give you this, my lady." Thomasin held out the silver cross. "And the most devoted love from your servant and friend, Sir Thomas More."

Catherine took it and smiled. "God bless dear Sir Thomas."

"May I do anything more for you, my lady?"

"Send Maria out to me, but otherwise, go!" The queen waved her hand and in a flash of diamonds and rubies, Thomasin was dismissed.

Thomasin approached the door in a sudden fever of excitement. Had Rafe come here, to find her? Surely he must be intending to seek the queen's approval for their match, or else he would not have been so direct. Did the Boleyns know he was here?

The sound of music and laughter reached her from beyond the doors. The guards in green livery threw the heavy wooden panels open to reveal a jolly scene, of musicians playing, Ellen singing and little Mary Willoughby walking through dance steps with their encouragement. She looked about wildly, seeking Rafe, but instead, standing before the fire, clapping in time with the rhythm, stood Sir Giles Waterson, resplendent in red and yellow velvet. Thomasin struggled to conceal the surprise on her face, and perhaps also a little disappointment.

"Here she is, just in time!" Giles cried, his face lighting up. "We had begun to despair that you had fallen into the Fleet and been carried out to sea!"

"And we would have to take a Spanish ship and sail after you, all the way to the New World," added little Catherine, "and fight monkeys and bears to get you back!"

Thomasin opened her eyes wide at the child. "That does sound like an adventure. Unfortunately, I was only at Blackfriars, and survived the crossing of the bridge."

Mary, Lady Essex, called for wine, asking Thomasin a hundred questions with her eyes.

"Yes, all is well," Thomasin reassured her, "nothing to fear."

"For now," said Mary, handing her a glass. "You will need this, after listening to all that talk!"

Thomasin sipped her wine eagerly, letting the spices roll across her tongue. Then, across the room, she spotted Ellen sitting with the second of the two gentlemen the queen had mentioned. He was a man in his thirties, with flecks of grey at his temples, a kindly face and twinkling eyes, but what Thomasin noticed most was the way he was smiling at Ellen. And the way she smiled back at him.

As if her cousin could feel her eyes upon her, Ellen turned and saw Thomasin watching them. Beckoning Thomasin over, Ellen gestured to the man at her side.

"Cousin, this is Sir Henry Letchmere from Kent. He came with Sir Giles."

Thomasin dropped a curtsey. "Very pleased to meet you, my lord."

"And I likewise. Please call me Harry." He rose and gave a short bow. He stood at about her height in grey and silver, and there was a pleasant air about him.

"Your cousin was speaking of you just a moment ago, anticipating your return."

"You were in court?" asked Ellen.

"Yes, I have given my report to the queen." Thomasin shot her cousin a look: she was not prepared to speak about this matter before a stranger.

"It is pleasant to be at court," said Harry, as if understanding her reluctance. "I have just returned after a long absence, and I forgot how good it is to be among merry people."

"Unfortunately, we are not as merry as we have been," Thomasin could not resist saying. "Great cares hang upon the king and queen, as you must have heard."

"News reached us even in Calais," confirmed Harry, "although we are not as close to the heart of things as you are here."

"In Calais?" asked Ellen. "What was your business there?"

"I was placed as a child in the household of Lord Berners, so I accompanied him when he became lieutenant of that city, serving with him on the Council."

"What is it like there?"

"Very much like England in many ways, but in others, very different. It is hard to explain; it has its own unique atmosphere, with the Channel on one side and France on the other."

"Were you not always afraid that the French would invade?"

"We worked hard to maintain good relations with our French neighbours, counting some of them as friends."

"I should like to see the place one day," said Ellen, "if I dared set foot aboard a ship. I am not sure how I would like to sail."

"Everyone did it for the first time once," Harry said with a smile, his eyes crinkling. "If you embark upon a fair tide, with the wind behind you, you will sail across and barely feel it."

"Come now," said Giles, striding up to them. "Catherine is going to talk me through the steps of the Almain. Do any of you know it?"

"Now that's something that didn't cross the Channel," admitted Harry.

"Are you so sure?" Giles laughed. "The north sea, perhaps, then. It is German, is it not? Allemagne?"

"A German dance!" exclaimed Harry. "Surely there is at least an Italian one instead? I'm not sure I'm heavy-footed enough for a Protestant dance."

"Thomasin, do you know it?" asked Giles.

The Almain was a dance Thomasin had learned during her time at court, but she was not really in the mood to join in.

"I recall it vaguely. I will direct you if I see you taking the wrong steps."

"You will not join us? It would be better if you were by our side to guide us." His blue-green eyes sent out a silent appeal.

"Go on, Thomasin," urged Ellen. "You must help them if you can, or else they will be all a-muddle instead of Almain."

Thomasin winced at her cousin's painful play on words. "Very well, but it is only to escape from your poor attempt at puns that I agree."

She joined Catherine Willoughby in the centre of the room as the musicians struck up their opening chord.

"Thomasin!" said the child. "You must follow me!" And she started her pattern of steps.

Laughing, Thomasin did her best to keep up, although little Catherine was so fast and nimble, twirling about and jumping like a hare. Opposite them, Giles did his best to partner her actions, but she left him behind, too.

"I see you need no assistance," he declared, "but only seek to make fools of your elders who cannot match your speed."

The girl laughed and twirled about again, following the steps through until the end of the song. Giles followed as best he could, his feet fumbling occasionally, and once he had to clutch at her arm to keep his balance. His laughter was infectious, lifting the mood of the whole chamber. Those ladies sitting around the outside started to laugh too at the sight of their antics, and one or two of the younger ones got up to copy their steps. With the last strains of the dance, little Catherine took them both by the hand and made them join her in an elaborate curtsey.

"Well, I don't know about you," Giles said to Thomasin above the girl's head, "but she has quite worn me out."

"Nothing German about that at all!" exclaimed Harry, mopping his brow.

The queen clapped from the doorway, where she had entered unseen during their dance.

"Excellently done, young lady. Now, gentlemen, will you dine in my chamber this day?"

Giles bowed low. "What an unexpected honour, my lady."

"We would be your most humble guests," added Harry, following suit.

"Then you kindly bring us more good cheer. Until then."

Presently, sounds came through the doors to the antechamber, where servants were busy preparing trestles and benches, laying cloth and setting out glasses and plates. More busy hands came to light candles and stoke up the fire, as despite the sunshine, the late spring evenings still could turn out a little chilly.

Thomasin found herself pleased that Giles was to dine with them, and she was interested to observe how Ellen and Harry laughed over a game of chess they had started. When the time came for them to take their seats at the table, she was not surprised to find Giles seating himself beside her, offering her his best smile.

"I have missed this," he admitted.

"Court?"

"Yes, being merry and in good company. Especially yours, Thomasin."

She blushed, spreading out her skirts.

"I lacked good company in the north. I thought often of my friends back at court."

"And now you are here."

"And I intend to enjoy myself, to balance the bitter business of the courtroom. Have you been very merry during my absence?"

He looked straight into her eyes. Thomasin sensed it was a challenge, to get her to admit that she had missed him, but the spectre of Rafe raised his head.

"It has been a difficult time," she said, choosing her words carefully, aware of Catherine at the head of the table. "The queen appears happier today than she has been in a long time."

"And you, Thomasin?"

"I am well enough, thank you."

"And your family?"

"As always, you know."

"I do. I remember that evening at your uncle's house in Thames Street. We spoke freely with each other then, openly, about many things."

Thomasin did remember that night, with its intimate confessions. But Giles could not turn up at court over a year later and expect the same from her. She kept her eyes on her plate.

"Much has happened since then."

"Are you still my friend?"

"Oh yes, of course." She looked up, hoping she had not hurt his feelings. "After all, we are cousins of a sort, are we not?"

"Cousins, yes." He reached for a plate of food before him, spooning out chicken in white sauce with almonds and baked dates. "Will you have some?"

Thomasin accepted the plate from him, hoping it would distract him from any further talk.

"I would have come south sooner, had it not been for my sister," he said.

"Your sister?"

"Felicia. She is a widow who lives at our old estate near York, and she has been quite unwell."

"I am sorry to hear that."

"Thank you, but it required my presence longer than I had anticipated."

"I do hope she is in better health now. I did not know you had a sister."

"She lives very privately. Since our mother died she has been much alone. Part of my time was spent attempting to engage a companion for her, but it had to be the right one."

"Of course. Did you find someone?"

"A bay mare named Shadow. She writes to me that she is happy, but she always tries to put on a brave face."

"A horse?"

"Yes, she likes horses and dogs far more than people."

"Could she not come to court, or to London, at least?"

"No, she would not. She has an absolute abhorrence of travel and cities. She lives largely out of doors, whenever she can."

Thomasin thought that Felicia Waterson sounded more interesting and unusual than these snippets suggested. "She is unmarried?"

"And likely to remain so. She is not overly keen on men and will only tolerate me for short periods!"

Thomasin laughed a little at this. "Sorry, I did not mean to sound rude."

"I know. She is quite the eccentric."

They ate steadily as Thomasin digested this intriguing information. Opposite, Ellen and Harry were deep in conversation about life at court.

"I had thought to write to you once or twice, Thomasin," said Giles suddenly, "but I was unsure. I apologise now. I should have done so. Would you have minded?"

"No," she said lightly, "not at all. But it is of no matter."

"Very well. I was thinking of calling on your parents and uncle soon, to pay them my compliments. Perhaps you would wish to accompany me?"

"Perhaps, if I am able to leave the queen. I only had leave a few days ago, though."

"Of course. You take your duties to her very seriously."

"Yes, I do," she said firmly. "Very seriously."

Their glasses were filled with wine again. Thomasin felt a little discomfort, torn between her loyalty to Rafe and her enjoyment of Giles's company, who clearly wished to re-establish their old connection. Yet something prevented her from speaking openly. Rafe was her secret. Until their engagement was announced, she felt she should not speak of it to anyone, save Ellen.

"Now look what we have here!" Giles's eyes shone to see the plate of suckets and gingerbreads set before them, stained with red and yellow dye and decorated with candied fruit peel.

When the meal was finished, Catherine rose to her feet to withdraw to her inner chamber. The candles were burning low and night was falling outside the lead-panelled windows, bringing down a blanket of deep blue velvet. Servants were clearing the table and guests were departing.

"Giles, we should be leaving these ladies in peace," said Harry, approaching.

"I am loath to leave when the cheer and food are so good," Giles admitted, "but as in all things, I should listen to your sage advice."

"Have you been friends long?" asked Ellen.

Giles nodded. "This past ten years, I believe, although I have not always been close enough to benefit from his wisdom."

"Wisdom, my teeth!" said Harry, laughing. "I have precious little of that to share, but he makes a good enough drinking companion."

"I believe that is our cue to depart. Come along, or else the ladies will think less of us for it."

Giles turned to Thomasin. "Does the queen need you yet, or can you see us off at the river?"

Catherine's door was firmly closed, with Maria and Mary inside.

"Of course we can," Ellen replied with a smile, taking Harry's arm. "But we must be quick."

It was only a short distance, through the court, under the archway to the riverfront where the boats awaited those departing from court. Thomasin allowed herself to be led by Ellen's enthusiasm, wrapping a shawl about her shoulders and heading out into the night air. There was a fresh, clean scent coming from the earth, and the stars spread brightly above them.

"Where are you lodging?" asked Thomasin as they entered the courtyard.

"Not far away, just down near Westminster. It's quite a nice place, really, with a garden and stabling, and less busy than the city itself."

"And will your work with the king keep you here long?"

"As long as the court convenes, I suppose, and after that, who knows?"

They were passing the sundial when the night suddenly seemed to become very dark around them and a figure emerged from the shadows.

"Thomasin! What means this?"

Rafe's face was glowering down at her, his eyes flashing.

"Rafe? I have been looking for you…"

"Who is this man?" He pushed Giles in the chest. "You look familiar somehow. Do I know you?"

Giles drew himself up straight, and Harry appeared at his shoulder.

"I am this lady's cousin, sir. Surely you mean no ill?"

"Have you forgotten me already?" Rafe said desperately. "Just a few days and I am replaced?"

"We were just walking. Nothing more. How can you be like this?"

"I saw you, laughing and smiling, your arm in his."

"As I often walk with my father. None of these things are a crime."

"I saw you, Thomasin, when you thought I was not watching. I saw you! Are you indeed so fickle as your sister?"

"No," she replied, horrified. "Are you so easily mistaken?"

He glowered back, chewing over more words.

"Come now," said Giles. "This has the appearance of a misunderstanding, nothing more."

But Rafe turned on his heel and disappeared into the darkness.

Thomasin wondered if she should run after him, but his accusations cut her to the bone. Surely by now he should know her better than that?

"I fear we have overstayed our welcome," said Harry. "We will leave you here and make our own way to the river."

"I am so sorry," said Thomasin, feeling Rafe's rage hanging heavily about her shoulders. "That was quite unexpected."

"We will bid you goodnight, with the hopes of a happy reunion soon," said Giles. He paused, then went on, "Perhaps I speak out of turn, but if you have intentions or feelings towards that young man, or any desire to unite your heart with his … then he should know you better, Thomasin."

His words so echoed her own feelings that she could only nod and bite back tears.

"We bid you farewell."

The pair waved and headed away towards the gate, leaving the women standing in the garden.

"Oh, Thomasin," said Ellen, laying a gentle hand on her arm. "What a horrible scene."

"I had truly thought us past all this. I thought he had left this childish suspicion behind."

"Had he been drinking?"

"I don't know. Perhaps. What I cannot forgive is that he compared me to Cecilia. Did you hear him?"

"I did. It was unforgiveable."

"I know he was angry, but…"

"But he had no cause to be, Thomasin, did he? He just saw you with another man and jumped to conclusions."

"And what must Giles and Sir Harry think of us?" Thomasin let out a groan. "Did you hear what Giles said when he left?"

"He was quite right. How can you wish to marry a man who knows you so little, or who disregards what he knows?"

"It is not the first time. He had the same reaction once before. To Will."

"Will Carey?"

Thomasin nodded as she remembered her old friend, lost to the terrible sweating sickness. They had grown close one summer, at Greenwich Palace, although Carey had still been married to Mary Boleyn at the time.

"I should try and speak with him when he calms down. Make it clear that I cannot tolerate this behaviour."

"That is more than he deserves, truly, Thomasin. He should be the one to seek you out. Let us sleep on it and see how you feel in the morning. Come, the queen will be seeking our assistance soon enough."

Thomasin threw one last look about the gardens, where night had settled into all the corners. All was so still and peaceful. Where was Rafe now?

EIGHT

Bishop Longland inclined his head towards the queen. Catherine was seated on the great chair in her antechamber, draped in finery of deep green and gold, in order to receive the delegate from the court. Beside Longland stood John Clerk, the Bishop of Bath and Wells, wearing his black and white gown.

Thomasin rested her hand against the wall beside her. She had slept little the previous night, tossing and turning with Rafe's angry words chasing around her head. Across the room, Ellen shot her a concerned glance.

Longland and Clerk had arrived early, soon after Catherine had broken her fast. Neither looked too pleased to be the messengers of the Papal Court, but they had a duty to fulfil, no matter how uncomfortable it made them.

"And thus, my lady," Longland proceeded, "the archbishops have sworn their oaths and under their scrutiny the court proceeds to examine the relevant documents and precedents in this matter. This will take a number of days before the evidence is assembled. Your good self and our most serene, diligent and devoted king must attend in due course."

Catherine's eyebrows rose at the adjectives used to describe her husband.

"If it please you, my lady," he continued, "to be present in the court on the morning of June the eighteenth, in order to state your case."

"It does not please me." The queen's voice was icy. "It does not please me at all, as you well know, Bishops. However, if I am summoned by the Pope's court, I am duty-bound to obey out of my deepest respect for his office."

The bishops nodded as if a concession had been reached.

"The king will be present in the court to hear you speak, and you should stick to the matter of your previous marriage..."

"Which was unconsummated."

"And..." The bishop faltered briefly. "And the matter concerning the validity of your present union. Present your understanding of the case as it stands and your reasons for..."

"Thank you, I need no instructions about how to speak on my own behalf."

"My apologies, my lady, of course not. Perhaps instead, I may ask if there are any questions you wish to ask of us ahead of your appearance?"

Catherine rose to her feet majestically. "I wish to ask what has become of the lawyers that were to have come out of Flanders to defend me."

"I believe they have remained in Flanders, my lady."

"How so?"

Longland looked anxiously at Clerk. The second man spluttered, "They were advised to do so, my lady, given that their presence in England may cause a threat to their persons."

"And who gave this advice? Who warned my lawyers to stay away?"

Neither man answered.

"Speak up, gentlemen. I can't hear you."

"I believe it was the Emperor, my lady," Longland offered, "but I might be wrong."

"My nephew? Charles? I cannot believe it. Why would he advise against them helping me?"

"Perhaps because he wants the king's assistance against the French," said Clerk bluntly.

There was a silence. Catherine absorbed this betrayal with a stoic expression, but Thomasin could see the information was turning to stone inside her.

"That is all. Leave me now."

She waved her hand, and the bishops bowed and made their way to the door.

Watching them depart, Catherine began to mutter under her breath, her voice rising after they had gone. "This cannot be. I will not believe it. Maria, fetch me paper and ink. I will write to my nephew at once."

She vanished into her room, and Maria went scuttling after her.

Thomasin flopped down onto a stool. The room spun, hazy and indistinct, before settling back into its familiar lines.

"Mistress, are you quite well?" Mary, Lady Essex, was standing above her.

"I didn't sleep so well. I'm a bit dizzy, that is all."

"Take this chance to rest then. Ellen and I will see to the room."

"That is most kind of you."

"Pay it no mind. You have often done the same for me, in my old age."

She bustled away to fetch the sewing basket.

Thomasin leaned her head against the wall beside her and closed her eyes. Gradually, the sounds of the room settled, and there was nothing but birdsong outside and the crackle of the fire.

She woke presently at the sound of footsteps gently approaching.

Ellen was looking down at her. "Sorry I woke you, but your father is in the antechamber."

Thomasin was suddenly alert. "Father?"

"Yes, he just arrived, asking for you. Shall I tell him to return later?"

"No, no." Thomasin adjusted her headdress. "I will be there in a moment, thank you. Did I sleep for long?"

"An hour, perhaps."

"So long! You should have woken me."

"It did no harm," said Ellen, smiling kindly.

Sir Richard was waiting in the window, looking over the garden. He turned as Thomasin entered the room, but she was relieved to see him not looking too concerned.

"Father, what is it?"

"Nothing to fear. I came to tell you about our plans."

"Plans?"

"Firstly, concerning Sir Hugh Truegood, my errant son-in-law. So far as I can see, he has left London. I called at his house on the Strand to find it quiet and dark, his stables empty. I am hoping he has come to his senses and returned to Sussex, but we will wait and see."

Thomasin didn't know if this was good news, or whether it was better that Hugh and Cecilia were apart.

"But your mother's melancholy increases. We have received a kind invitation from dear Thomas to visit him at his home in Chelsea and stay a few days, which I think would do her good. He has the most wonderful physic garden there, which your mother would like to see, and it might distract her from Cecilia's plight."

"How kind of More."

"He is all kindness. I hope to meet his wife, Alice, of whom I have heard many good things."

"How I envy you the prospect."

"Well, this is what I have partly called to ask you. The invitation includes you, if you think the queen might spare you. The Papal Court will not sit tomorrow, so you would not be needed there and you might return the following morning by barge, so you would scarce miss a thing. I'm sure the queen would understand."

Thomasin's mind ran in conflicting circles. How good it would be to visit the More family home, where perhaps she might see Margaret again. But she knew how far Catherine relied upon her.

"When can you give me an answer? We intend to leave in the morning, if that buys you a little time."

"I will speak first to Maria, who knows the queen best, to see how she really fares. I do not wish her to feel that I am leaving her when she has greatest need of me."

"Of course not. You must go where your duty lies. There will be other occasions to visit Chelsea, I am sure."

"I will send word to you tonight, I promise, with my decision."

"Tonight then, and you must not fret either way." Sir Richard paused and shot a look towards the door. "How fares the queen? She was visited this morning by the bishops, I believe?"

"Yes, during which she learned that it was her nephew, the Emperor, who has withdrawn her Flanders lawyers. I think she feels that keenly."

"Yes, she must." Her father lowered his voice. "She has been clinging to him as something of a saviour, but I fear he is placing political alliance above family. At least she will have Fisher and More, and no doubt others to speak for her. And myself."

"Cromwell has not yet understood your intention?"

"We spent time yesterday closeted in his chambers, going through various letters and arguments. I am very tactful, mostly silent, but am absorbing it all. I will speak my mind when the time comes, not before."

"How do you think he will react to your departure?"

"I will send him word when I am at Chelsea. Then there will be little he can do."

"Be careful, though. He is a powerful man, determined to succeed. He will let nothing stand in his way."

"I think he does not see me as the enemy. His sights are set firmly upon the Pope. He will meet Wolsey again tomorrow, to prepare more arguments. I am just a small fish in their pond."

"I hope so."

"I had better get back to your mother now. You know how she grumbles."

"Oh, wait." Thomasin remembered she had gathered a little packet of cloves and hurried back into the great chamber to collect them from the chest. She brought them out and laid the small bundle in her father's hand. "The queen was happy to spare these for Mother's sake."

Sir Richard pocketed them. "She will be most grateful. Now, I will be off."

He strode towards the door, when a thought flickered through Thomasin's mind.

"Father, one thing before you depart, I pray you. Have you seen the Boleyns at court? I do not know where Rafe is staying."

"I hear they are at Durham House, and will remain there for the duration of the court, although I believe Mary is to take Lady Boleyn back to Hever shortly. Anne, her father and brother will remain. I imagine that is where Rafe is. I am sure he will get word to you soon."

Thomasin put on a wan smile. "Yes, I am sure."

In that case, what had Rafe been doing here at court last night? She shuddered to think he had come especially to seek her out, only to be faced with her laughing together with Giles.

"Farewell for now." Sir Richard leaned across to kiss his daughter's cheek. "Have I told you recently just how very proud your mother and I are of you, Thomasin? So very proud."

Tears welled in her eyes as she waved him goodbye. His kind words, and Rafe's outburst, suddenly made her feel emotional.

"What is it?" asked Ellen, who had entered the chamber upon hearing the outer doors close.

"Only my foolishness," Thomasin replied, wiping away her tears. "Does the queen need us yet?"

"Yes, she wants to attend chapel, so we must put on her cloak and change her headdress."

"Very well."

Thomasin followed Ellen, knowing from experience that the best way to forget her troubles was by serving another.

The church of St Bride was quiet, as if had been cleared especially for the queen. Bright sheafs of country flowers, brought from the fields outside the city walls, brightened the place and candles burned on the altar and in niches at the side.

The train of women followed the queen down the aisle towards the front of the church, where Cuthbert Tunstall, Bishop of London, awaited them. Thomasin dropped to her knees, close beside the rippling dark edge of Catherine's cloak, and copied the actions of her mistress, clasping her hands together in prayer.

"Bless you and welcome you, my child," he began, "on this and every day granted to us by God's mercy."

Catherine raised her eyes to the splendid stained-glass window behind his head, where the light streamed through, brightening the halo of the infant Jesus. At times like this, thought Thomasin, it was quite possible to believe in God's mercy. But what if the court did not find in the queen's favour? What would that do to Catherine's faith? Her belief in her nephew had been shaken. She had lost her husband. Through the dim, filtered light of the church, it looked as if the queen's thin shoulders were shaking. She was trembling, despite the weight of her cloak, trembling before God, fearful of her fate.

At that moment, Thomasin knew that her place was at the queen's side. She would go to Chelsea another time. Right now, Catherine needed all her friends around her.

NINE

Catherine wielded the piece of paper, standing before the hearth in regal purple and white.

"Alive!" she cried. "The Pope is not dead, he is alive and well! Confound these infernal rumours. What absolute nonsense."

"He is alive?" echoed Maria.

"I have it here, by my messenger, who saw him in Rome just four days earlier. He has recovered from his illness, God be praised. The court may continue."

Thomasin shot Ellen a look, partly of relief, partly of disappointment that her duties must resume.

"Call my supporters!" demanded Catherine. "Call them all here — Fisher, Clerk, Tunstall, Warham, More, Dudley, West, Standish, Shorter. All whom I can trust to speak for me. Summon them here this afternoon and let no others be admitted."

A few days had passed since the opening of the Papal Court. With her father at Chelsea, and no sign of Rafe, Thomasin had whiled away the time in service to her queen, helping her in and out of her heavy dresses, lacing her undergarments, draping her with jewels and pinning her headdresses in place. The hours had passed in prayer, reading from the lives of saints, embroidery and cards, until the women in the queen's chamber began to wonder whether the outside world still existed.

Thomasin and Ellen had made a game of spotting people from the window: the occasional stable boy, or a maid carrying wood. But the court felt very quiet, despite the presence of many important people under its roof.

That morning, Catherine had emerged from her chapel with a mission. Inspired by her prayers, she was calling a meeting of her closest counsel and learned friends. Lately her prayers had been full of her daughter, and Thomasin could not help but wonder if this action had been prompted by concern for Mary's welfare.

"They must be here at one of the clock, or as soon after as possible, unless they are from the city. Send messengers at once, and prepare my great chamber."

Thomasin pictured the letter being carried through green fields and along leafy May lanes, towards Chelsea. It would interrupt More in his garden, where he bent over herbs and flowers, and offered up their scents to her parents. But the queen's will had to be obeyed.

Maria approached Thomasin, her face concerned. "Take the order down to the kitchen for wine and spices, and a few plates for good cheer. You know the kind of things the queen likes — Spanish cheeses, marmalade, figs and strawberries if they have any in season. Saffron and honey cakes, whatever can be produced at short notice. Have them delivered up here at one."

Thomasin hesitated, unused to such a request, which was usually passed to the guards outside.

"I want to be certain that this goes well for her," explained Maria, "as well as possible. I don't trust the guards to make the right requests."

"Very well, I understand."

"Ellen, I am sending you to the laundry for fresh linen and then to the cellar for more wine, both to arrive by one."

Ellen nodded, understanding at once.

They headed out, closing the door upon the bustle inside.

"If this meeting can give her a little hope, a little courage," mused Thomasin, as they parted ways, "I would venture into hell itself to bring back logs for the fire."

Thomasin was crossing the courtyard when she heard the sound of footsteps. Echoing under the archway, they rose up from the river landing, where the special visitors to Bridewell alighted. Yet there seemed to be something secretive about the way they were moving, with muffled voices and quick steps. She guessed there might be four or five of them, and drew back as they approached the arch.

In silhouette, Thomasin saw them appear: an unmistakeable woman in green, and a group of tall men, walking tall and proud, knowing where they were headed, certain of their welcome. Anne strode at the front, with a waiting woman beside her, perhaps Nan Gainsford, Thomasin thought, although she had a hood pulled over her face. Flanking them were George Boleyn and Francis Bryan, as might have been predicted, as well as the new French ambassador, Jean du Bellay, his lips set in a wry smile. Behind them came the distinctive figure of Rafe. Her heart leapt when she saw him, although his dark brows were furrowed and his lips pursed.

They quickly paced through the court, past the place where she stood in the shadows, and hurried up the steps to the king's apartments. Of course, Anne was visiting Henry, Thomasin realised. That meant she might steal a few moments with Rafe when the king's head was turned. And she had to see him soon, in order to get this nonsense between them resolved. When their feet were out of sight, she cautiously climbed the first step, looking up to where torches burned bright in the darkness. At the top, the figures entered the outer chamber, and the hum of noise within floated down the steps.

Thomasin was left with a dilemma. She could either turn away and deliver the queen's messages, which would summon their recipients to the palace by one, or she could follow. As one of Catherine's ladies, she could probably talk the guards into letting her inside the king's antechamber, on the pretext of delivering some news. Should she play safe, she mused, or take a risk? Should she let herself be carried along by events, or take charge of them herself? When she put it like that, she considered, there was no choice but to follow up the stairs.

And then it struck her. If she was lucky, she might kill two birds with one stone and need no excuse at all. Here in her hands were letters addressed to Bishop Fisher, John Clerk and Archbishop Warham. Whilst Fisher was probably at prayer, there was a good chance that Clerk and Warham were in the king's apartments. Destiny and desire had collided. She hurried up the steps.

"What business?" The guards looked at her with tired eyes.

"I have letters to deliver to those within."

"Who for?"

"Oh, quite a few, who are probably with the king. You know me — I'm a gentlewoman of the queen."

"Thomasin Marwood isn't it?" said the other one, a shorter man.

"Is it?" said the other.

"I know those pretty eyes. You got a sweetheart, Thomasin?"

"I need to deliver the letters. Please let me in."

"Is that a no? You can be my sweetheart if you want. I'll meet you in the gardens after dinner."

"When the queen hears of this, she'll have you strung up for your insolence!" Thomasin warned, fixing him with her steeliest glare.

"Oh, let her pass," said the other, standing aside.

Thomasin didn't wait to be asked twice.

The antechamber was lit by a roaring fire in the grate and torches around the walls. Tapestries and cloth of gold made the place seem rich and colourful. A few people stood about, talking in groups or playing cards on a trestle, while a lute-player strummed softly in the corner. Anne and her party had passed straight through into the next chamber. Thomasin caught a glimpse of her green dress as the doors ahead of her closed. She had come this far; it would be a shame to turn back now.

"I have letters to deliver, sent by the queen," she said boldly, lifting her chin.

To her surprise, the guards stepped aside at once. She hurried past them into the next room, which was much busier with people waiting to see the king. A little pang of fear gripped Thomasin's stomach: it reminded her of her family complaining to Henry at Greenwich last Christmas, on the occasion of Cecilia's disgrace.

She was relieved to see Archbishop Warham seated on a chair by a low table, where a clerk was copying down a letter as he dictated. Striding across the room boldly, she curtseyed before him. Warham looked up, his ancient, pale eyes rimmed with red. Approaching eighty, he had lived through decades of conflict, through the reigns of five kings, through famine, plague and fire, and now the weight of the world seemed to settle on his shoulders.

"Forgive the interruption, my lord."

"You are the queen's lady, are you not?" His voice was thin and reedy.

"Thomasin Marwood. She sends you this."

She came closer and held out the letter. The back of the archbishop's hand was a knot of blue veins. He took the paper and broke the seal.

"Tell her I will be there."

Thomasin curtseyed again, then cast a look towards the next pair of closed doors, through which Anne had passed. "I was wondering if John Clerk or Bishop Fisher might be within."

"I doubt it," said the old man. "The king is at pleasure this morning, not the business he professed."

Thomasin did not respond to the air of judgement, and just at that moment, a woman's laugh was heard from within. This was really the point at which she should turn around and go and seek the others to fulfil her commission, but she had come this far.

She knew one of the men on the door. He was John of Hampshire, whom she had once spoken with in the stables while waiting for Catherine to mount her horse.

"Good morning, John," she said with a smile, casting her eyes up at his tall frame. "Might you do something for me?"

He gazed at her, half interested, half suspicious. "Will it get me in trouble?"

"Not at all, or I should never ask. I just wondered if you might call Rafe Danvers out for me, for a moment. Say there is someone wishing to speak with him."

"You've come a-courting here, in the king's chambers?"

"No!" Thomasin said defensively, flushed with annoyance. "I just need to speak with him, if you would be so kind."

"Very well, one moment."

But at that moment, the doors swung wide. In a flurry of skirts, a vision of green came striding through and then stopped abruptly.

Anne Boleyn looked Thomasin right in the face. She was bold and dazzling as ever, holding herself with an ease and grace that surpassed all but royalty. Her cheeks were flushed and her dark, dancing eyes, framed by long lashes, caught the intruder.

"Well, well, what do we have here?"

Thomasin immediately dropped a curtsey.

"Thomasin Marwood. What on earth are you doing, creeping around the king's apartments uninvited, listening at doors?"

The words came rushing to her defence before she could stop them. "It wasn't that. Ask the guards — I was awaiting admittance."

"But what on earth for? What business can you have here?"

Thomasin lifted her chin, refusing to be intimidated. "The queen's business. I have letters to deliver."

Jean du Bellay crept alongside them and stared down at the letters in Thomasin's hand as if they might go up in flames. He leaned close and whispered something to Anne.

Anne's hand shot out. "Give them to me and I shall see that they are delivered."

Immediately, Thomasin drew the papers close to her chest. "Forgive me, madam, but I was enquiring of the guards whether the recipients are within. If they are not —" and she knew they were not — "then I must carry them away to deliver elsewhere."

"Who are they for?"

Thomasin hesitated but could not ignore a question from someone of Anne's status, no matter how much of the queen's authority she carried with her. "John Clerk and Bishop Fisher."

"Indeed." Anne raised her eyes. "Give them to me and I shall see whether they are in the room."

"I beg your pardon, madam, but I hope you would already know that, as you were in the room yourself."

"But you will never know, will you, whether or not they are here?"

Anne's eyes narrowed; she was clearly determined to have her fun. She caught du Bellay's eye and some communication passed between them.

It was then that King Henry appeared beside her, tall and wide in royal blue and gold.

"Who is it? What is this talk? Have you given the order?"

Anne demurred, lowering her lashes. "An unexpected visitor."

Henry stared down at Thomasin with his small, pale blue eyes. His presence was always imposing, but it no longer had the power to overwhelm her as it had when she'd first come to court.

"Mistress Marwood."

"My good lord, forgive my intrusion."

Behind Henry, Thomasin could see Rafe, hovering inside the chamber. He frowned as he saw her kneeling before the king and her heart sank. Her risk had been misjudged after all.

"Come," said Henry, turning to Anne, "I intend to reach the bridge before high tide."

He strode past the spot where Thomasin crouched, trying to make herself as small as possible, and Anne followed him without another word. Thomasin smoothed out her skirts and rose to her feet as they swept out of the chamber.

Rafe was left staring at her through the open door. Once the king had disappeared, he came forward.

"What are you doing here?"

There was a strain of annoyance in his voice that wounded Thomasin. She decided not to admit her true motives.

"I am delivering letters for the queen."

"Who to?"

"Bishop Fisher and John Clerk. I had already found Archbishop Warham here, so I thought it best to ask before I went on my way."

"What letters?"

"Private letters from the queen."

"Well, they are not here."

"No, I gathered that."

They stood in awkward silence. Thomasin waited for him to speak, perhaps to offer a gentle word or an apology for the other night, but his mouth was set firm. His chestnut eyes were hard. He seemed so contradictory to her, as if there were two Rafes, one kind and warm and the other hard and cold. Shaking her head, she turned to walk away, still hoping to be called back. He said nothing.

As she reached the final set of doors, Thomasin was choking back the tears that had risen in her throat. Just a few days before, they had been set to announce their engagement. She had believed all these difficulties between them to have been resolved: Rafe had seemed to get past his insecurities and immaturities, but perhaps he had just been trying harder to conceal them. How could he treat her this way? Was her heart, and her future, even safe with him?

TEN

Thomasin, Ellen and Mary, Lady Essex, were sent out to gather cherries from the orchard while Catherine met with her supporters. The orchard was a small, walled enclosure, attached to the side of the palace complex, best placed to catch the sun. Mary grumbled as they trod the path, placing her hand upon the small of her back.

"It's bad today. Shooting through my hip and all down my leg." She eased herself down onto a stone bench. "You two make a start. I'll help when the pain has eased."

"Is there anything we can fetch you?" Ellen asked.

"Nothing, but a few moments' rest, I thank you. It's what you get after having children, you mark my words — your body will never be the same again."

She arched her back and rolled back her shoulders, turning her face towards the sun.

Thomasin and Ellen took their baskets and picked their way through the long grass, which was dotted with wildflowers. The trees were spread out, with their little packages dangling enticingly between clumps of leaves.

"I fear it is too early in the season for many," Ellen said, pulling down a nearby branch. "There are one or two, but most will be too hard yet."

"Some are pale," Thomasin admitted, inspecting a tree, "but there are a good few here. I think the orchard being so sheltered brings them on early." She plucked a few firm, pale red fruits and dropped them into her basket.

"I suppose they could always be candied, or made into a conserve," said Ellen, following her lead.

"I wonder what they are saying in the queen's chambers right now," Thomasin mused after a while.

"Not the truth, that is for sure," Ellen replied swiftly.

Thomasin paused, her hand upon a branch. "What do you mean?"

"Well, no one is being brave enough to tell her the truth, are they?"

"What do you mean? What is the truth?"

Ellen stopped and looked at her cousin. "That she cannot win this. The king will have his way. He always does, no matter what the court finds. It can only cause more heartache and pain for the queen the longer she fights it."

Thomasin looked at her cousin aghast.

"What?" said Ellen indignantly. "Surely you must see that? You don't think Henry is ever going to return to her bed, when there is Anne, and a thousand others like her ready and willing?"

Thomasin swallowed. "I know, but it's just … the way you put it, it's so harsh."

"But that's the problem. No one is telling Catherine the truth. No one is being direct. She can't win. Not for all the Popes and Emperors and foreign lawyers. She can't win because Henry doesn't wish it. And while they explore new legal arguments and find new biblical quotations, it only draws out her suffering."

"Would you be the one to tell her, like this, as bluntly as you spoke to me?"

"Not for the world."

"There we are, then."

Thomasin turned back to the cherries, but Ellen had not yet finished.

"But someone must. She is living with false hopes, breaking her own heart."

"I think the king has already done that for her."

"Indeed. But the time has come for her to recognise the truth."

A silence fell between them. Thomasin gazed at the dancing green leaves before her.

"What has brought about these thoughts?" she asked Ellen eventually.

Her cousin sighed. "Seeing how the queen suffers daily. How the king acts. Anne herself. It has gone on too long. He will never return to her."

"But she will never give up her queenship."

Ellen made no reply.

"What? You think she should step aside and admit that the marriage was untrue, and live as the dowager princess of Wales that she was twenty years before?"

"It may be the only way. I do not think Henry will wait much longer."

Thomasin thought of the impatient king striding past her this morning. She could not deny he was a man who got his own way.

"He and Anne are so close now, together so often," Ellen continued. "What if she were to conceive a child? What then?"

"There is no point speaking of things before they have happened."

"I disagree," said Ellen quietly. "Sometimes it is better to be prepared."

Mary was rising from her seat and approaching them among the trees.

"Have you many?" she asked. "Shall I pick more?"

"If you can find any ripe ones," Thomasin suggested. "We can take a few more. The queen doesn't want us back yet."

When their cherry baskets were full, they sat on the benches and turned their faces towards the sun. The peaceful moment did not last long, as a figure appeared in the orchard doorway.

Ellen got to her feet at once. "It's Sir Henry Letchmere. I'll go and speak to him."

Thomasin watched her go in surprise. The pair greeted each other politely, then he offered her his arm and led her into the rose garden beyond the gate.

"Is he her sweetheart?" asked Mary.

"I don't know," confessed Thomasin, wondering at this new Ellen. "She has not spoken to me on the matter."

"No, but she keeps her feelings close, that one," Mary observed. "She conceals her griefs and joys, but that doesn't mean she doesn't feel them."

Thomasin suddenly felt that she had quite overlooked her cousin, accepting her assurances of stoicism without probing much beneath the surface.

"I fear," she said softly, "that I have been so concerned about my own matters that I have not been the cousin she deserves."

Mary patted her knee. "You are both young. It is natural. Plenty of time to put it right."

"Is life really this hard?" Thomasin turned to her companion suddenly, thinking of Rafe. "Why can't it be happy and simple, without disagreements and pain?"

"It is the way of the world. These things are sent to try us."

"But how much do we need to be tested? The queen, in her situation, surely has already suffered enough?"

Mary looked down into her cherries. "You would think so, wouldn't you?"

"Then what is God's purpose, in making us suffer this way?"

"I am an old woman now, my girl. I have lost loved ones, weathered storms, survived illness and hard times. What I have learned in that time, is that it is impossible for us to understand his plan. We must be accepting of our situation and do the best we can with the cards we have been dealt."

Thomasin's indignation rose at this. "But what then, of our own will? Do we just give up and not fight to make things better? Must we be passive victims of our destiny?"

"No, child, you did not listen to my message. That last line in particular: do the best we can with the cards we have been dealt. We must accept what we cannot change and use all our strength, cunning and wisdom to play the game."

"It is hard sometimes to think of it as a game."

"Not a game, then, as children play, but a battle of wits. Like a game of chess, where we stand to gain or lose, depending upon which move we choose to make."

Thomasin nodded, thinking again of Rafe. But what card should she play now? Should she fight again for their relationship, or wait for him to come to her, having realised the error of his ways?

Presently, Ellen returned to the orchard, her cheeks flushed. She quietly collected her basket of cherries from the foot of the bench.

"How does Lord Letchmere?" asked Thomasin.

"Very well, thank you. He has asked me to attend the dancing tonight. Will you come too, Thomasin, if the queen permits?"

It was an opportunity to see Rafe, even if things were difficult between them. Perhaps they could clear the air.

"Yes, queen permitting. I had not realised you had established that kind of friendship with Lord Letchmere."

Ellen thought for a moment. "Nor did I. But I think we just did."

On their way up to Catherine's apartments, after delivering the cherries to the kitchen, they met Thomas More and Bishop Fisher coming out.

"Ladies," said More, "good afternoon. I trust you are in good spirits?"

"Well enough, my lord," said Thomasin, pleased to see her friend. "But you have been summoned from Chelsea, I fear?"

"It is no trouble. I will catch the return tide and rejoin your parents."

"I'm sorry for your trouble. They are well?"

"Very well indeed. I left them enjoying the peace of my physic garden."

"How fares the queen?" asked Mary.

"Somewhat ill, I fear. She is confronted by a stalemate with little more than her faith to comfort her."

Thomasin and Ellen exchanged glances.

"She will be grateful for your company," More continued. "Do whatever you can to cheer her. God keep you, ladies. I must away. Will you come, Bishop?"

Fisher nodded a similarly grave adieu and followed.

They found Catherine before her fire, her hands outstretched towards it. She did not turn or speak as they entered, and a warning look from Maria was enough to deter them from approaching. Quietly, Thomasin and Ellen slipped into the furthest chamber, where the queen's bed stood waiting, and set about the business of making it fresh and dusting down the hangings.

"The signs don't look good for dancing," Thomasin whispered to Ellen, as the gloomy mood penetrated the walls of the queen's apartments.

"Let's light some more candles and stoke up the fire in here," Ellen suggested. "A little brightness often helps."

But Catherine seemed to take no notice of their efforts. They strewed herbs on her bed, placed a scented pastille in the hearth and scattered rose petals in her water bowl, to no avail. Dinner was served in the main chamber, a modest spread of which the queen ate little. Thomasin watched her picking strands of meat delicately off the bone and sipping wine so that it barely came into contact with her lips.

Afterwards, she rose and announced her intention to retire early. They assisted her in removing her heavy pearled headdress and drawing out her long, thinning hair. Its ends were frayed and weak, like the feathers of some aged, momentous bird. Their careful fingers found the pins in her sleeves, unlaced her bodice and removed her chains and brooches. Thomasin placed them carefully upon their velvet boards. Ellen slipped the soft kidskin shoes from the queen's feet and packed them away with lavender.

They joined Catherine as she knelt in prayer, her knees bare under her night smock. The moments seemed to drag as she mouthed her way through her devotions, the night deepening around them. At one point she paused, and Thomasin waited for her to rise, but she stifled a sob and resumed her prayer. Finally, she rose to her feet, moving painfully back into the chamber, where little Catherine Willoughby had lit many candles to cheer her. A very faint smile raised the corners of her lips when she saw the girl awaiting her with bowed head.

Thomasin and Ellen assisted Catherine as she climbed into bed, pulling up her sheets and smoothing them over her. Ellen fetched the prayer book she always kept at her bedside, along with the small silver cross she had brought from Spain all those years ago. Often she would hold it in her hand before sleep. With a sigh, the queen called Maria to her side and dismissed the rest of the women with a wave of her hand.

Thomasin followed her cousin out of the chamber on soft feet.

"Do you think…?" whispered Ellen.

Thomasin knew exactly what she was about to say. "It is still early. We might slip out for an hour or so, as we are no longer needed."

"Mary will cover for us."

"Quickly then, before I change my mind!"

Feeling daring, Thomasin slipped out of the outer doors, where the guards eyed her in surprise. She pressed a finger to her lips.

"We won't be long, promise."

ELEVEN

The queen's portion of the palace was dark and quiet as they crept away. Torches burned on the walls and guards stood idly, like dignified statues in the alcoves and doorways. But soon they left the peace behind them, heading out towards the king's rooms, where life and colour crept back in.

Almost at once, Thomasin ran into Sir John Dudley and his wife Jane.

"Thomasin Marwood," Jane greeted at once, having not seen her friend for a long time, on account of her latest pregnancy.

"You stay," whispered Ellen. "I'm going in."

Thomasin watched her slip into the hall, no doubt looking for Lord Letchmere, and turned back to Jane. Her friend was looking well, in a new gown of green and cloth of silver, although she was pinched about the eyes from lack of sleep. By the time Thomasin had finished hearing about Jane's lying-in, and the baby's little habits, Ellen had disappeared amid the crowd.

"Are you coming to dance?" Thomasin asked.

"No, I'm afraid we're just leaving," explained John. "Our carriage is waiting. But while you are here, have you heard my news? My stepfather Lord Lisle is to be married, here in the palace next month. I fear the king will favour Anne and her family in attending, so that the queen will not be informed of it, but I should like you to come."

"How lovely to have a wedding to celebrate," Thomasin replied, smiling. "Who is the bride to be?"

"Lady Honor Grenville, a young widow from the West Country, although her father served at court in the days of the old king. She is quite a fascinating woman."

"I should be delighted to come, and to make Honor's acquaintance. Thank you for asking me."

John nodded, then paused and looked around to see whether they were being observed. "And, Thomasin, I should not say this, but I heard it whispered today that Cromwell will try and bar you from the trial, as you are the queen's eyes and ears."

"Bar me?"

"He intends to find some pretext to expel you from the court, so give him no cause. Do not let him intimidate you. He wants to control the means by which Catherine is informed of proceedings."

The shock of this news took hold of her. She had not realised that Cromwell had even registered her presence.

"Thank you, John. I do appreciate your warning."

"Take care, Thomasin. I hope we will meet again soon. God bless you."

Then he offered Jane his arm and they disappeared into the night. Thomasin stood for a moment, still trying to compose herself. But she was determined that Cromwell should not get the better of her, and now, thanks to John, she was forearmed.

As soon as Thomasin stepped through the doors, the music and bustle chased away all her other thoughts. In their gallery high above the crowd, the musicians were halfway through a lively tune and couples dressed in bright colours were following a complicated pattern of steps that saw them fall into lines, form circles with their hands joined in the centre, then fall back into smaller groups. There was no sign of Ellen, but Thomasin did spot a few familiar faces, as the Duke and Duchess of Suffolk had taken the lead, with their group of friends around them. George Boleyn whirled past her, followed by Francis Bryan, George Zouche and one or two others Thomasin had known before. She turned away in distaste at the sight of William Hatton, her sister's former lover, laughing heartily as he conversed with some of Anne's women.

Thomasin headed to a space at the side, from where it was possible to see the whole hall. It was then that she spotted the king, not dancing, but seated on a chair on the dais, under the royal canopy. Perched on a stool drawn up to his side, Anne was leaning into Henry, whispering something in his ear that made him roar with laughter. Thomasin turned away.

Across the heads of the dancers, Ellen was speaking with Lord Letchmere, a smile on her face the like of which Thomasin had not seen in many months. Not since before the debacle of Cecilia marrying Sir Hugh. She began to wonder again about her sister's behaviour and what the outcome might be.

"Mistress Marwood, might I have this dance?"

Unexpectedly, Sir Thomas Boleyn was looming over her, his steel-grey eyes bearing down upon her like a hawk examining its prey. The final chords of the tune sounded, and the dancers broke up and regrouped. There was no polite refusal to be found. Without a word, she inclined her head and offered him her hand.

Sir Thomas led her into the centre of the space, as if reclaiming his natural position. The king and Anne also rose to take part, and Ellen stepped forward with Letchmere, making a four with the Suffolks. Mary, Duchess of Suffolk, beautiful but recently frail due to illness, smiled graciously at Thomasin on account of their old acquaintance, yet although she admired the duke, Thomasin could not bring herself to fully forgive him for his role in Cecilia's marriage. He was newly returned from France, where he had been on the king's business, and was dressed finely in a doublet of Parisian watered silk.

As the music began, the crowd was jolted into action. A few graceful steps and hand sweeps to the right and left, then a pace forward brought her closer to her partner.

"You are looking well, Thomasin," he said softly, his voice smooth and deadly. She had never been able to shake the sense of him being vulpine.

"Thank you, my lord."

"And your family?"

If he was hoping for gossip about Cecilia, he was not going to get it. "Well enough, thank you."

"Your parents are in London again?"

"For the court."

He said nothing but gave a curt nod, before the music parted them again.

As Thomasin followed her route, Ellen crossed her path, but her cousin's eyes were fixed upon the face of her partner and she did not notice. Thomasin turned back, past the duchess, and rejoined Sir Thomas.

"How fares your wife?" she asked politely.

"She is at Hever, the best place for her health. She will be glad to hear you have asked after her."

Lady Elizabeth Boleyn had become rather fond of Thomasin, despite disliking the court and what seemed to be the start of some confusion in her mind. The last time Thomasin had seen her, she had been looking lost and troubled, so it was reassuring to picture her at home, walking among her gardens.

"Please send her my best wishes."

"I am sure she would be pleased to hear a few lines from you, if you can spare the time."

Thomasin was surprised. "Yes, of course. I shall write to her."

Sir Thomas turned her around to the left, in time with the music, so that the dancers whirled about her.

"My daughter looks well tonight," he said proudly. "I have never seen her more beautiful, more alluring, don't you think?"

Thomasin wanted to laugh. Was he really expecting her to offer some praise for Anne?

But Sir Thomas hadn't finished. He leaned closer to her ear, so she could feel his hot breath, adding, "She languishes with the waiting. Her best years are withering away; her freshness will soon fade, as it does for all women. The sooner this matter is resolved, the better it will be for us all."

Thomasin knew what he meant about women withering and losing their freshness, especially when it came to fertility, but his tone annoyed her. Even Anne was worth more than that.

"Don't you agree?" he asked, when she made no reply.

"I cannot disagree with you," said Thomasin carefully.

"As a woman, you must see her predicament, as it is your own, too."

"Please do not give my predicament another thought," she replied pertly, "as I intend to find a husband whose understanding of my worth far exceeds my freshness."

"Ha!" Sir Thomas laughed. "Anyone in mind, in particular?"

"Not that I wish to divulge. Excuse me."

She turned her back on him in a slightly more exaggerated manner than the dance required, and moved back into the final line.

When the dance ended, Sir Thomas bowed low. Thomasin prolonged her curtsey to allow him enough time to leave before she had to rise again, then turned away in relief. Perhaps she might find Ellen now. Henry and Anne were surrounded by a ring of admirers, complimenting their dancing.

"Thomasin! I was glad to see you across the room." Giles was before her, his smile lighting up his eyes. "I had not thought to find you here."

"The queen is abed already, so I have a brief respite."

"Well, I am glad of it. You had better make the most of it and dance with me."

Thomasin saw Ellen was still attached to Lord Letchmere, waiting for the next dance to begin, so she offered Giles her hand. His company was far more amenable than that of another partner from the Boleyn faction.

"Play a French dance!" Anne's voice rang out over the heads of the assembly. "A brangle, with the dancers in two lines. Strike it up!"

She waved her hands to direct those near her into position. Thomasin and Giles fell into line, with Ellen and Letchmere ending up opposite them. Ellen gave her cousin a shy smile and Thomasin couldn't help noticing that Letchmere seemed to be livelier, even warmer, tonight.

It was a lively tune. Thomasin had seen it danced before, among those in the Boleyn circle, but had never learned the steps herself. Now she followed Giles's lead, keeping one eye on Anne, and managed passably well with the little jumps and steps, and even the funny little turn at the end of the line.

"That's it, you've got it," said Giles, who had somehow intuited that she was guessing as she went along.

"Was I that obvious?"

"Not at all, except to someone like me who happens to be a connoisseur of every new dance move," he joked. "No, really, it's a rare dance. You covered it well. Now turn to your right."

Thomasin turned away as instructed, followed the circle behind Ellen and redoubled to face Giles again.

"There, now you have it. We just repeat those movements and then swap sides."

"You've made it so easy."

He laughed. "Call it beginner's luck."

"Beginner? So you've not danced this before either?"

"It's my first time too. Now swap."

She crossed over with Ellen, circled and returned, impressed by her partner's nimbleness.

"But how did you pick it up so easily?"

"I've been following the king!" He nodded behind Thomasin, and she looked quickly over her shoulder to where Henry and Anne were leading the crowd. "Besides," he added, "how would you have known if I had set a foot wrong?"

Thomasin laughed. "I could have been following your wrong steps all the time!"

He turned about her neatly. "Indeed, I could have been leading you through some strange northern dance."

They straightened out into a line, facing each other. The final chords of the music sounded, and she dropped her curtsey just as Giles made his bow.

It was when Thomasin straightened up that she saw, across the floor, the dark figure of Rafe, who had been watching them intently. A jolt of something raced through her. Was that nerves, or fear? Immediately the moment changed.

"What is it?" Giles read her face and followed her gaze. "Oh, this fellow again?"

She was torn. Stay here with Giles or follow Rafe?

"Thomasin, did you see me dance?" Ellen appeared at her side, glowing with happiness. Lord Letchmere was a little behind her. "We danced so well; Harry knows all these new ones and I just followed him. It was easy!"

"Unlike us," added Giles, "because Thomasin led me the entire way!"

"Honestly, I did not!" she was forced to admit. "It was my first time."

"And how very well you did, too," said Giles, his eyes twinkling.

When Thomasin looked up again, Rafe's glowering face was gone. Her stomach flipped.

"What is it?" said Ellen.

"Nothing." Thomasin tried to force a smile but knew that her cousin was not convinced.

The music started up again for the next dance.

"Come," said Lord Letchmere, holding out his hand to Ellen, "if you can bear another turn about the room with me?"

But Ellen lingered. "Will you dance again, Thomasin?"

"I must be getting older, as I need to rest my aching limbs for a turn," said Giles, bowing as he stepped away from them.

Thomasin felt shame flood through her. He had understood her feelings and given her an opportunity to escape.

"You dance," she said to Ellen. "I may just take a breath of fresh air."

"Very well, but don't be long. And you and Giles made such good partners, too!"

Thomasin smiled wanly and headed towards the door.

The night air streamed down coolly, smelling fresh and clean. For a moment, Thomasin thought of Catherine, lying alone in her bed, fears for the future looming over her.

Her eyes scanned the darkened courtyard. Where might Rafe have gone? Back up to the king's quarters, or down to the river to take a barge to Durham House? It was more likely that he was lurking close by somewhere, perhaps even hoping to speak with her.

In her heart, Thomasin knew why she still clung to him. She had let down her defences and was prepared to commit herself to him. After all her doubts and his many wrong turns, she had finally thought that Rafe had mellowed, matured, and become the man who she could be happy with. She had decided to trust him. To have this happen now, after she had chosen him, was disappointing and exhausting.

Surely he would not have gone far? He must be wanting to speak with her, to sort out this quarrel, rather than running away. That was not in his nature, so far as she had understood it.

Something stirred in the darkness ahead. And as if she had called him, Rafe stepped out of the shadows and onto the path. Her fears were mingled with a twinge of relief. She hadn't misjudged him so much, then.

"Tired of dancing already?"

His tone was bitter, mocking — not the Rafe she had hoped to encounter. More like the old Rafe.

Thomasin took a deep breath. She must approach this carefully, sensibly, with love. "I was dancing; there is nothing more to it. I went with Ellen while the queen sleeps; please don't make something of it."

"With him again?"

"With Giles? He is my distant cousin. It is the first time we have danced together since he returned to court. Surely I am permitted to dance?"

"Oh, but it is how you dance, Thomasin. Laughing and casting eyes at him, as if you would throw yourself at his feet."

She was taken aback by this. "No, that is not true at all. I was simply dancing, along with Ellen. There was none of what you describe."

"I saw you laughing."

"I may have laughed. That is not a crime."

"There, so you admit it."

"I admit nothing. There is nothing to admit." She took a step towards him. "Rafe, what is this? Suddenly you don't trust me?"

"I saw you."

"Dancing. That is all you saw. Openly and publicly. There are no secrets. I thought we had moved past this? Why have you decided not to trust me all of a sudden? How have we moved so far away from that night, just last week, when we were to announce our engagement?"

"I know what men are like. I saw the way he looked at you."

"Nonsense. He is my cousin."

"He is in love with you. I saw it."

"He has just returned to court, after having been away for more than a year."

"He is in love with you and now you have given him encouragement."

Was he? Was Rafe correct and Giles was in love with her?

"I merely danced with my cousin. Rafe, this is unreasonable."

"You should not have!"

"Not danced? Am I never to dance again, or only to dance with those partners you approve? And what about when you're not there?"

"He will appear soon, you wait and see. He will come out looking for you, hoping to take you into the bushes."

"Rafe! This is nonsense."

He stepped closer and made a little growling noise in his throat. That was when she realised he had been drinking too much again.

"You can't believe this. I do not believe this is you," she said, drawing herself up to her full height and looking him in the eye. "You should reflect upon your words. You will regret speaking to me this way in the morning."

"Will I?" he said. "Will I indeed?"

And in a flash, the realisation broke inside her that it would never work out between them. Rafe would never change. There would always be terrible scenes like these.

"You are drunk. You know that drink affects your judgement. You should not drink so much."

"Here we are," he said, leering. "Already playing the part of the nagging wife before the wedding has even been announced. Do you think I will be content as the henpecked husband all my life, at your beck and call?"

Thomasin was stunned. "What a terrible thing to say, and so far from the truth, as you well know. I will not speak with you when you are in this state. You are doing yourself damage and you will rue your words."

She turned to go, but he caught her by the arm and held it tight.

"Let me go! You are hurting me."

"Why don't you call him then, your cousin-lover? Call him to help you!"

"Rafe?" Her fury mingled with shock, tears flooding her eyes.

"And now you turn on the tears for him."

"I do no such thing! It is your barbarous treatment that provokes them."

He looked her in the face. "You are just like your sister."

Those words were the last straw. Thomasin felt the rage course through her as she lifted her hand and slapped him round the face. The contact stung her palm. Rafe dropped her at once, his hand flying to his cheek. His eyes widened in surprise.

"Don't you ever," she said, with the power of her anger suffusing her words, "don't you ever speak to me like that again. Ever."

She did not give him the chance to answer, but turned on her heel and hurried away. Straight into Sir Thomas Boleyn.

He caught hold of her to prevent her from falling. "What is this?" He looked from Thomasin to Rafe, glowering in the background. "Some sort of lovers' tiff?"

"No," she replied angrily, "nothing of the sort."

Thomas frowned. "Has he hurt you?"

"Not in body, no."

"But in heart, in mind? I admit he can be a brute." Thomas looked again at Rafe, then back to Thomasin. "There is no other matter? No delicate concern?"

Thomasin wondered what he meant. Delicate concern? Surely he could not be asking what she feared he was: that their argument had been occasioned by her expecting a child?

"Nothing of the kind!"

"Well, then. You should not be out here, alone, with a young man. Both of you should be about your business. Go to it."

He stood aside to let Thomasin pass, burning with indignation, then summoned Rafe with an imperious wave.

Thomasin felt as if her insides were on fire. The indignity, the shame, of Thomas Boleyn suggesting she might be with child! That she might have already surrendered herself to Rafe! Oh God, let him not tell Anne of his suspicions. The cool night air stung the tears upon her cheeks as she headed back up towards the queen's apartments. So many times in the past she had considered taking that final step with Rafe, and reasoned her way out of it, letting her head rule over her heart. What a good thing it was that she had been so wise. How relieved she was now that the predicament Lord Thomas suggested had not come true. To be pregnant and dependent upon Rafe for her welfare and her happiness: the thought sent a shudder through her. No, it could never be. He would never make her happy. The engagement, along with her hopes and dreams, was over. She must break with him, once and for all.

TWELVE

Thomas Cromwell stood barring the door with his wide, fur-lined bulk. With a hand on each hip, he surveyed the woman standing before him, who only reached up to his shoulder in her pearl headdress.

"The court is full enough. Your presence before was an oversight."

But Thomasin was forearmed, remembering John Dudley's words. She thought of all the times Cromwell had put pressure on her father, even coming to her uncle's London home for the purpose. She took a deep breath.

"I am here on the authority of the queen, whose vested interest in the outcome of this court overrides all other concerns. As the queen's representative, I demand that you admit me to the chamber."

Cromwell's eyes shifted from left to right. He had clearly thought he could intimidate a mere girl, but he had seriously misjudged Thomasin Marwood.

She pulled a paper from her gown. "Here is the queen's permission, written in her own hand, confirming her desire for me to attend. See, her own seal. Would you deny the queen's direct command?"

Cromwell muttered something under his breath.

"Was that your answer, my lord?"

"This is most irregular," he began, "most irregular to have random women of the court in attendance as if this were some sort of dance."

"I have not come here to dance, nor am I the random woman you describe. This court has summoned the queen to attend and she has appointed me in her absence to hear the proceedings. Or do I have to appeal directly to the king?"

Thomasin had chosen her words carefully that morning. She had risen with the light, splashing rose water on her face and taming her long, unruly locks with a wooden comb. Her hand-mirror told the story of tears in the night, and secret, silent resolutions, but she was determined to start the new day afresh. With the queen's blessing, and fortified by bread and curds, she had made her way across to Blackfriars, knowing exactly what to expect. It was pathetic really, she thought, looking at Cromwell, when men's devices were so transparent and illogical. And such a waste when their talents could have been turned to improving the world.

"Is there a problem here?"

The dear, welcome face of Sir Thomas More appeared at her shoulder.

"Good morning, my lord. Unfortunately, Master Cromwell is attempting to refuse my entrance into the court's chamber this morning."

"Surely not?" More turned his scrutiny upon Cromwell. "Upon what grounds?"

"Apparently because I am female."

"Is that so?" He raised his brows. "And what qualification does that bestow? For sure, many females of my acquaintance have twice as much common sense, good manners and sharp wits than many of the men already assembled within. Surely that cannot be the reason."

Cromwell sighed, attempting to ignore them.

"And he tells me that the court is full," Thomasin continued, "although looking over his shoulder, you and I can both see that there are plenty of empty places within."

"Well, it cannot be that, then," said More, playing along.

"The only thing remaining is that he does not accept that I have a legitimate reason for attendance, but here, in the queen's own hand, I have her written instructions to attend as her representative. So he chooses to disregard the queen's word. I fear I must appeal directly to the king, or to the cardinals."

Upon that, Cromwell snatched the letter out of her hand and broke the seal. He scanned the contents quickly.

"And now I have read the letter, and am pleased to allow you admittance," he said in oily tones, turning his back upon her.

Thomasin decided not to argue further. She had won her point, but Cromwell was not a man she wished to make a worse enemy of. The court had already begun its formal opening proceedings, so she hurried inside and took a seat beside More. There was no sign of her father, though, only Wolsey and Campeggio on the dais, surrounded by officials making notes, Bishop Fisher, the king's clerks and a few others, listening to the pronouncements of various authorities on the matter.

"All that and I fear it will be dreadfully dull," More whispered.

Thomasin knew he was right, but having established her right to attend, she could at least anticipate being present when things finally started to liven up.

Wolsey was speaking at length, establishing legal precedents for the case, and Thomasin's mind began to drift. She could not help revisiting the painful scene of the previous night, with Rafe's cruel words and Thomas Boleyn's assumption. Both men had thought her like Cecilia in some way, accusing her of immoral conduct. Their crudeness made her feel stronger. Boleyn, Rafe, Cromwell and even the king were men trying to judge women according to their own tawdry standards, to bend them to their will. She would not accept it. Alongside the queen, she would stand against such monstrous treatment. Rafe would find her dignified and distant. She would dance with whomever she pleased, laugh with whomever she pleased, and find a man cast in the same inspiring mould as her good friend Thomas More. But where might she find such a man?

Wolsey rose to his feet, drawing her attention back to the court. She spotted Cromwell on one of the benches, looking at her out of the corner of his eye. Behind him sat her father, Lord Richard Marwood. He was listening intently to Wolsey's closing speech and had not yet seen her. No one else but her could have read the conflict behind her father's eyes. She knew he was walking a fine line, allowing Cromwell to believe in his support, but intending to contradict him in his evidence. The Marwoods' support for the queen might mark them out as targets: they would both have to be careful.

Wolsey was rising to his feet. He fumbled with a packet of letters and looked around at those gathered before him. Thomasin sensed a note of hesitation in his manner: no, Wolsey could not fail now, not at this crucial moment. The French ambassador, Jean du Bellay, seated to the right, shifted expectantly in his chair.

"Our king is of an age where another marriage may furnish him with the son and heir the kingdom requires. Our ally and brother, King Francis of France, has given his personal assurances that his own sister-in-law, Princess Renee, is sound in body and health, making her an excellent choice for marriage. Once this matter is concluded, she can be brought to England with the greatest haste and I myself would officiate at the wedding ceremony. God willing, the king might be blessed with a male child by the end of a twelve month."

Thomasin could hardly believe what she was hearing. No one believed that Henry was interested in a French princess. She nudged More.

"Is Wolsey mad? Henry would marry Anne straight away."

"But Wolsey still won't believe it. He ascribes the king with purer motives."

"But it is plain for all to see."

"He has always favoured France and has spent too much time there lately. And he has guided the king for so long that he can't accept that they may not be of one mind."

"France would be supportive of a marriage alliance to strengthen our mutual position against the Emperor," Wolsey continued. "Some English privileges in Spain and Flanders might be lost, but this is nothing compared with the potential gains to us through an alliance. Nor would the Emperor wish to risk war or jeopardise our important mutual trade. Now that the Duke of Suffolk has returned from France, he will speak to us on this matter."

Suffolk rose and surveyed the chamber with a detached gaze. He was looking older, Thomasin thought: still handsome, but greyer in the beard. "I met with the King of France at Blois, where he was as gracious and hospitable as ever. He is most eager for any match that would unite him with England, especially a match between King Henry and Princess Renee, which would make him a brother to our most excellent king. According to the terms of the League of Cognac…"

"Is Francis still intending to marry the Emperor's sister?" Fisher interrupted.

Suffolk frowned. "I am sure you are well aware that those promises were extracted from the French king under duress, whilst he was a prisoner of the Emperor, and cannot be held binding."

"Yet he has not refuted them," Fisher added.

"Again, you will know that the king's own two sons are still being held in Spain as hostages for their father's compliance. It is in their interests that he does not break openly with the Emperor until their return, or until he has sufficient support behind him to do so. An alliance with England might weigh upon the Emperor and effect their release."

"But this means a promised alliance in secret. Can we expect the princes to be returned to France imminently? If not, your time scale of an English heir within a year cannot be met."

Suffolk looked angry. "It is a matter of urgency, upon which our ambassadors are engaged as we speak."

"What say you, de Bellay?" asked Wolsey, motioning towards the ambassador.

"I have little to add," the man affirmed, with waspish eyes. "All that Suffolk says about the position of my king is true. He awaits the return of his sons eagerly, but does not wish to jeopardise English plans. But is it not that king whose life is under investigation in this courtroom."

"This is very true," said Wolsey, "but it is the place of this court to establish the likelihood of a French match occurring in the event of it declaring the king's present marriage null and void."

"Surely," snapped du Bellay, "the marriage is either null and void in the eyes of the court, or it is not. This should not be affected by the potential outcome. The king's marriage is not yet broken, so any discussion of his next one is immaterial."

Wolsey's face assumed a tired expression and he sat down heavily in his seat. He motioned to Campeggio to continue.

"Setting aside the details of such a marriage," continued the second cardinal, "the matter in hand is urgent precisely due to the king's desire to father a son in legitimate wedlock. That cannot be denied. So, to turn back to the marriage and its dissolution: there are precedents in such cases. As we are already discussing France, I would cite the example of Renee's own father, Louis the Twelfth, late of fame, who set aside his first wife Joan in the case of childlessness and went on to produce issue. There was also Henry the Fourth of Castile, whose first wife had failed to arouse him to, shall we say, the necessary act, so the marriage was annulled by the Bishop of Segovia."

Beside Thomasin, More spoke out. "The Castilian marriage was annulled on the basis of the king's impotence, supposedly as the result of witchcraft. Surely you do not suggest a parallel case here, with all the implications for a lusty king who has already fathered children?"

"I do not," replied Campeggio steadily. "I merely say there are precedents for annulment where there is good cause. And the common cause in both those examples is the need for an heir. Or would you have the country descend again into the civil war and chaos that many of you present still recall?"

"Nobody wishes for that," said Archbishop Warham, who had lived through the duration of the struggles between York and Lancaster, "but the country is stable, the nobles are not in conflict and the king has dealt severely with any rebels. Nothing suggests that we are on the brink of such a return. This dramatic rhetoric is unhelpful."

"It is scaremongering," called out More.

"And what of the Emperor's reaction?" Campeggio fought back. "Do you think he will sit calmly by while his revered aunt is thus cast aside?"

"The Emperor who has done little yet to alleviate her situation?" said Fisher. "Who recently advised her lawyers from Flanders not to attend this court due to the potential dangers? We cannot govern this country by living in the Emperor's pocket."

"Perhaps," added Wolsey, "we should all do well to remember that it is the king who governs this country, not us. We are merely his humble servants, employed to carry out his will."

At that, the court fell silent. There was no arguing with the hierarchy that placed them all under the rule of King Henry.

"Gardiner," said Wolsey, turning to his new assistant, "what say you, as a doctor of civil and canon law?"

"Your Holiness has spoken truth," replied the man in a high, reedy voice. "But while there is one king governing this country, we would do well to remember that there is another above us, in heaven, whose word is final."

Something about his pronouncement sent a chill down Thomasin's spine. Gardiner was not wrong. God would judge them all, no matter how right or wrong they believed themselves to be.

Presently, Wolsey returned to the virtues of the French match, and More rolled his eyes at Thomasin.

"Over the years, I have come to suspect that the cardinal is actually a subject of the King of France, rather than a true-born Englishman," he whispered. "Perhaps he should go and live there and spare us his misguided views."

When the court was over, Thomasin and More waited for Richard Marwood outside in the courtyard. As her father approached, Thomasin could see at once that he was troubled.

"This bodes ill," he said, as soon as they were out of earshot. "Wolsey is living in a fool's paradise. How can he be so blind as to the king's true intentions?"

"He has seen the king's mistresses come and go," explained More. "Mistress Blount was cast aside even after she had borne him a son. He believes that Henry will tire of Anne before the match can be made, or that some new face will draw his fancy. He believes that the matter is the marriage, not the woman."

"He has built a career on carrying out the king's wishes; I do not see how he can be so blind as to this one. Surely Henry has spoken with him directly?"

"I would imagine so, but in this he has proved to have cloth ears. They will be his downfall."

"I think he cannot accept Anne due to her status. He cannot see that the king would choose another wife who does not equal his first, from a royal house. The blood of the Boleyns is hardly a match for that of the Hapsburgs."

"He is well past that now," More said, shaking his head. "I think he would marry his laundress if she would promise him a son."

"Shh," Thomasin warned them, as Wolsey and Campeggio emerged into the courtyard with their entourage. Campeggio was leaning heavily upon his stick, heading straight for his room and cures for his legs, while Wolsey looked tired and unsettled.

"The Italian is, well, an Italian," said Sir Richard quietly as the group passed along the path, "but I wonder whether someone should warn Wolsey, speak with him about the dangers. Open his eyes, if we can."

"You think he would listen?"

"I have no idea, but it is worth a try, surely? All this nonsense about a French marriage is making him look like a fool."

"Do you think that it might just be a formality?" asked Thomasin. "He might be offering the king a noble way out of his present marriage, while knowing his true intentions."

"It's possible," More replied, "but he seems overly committed to the idea. He has lashed himself to the French mast, but that ship is sinking."

"It cannot help to try, surely? What can we lose?" asked Sir Richard. "I have known Thomas since his early days at court, when he was in the household of Richard Nanfan, serving the old king. I might appeal to him to hear me, on account of such a long history between us."

More was thinking. "And how does this fit with Cromwell's plan?"

"Master Cromwell need not know. He watches me like a hawk in court, but he must permit me my freedom once in a while."

"What says the queen about Wolsey?" More asked Thomasin.

"Like father, she has known him since her first arrival in England. She had hopes of him, truly, but he has always been the servant of the king above her. This was not a problem when her wishes were the same as her husband's, but now he cannot be trusted to serve her cause."

At the far end of the court, the cardinals parted ways. Thomasin watched as Campeggio hobbled towards the bridge that led to his Bridewell lodgings, while Wolsey retreated into the house of the Blackfriars.

"Now would be as good a time as any," said her father. "Will you accompany me, More? He would listen to you, too."

"I suppose it can do no harm."

"Thomasin?"

"I must return to the queen, while the proceedings are still fresh in my mind. And I do not think that the cardinal would take kindly to being advised by one such as me."

"Your sensitivity does you proud, although you are wrong about the advice, as you speak much wisdom, Thomasin."

"I shall see you again presently, in the court, but the queen's appearance there comes ever closer. Surely then we shall have some kind of conclusion?"

"We will direct our prayers to that hope. God speed you."

THIRTEEN

Ellen was waiting just inside the queen's antechamber, looking out for Thomasin's return.

"You will not believe this," she said, with incredulous eyes. "We are expecting the arrival of the Duke of Norfolk's lady."

"I thought the duchess had left court," said Thomasin, remembering the woman's waspish and tiresome ways.

"Oh, she has. It is not her whom we seek. In the duchess's absence, Norfolk has brought his mistress to court!"

"What?"

"That Bess Holland who used to work in the Norfolks' household. Some say she was the children's laundress, but that is unlikely, surely? She was the daughter of his secretary, we know that much, and she has come to court and intends to pay her respects to the queen. Can you imagine?"

"How does Catherine take it?"

"Very ill. While the duchess is no great favourite of hers, the idea of receiving the duke's mistress fills her with horror. She says it is akin to Anne Boleyn visiting her. Anne's position has made this Bess woman bold."

They entered the central chamber, where everyone turned round to look.

"Oh, it is not her yet, then," said Mary, looking up from her darning.

"It will not be long," Ellen told Thomasin. "Norfolk's servant brought word to expect her within the hour. I wonder what she will look like and how she will conduct herself."

"We shall find out soon enough, by the sound of things. I should go and report to the queen of today's events in court while they are fresh in my mind."

Thomasin found Catherine staring out of her window at the late afternoon sky. The queen did not notice her arrival at first, but eventually she turned and nodded, holding out her hand for Thomasin to kiss.

"Mistress Marwood, you've come from the Papal Court?"

"Yes, my lady, with little pleasant to report."

Catherine's eyes looked tired. "Do proceed."

"Initially my way was barred by Master Cromwell, who tried to argue against my presence on various flimsy accounts, but I was prepared for him, so made my way inside. The discussion was mostly concerning a potential French match that Wolsey intends the king should make, and the legal precedents for separation. Nothing was resolved and little progress made. My apologies, my lady, that I am unable to bring you better tidings."

"You have reported fairly, as I knew you would, Thomasin. It is not for you to set the matter of the court's proceedings."

"I would add, my lady, that the thinking among some of those assembled is that Wolsey is out of touch with the king's intentions. He continues to push for an alliance with the French and is likely to lose the favour of the king on account of it."

"That may be the case," Catherine agreed. "I have sometimes wondered why he is such an ardent supporter of France, but it is no concern of mine. How fared Campeggio? Of him I have greater hopes."

"It was merely routine business on his part. Tomorrow, the court will hear from those speaking in favour of your marriage.

I hope I shall have better news to offer after More, Fisher, the bishops and my father have given their views."

"I have submitted letters from Vives and Erasmus to the court on this matter. I believe even the great heretic himself, Martin Luther, supports my case, so we shall see. Make sure you are at the court promptly."

"Of course, my lady."

The sound of voices from the outer chamber reached them. Catherine looked up, her head on one side, trying to make out their words. Thomasin thought this must be the anticipated arrival of Bess Holland, but it was not her place to speak of this unless the queen herself raised it.

Catherine swept out through the main doors, with Thomasin at her heels. But it was not the Duke of Norfolk's mistress who greeted them, but Sir Richard Marwood, clearly agitated.

"Lord Marwood," said the queen in surprise. "What is the matter?"

"My lady, I have come to speak with you directly, as I scarce know what to make of this, or what to do. It seems that Cromwell has got wind, somehow, of my intention to speak in your favour tomorrow, in court. Now, under some pretence, he intends to send me into the country on a fool's mission, in order to prevent me from offering my defence."

"What? He cannot be so bold! On whose authority does he override mine?"

"It can only mean that he has the king's support, whether directly or tacitly, but I am commanded to leave court at once and deal with some trivial matter arising in the Suffolk assize court. He claims it is of the utmost importance and I must be gone by the morning."

Thomasin could see the queen's anger rising. Her back stiffened and arched; her head flew back. She gripped the back of a chair before her.

"That upstart nobody, that low-born servant, a blacksmith's lad plucked from the streets — how dare he cross me! I am of a mind to find him and speak with him at once."

"He is currently with the king," added Sir Richard.

"My lady," offered Mary, Lady Essex, "I do not think there is anything to be gained by confronting the man. It will only serve to show he has raised your anger, which he might take as a sign of success. Perhaps there is a better way around this. Sir Richard, was the instruction given to you in person?"

"No." He held out a piece of paper. "It came from this damned letter."

Mary crossed the room and plucked it from his hand. "What letter? Who delivered it?"

"A young man in his employ, one Rafe Sadler."

"Did you open it in his presence?"

"No, he departed at once."

"Then let the trouble fall upon his head, or that of chance. What if the letter went missing before you had a chance to read it? And circumstances today kept you so busy, with Cromwell closeted away, that you were unable to find him to enquire of its contents. After all, had it been a truly important matter, he would have spoken to you directly."

Thomasin saw where Mary was going with this. "So you counsel us to pretend ignorance? That the letter was never read, and so its contents cannot be acted upon?"

"I don't know," said Sir Richard. "It is still a deception."

"A small deception for a greater good," said Mary. "And if I have the letter, you can honestly say that it is no longer in your possession. And if I place it somewhere unknown to you, you can tell the truth and say you have no idea what has become of it."

"And if Cromwell makes trouble tomorrow, I can still offer to leave straight after the court, if the matter is so urgent, except I will have already given my evidence."

"He will try and prevent you from entering," Thomasin added, "as he did to me today."

"Then I must ensure I am present before his arrival, even if I must bribe my way in and conceal myself behind a tapestry!"

"There is a servants' passage that passes behind the dais," said Ellen, "with a door opening behind the depiction of Moses. You could enter that way."

Thomasin nodded. "And you'll appear in court, before his very eyes! If you wait there until just before Wolsey and Campeggio appear, he can hardly have you thrown out before them, as he would need to give good reason."

"And Campeggio would not stand for that. His papal authority would override any decision made by the king," added Catherine. "It is an excellent plan, although I am sorry that we must go about it in this manner. And you are always under my protection, Sir Richard, whether in court or countryside."

"I thank you, my lady." Richard gave a low bow.

"I shall meet you early," said Thomasin, "not in the courtyard, as that is too public, but by the stable, where no one would expect us to be, and we shall go to the servants' passage together."

A sound at the outer door interrupted them. One of the guards appeared to announce Mistress Holland.

"Good grief," said Mary. "Brace yourselves."

"She can't be much worse than the wife," muttered Ellen.

All turned towards the doorway to catch a glimpse of the controversial new arrival. To their surprise, however, she was accompanied by Norfolk himself, who strode majestically into the chamber and made his bow before Catherine. The woman at his side was young and slight, with pale colouring and bright red hair pulled back beneath her French headdress. She looked demure, rather than brazen.

The duke drew himself up to his full formidable height. "My lady, may I present Mistress Holland."

The woman curtseyed slowly and deliberately, as if she had been practising.

"Mistress Holland, is it?" Catherine asked, almost through gritted teeth. The Duchess of Norfolk might have been a horror, but at least she was the duke's lawfully wedded wife.

"Yes, my lady." She spoke sweetly, unassumingly.

"We must bid you welcome to court, as convention demands," said Catherine, tempering her welcome with all the reluctance that she could. But the new arrival seemed oblivious to her coldness.

"Thank you, my lady. It is an honour to be here, and to meet you."

Norfolk cleared his throat warningly, as if she had overstepped the mark. The woman smiled shyly, and her cheeks dimpled.

"What do you intend to do, whilst at court?" Catherine persisted. "What is your purpose?"

Mistress Holland's dimples deepened as her blue eyes lighted upon Norfolk. "To serve my good lord, of course."

"We have come, out of courtesy," said Norfolk stiffly, "as custom demands, to enquire about positions. Should there be a place in your lady's household whereby Mistress Holland might fulfil some simple tasks and earn her board and lodgings, as she has many practical skills? Only if it suits you, my lady."

But Catherine was not in the mood to do a relative of Anne Boleyn's any favours. "As you can see about you, my lord, I am already generously provided with women."

"Indeed you are, but I should not have dreamed of asking any but you first."

"I wish you well at court, Mistress Holland. Alas I have no words of advice for you, nor suggestions, as it can prove a dangerous and misleading place, but you may depart with my best wishes nonetheless."

Norfolk glowered as he bent his head in acknowledgement and offered his arm to the lady beside him. But she, oblivious to the undercurrent, threw a beatific smile about the chamber and walked out with her head held high. Thomasin could not help feeling a pang of sadness that this untouched country girl would soon be disillusioned about the true nature of court life.

After they had gone, Catherine turned and retired into her chamber, calling for wine and Maria.

"What will become of that woman now?" asked Sir Richard.

"Straight into the Boleyns' household," said Mary. "That is what they wanted all along. It was mere courtesy to ask the queen first, a formality, before she returns to the fold. We shall see her among Anne's ladies soon enough."

"It would have been a surprise to them had the queen accepted her," said Ellen. "I do wonder how they would have taken it."

"It would have thrown the cat among the pigeons," said Thomasin. "But I am glad how it worked out. It is best for all this way. The more distance between the two households the better."

"She seemed a pleasant little thing," said Mary. "It's a pity she has fallen into Norfolk's hands."

"At least she will be provided for," said Ellen.

"For now." Mary looked towards the queen's closed door. "It reminds us again how our fates are tied to the men who choose us. We rise or fall with their favour."

"What do you really think of this plan?" asked Sir Richard, as Thomasin walked him to the outer door. "Should I attempt to dissemble before Cromwell?"

"You are serving a higher authority in doing so," said Thomasin. "What is giving you cause for doubt?"

"I was never a good liar, Thomasin. It was for this reason that I left court the first time around. I could not hide my true feelings."

"But this time it is in service of the queen, whose need is greatest. Tell yourself that and avoid Cromwell as much as you can."

"There is something about the man that troubles me. There always has been. It is his lack of scruples. I am sure he would happily see me at the bottom of the Thames before I give my testimony in court."

"Do you think?"

"I am sure of it."

"There are others who will testify for the queen: More, Fisher, Tunstall and Gardiner. If you truly fear the consequences, nothing is more important than your own life." She lowered her voice. "Not even the queen."

"I am probably being foolish. Overreacting. I would not wish to cross Cromwell, nor displease the queen. This is a hellish situation we find ourselves in. I will pray to God for guidance."

"It rather depends," said Thomasin, "whether this instruction comes from Cromwell himself, or the king."

"Surely not the king?" said her father at once. "I cannot accept that he would block my appearance, or that any threat comes from him. Above all, we must follow our consciences, but when those differ from the wishes of the king, I know not what to do."

"All will be well, Father, I am sure. The court will summon you tomorrow. You cannot refuse to appear simply because Cromwell wishes it otherwise. You are bound to obey the authority of the Pope."

"I do not believe Master Cromwell gives a fig for the Pope!"

A knock at the door brought in a messenger boy. He saw Thomasin first.

"Mistress Marwood, a letter for your father," he said, then turned and saw Sir Richard. "My lord, what fortunate timing."

Sir Richard took the paper and broke the seal. "It's from your mother at Monk's Place. It seems that Cecilia has turned up there."

"Cecilia?"

"Apparently she has left Sir Hugh in Sussex and come to London, to throw herself upon our mercy."

"Goodness. Well, at least she has arrived safely and will come to no harm under your roof."

"But your mother writes of the shame of it! We must give out some report that she is staying with us while Hugh is abroad, just so long as Hugh remains out of sight!"

"She could return to Suffolk with you and deliver her child there. She is a married woman, after all. No one would question it there."

Sir Richard ran his hand through his hair. "It is possible. But I must go back to Monk's Place now and calm this situation. Your mother appears distressed. All being well, I will return in the morning and meet you at the stable as planned."

"So you will testify?"

"I must answer to God for it, if I do not."

FOURTEEN

Thomasin woke early. There was soft light outside the window, and birdsong, but the day had not yet begun. It had been her turn, along with Ellen, to lie on the pallet beds in the queen's chamber, but for once Catherine had passed a peaceful night and was still breathing softly inside the closed curtains of the great bed.

Had it been cold, Thomasin would have got up and started building a fire, but the summer morning was pleasant enough. She rolled onto her back and stared up at the ceiling, with its carved wooden roses. So many questions flooded into her mind, mixing with the promise of the day ahead. She thought of the court, Cromwell and her father, the king and queen, Rafe's behaviour, and strangely enough, she thought of Giles, too. He appeared in her mind unbidden, with his gentle ways and short bursts of laughter as they had danced the other day. How differently that evening might have ended, had Rafe not come up to court from Durham Place. She might simply have enjoyed the dance, come away bright-cheeked and pleasantly tired, and slept soundly.

Mary's comments from yesterday returned to her, that as women, their fates were tied to the men who chose them. But what about a woman's choice, thought Thomasin? What about shaping your own path, instead of simply following?

As she dressed, swallowing down bread and cheese to stave off her hunger, Thomasin felt her nerves rising in her chest. Today was an important day for the court; leading figures were to give evidence in opposition to the king's desire to annul his marriage. Legally, they might be correct, but as Ellen had reminded her recently, they were merely delaying the inevitable. Henry would get his way, no matter what; it was just a question of how he would justify it.

Sir Richard was waiting at the stable door, just as he had promised. His face was full of concern, but this lifted when he saw Thomasin approach, her hood pulled over her headdress to avoid detection.

"Good morning, daughter, I hope!"

Thomasin met his greeting with a certainty she was determined to cling to. "It will prove a good morning, I am sure. How fare things at Monk's Place?"

"I have only left there under duress this morning. It was as much as I could do to escape the wails and complaints of your mother and sister, even after I had explained to them the summons of the court! But Cecilia is well enough, although she will not leave off crying and calling for me to fight a duel with Sir Hugh. A duel? Me? Can you imagine it?"

"What happened?"

"Apparently Hugh arrived back at Raycroft and there were cruel words between them. As far as I understand, she left of her own accord before he could insist upon it, but he threatened her with divorce or a nunnery, which has quite sent her into a state. It is not good for her health at this point. I left your mother calming her as best she could."

Thomasin thought of the elegant Lady Elizabeth tending to her distressed daughter.

"The whole matter is absurd, of course," her father continued. "Cecilia's bad behaviour means she is being held to account, and justly so, but it is the severity of the accounting that concerns me. I have counselled her to remain with us, and

I hope she will be wise enough to do so for the sake of the child. She must rest and be quiet for her final few months."

"There will be time enough to worry about them later," said Thomasin. "At least Cecilia is safe for now. We must turn our thoughts to the court today."

"Indeed, you are right, although I had been doing my best not to do so."

"People are assembling at the far doors, so we should take our place to be present in time for Wolsey's arrival."

"You do not think Wolsey is privy to Cromwell's plan?"

"Certainly not. He is answerable to the Pope only, not some common upstart."

"Quite. And you have your speech ready?"

"I have been working on it for weeks, unbeknownst to Cromwell, of course, but I dared not commit it to paper, for fear that he would see it."

"That is wise."

"Last night, I examined my conscience and prayed to God. I was here, at court, in 1509, at the time of the wedding. I well recall the concerns raised by Archbishop Warham back then about the validity of the match, but these were well answered by the dispensation issued by Julius the Second. Once a Pope has ruled in favour of a marriage, it cannot be undone, no matter what the king wishes."

"Then it sounds like a strong case."

"The original dispensation was in the hands of the queen's parents, Ferdinand and Isabella, God rest their souls. Imagine how they would react to this situation, were they here to see it! But a copy of it was sent to England, and the original was seen by our ambassador. There is no doubt about its legitimacy."

"The king will not like it."

"Then the king does not like facts."

Thomasin nodded. "Come, let us head for the passage. It will soon be time for the court to open and we must be inside first."

She led her father in through the servants' wing that ran alongside the departments of the kitchen. Sounds of chopping and fires roaring reached them, with the heat flaring through the open hatches. Thomasin caught sight of the activity within as bodies moved back and forth.

Partway along the corridor, a door led them into a waiting room, where trestles and benches were stored, and from which led the passageway.

"It is not long, but it is narrow," Thomasin warned. "I looked at it earlier this morning, but there should be no one around now, as the service hour is still a good way off."

"It will serve its purpose," said her father. "I will follow you."

Heading towards the opening, Thomasin pressed her finger to her lips. There was already a slight hum from behind the curtain, where the officials were setting things up. Very carefully, she parted the two panes with her fingers, so she could see through a narrow gap into the chamber. They were right behind the dais. The table stood before them, but neither cardinal was present yet. Papers were being carried in, ink and quills were being supplied and the benches straightened and swept down.

"Any moment now," Thomasin whispered.

There was an air of expectation in the chamber. It was strange to see the place so empty. For a moment, the future hung before them, tremulous and unwritten. Dust motes swirled in the air as a ray of sunshine shone down through the windows and hit the stone floor.

Presently the cardinals would take their places; the benches would fill up with bishops and statesmen, legal experts and witnesses. People would be called to swear the oath to speak the truth, and their experiences and opinions would be given to the court. Thomasin could see the place where she usually sat, towards the back on the left.

The opposite doors opened, admitting Cardinals Wolsey and Campeggio draped in their red cloaks. Behind them, a sea of heads showed those outside in the courtyard, waiting to be admitted. Thomasin wondered if More and Fisher had had the opportunity to speak with Wolsey yesterday about his French aspirations, and whether they had been able to convince him of the king's true intentions. Hopefully she would have the opportunity to ask them later.

"Now," Thomasin whispered, "we must sneak in quietly and take our places."

They pushed through the curtain and round the side of the table, close to the wall. Sir Richard squeezed Thomasin's hand, then headed to the row of witnesses, just as Gardiner was approaching the same spot. Thomasin kept going, merging with the arrivals, towards the seats at the back. Soon so many people had entered the hall, that their strange isolation was no longer regarded. As More passed her, with a good morning, and Fisher took his seat, Thomasin breathed a sigh of relief.

She had not yet seen Thomas Cromwell enter, but after a moment, the bulk of his grey cloak passed her, causing her to shiver. He did not look down at her but proceeded through the chamber to the place where her father sat, two guards following in his wake. From her seat, Thomasin could not hear what was being said, but after a moment, one of the guards laid a hand on Sir Richard's arm and caused him to rise. Her father looked confused, then angry, before Cromwell spoke with him again. Then, suddenly, both guards seized him and started to walk him out of the chamber. Sir Richard looked round wildly, seeking support.

Thomasin was on her feet at once. "What is this? What is happening?" She moved to block their way.

Wolsey, at the front, had also noticed, and raised his hand to halt their departure. More had already reached them.

"What is this disruption?" asked the cardinal.

Cromwell turned and approached the bench, speaking quietly to Wolsey, who frowned but nodded his head.

"I am being arrested," stammered Sir Richard, still held by the guards, "for failing to follow orders. Fear not, this is all a misunderstanding. Tell your mother!"

"What is this nonsense?" asked More, appealing to Wolsey. "Stop this; it cannot be right. By whose authority is this happening?"

"By the king's," snarled Cromwell, who had drawn level with them again. "Take your arguments to him."

"By God's blood, I shall!" More replied. "Arresting an innocent man obeying a summons! Do you think yourself above the law, Master Cromwell?"

"No," he replied, with a glint in his eye, "I am the law." Then he motioned for Sir Richard to be led away.

Thomasin felt the rise and fall in her chest but could not seem to be able to catch her breath.

"Do not fear," More urged. "This is more for show than serious intent. It is Cromwell's way of making an example of the king's opposition. I am surprised that Wolsey allows it, as it is his court. Wait here; I will speak with him."

He hastened forward and leaned over the raised table. Both cardinals listened but neither spoke. Eventually Wolsey shrugged his shoulders and More looked defeated.

"It is as I feared," he said to Thomasin on his return. "The court may be governed by the Pope's law, but the palace is run for the king's benefit. They have no say over matters of security."

"Security? How has my father offended?"

John Dudley had reached them through the crowd. "This is terrible," he said. "What on earth is the reason given?"

"Failure to follow orders, apparently," said Thomasin.

"What orders?"

She was torn between confessing about the letter and maintaining the fiction that her father must now rely upon. Yet she had no wish to lie to friends.

"It all happened so quickly. It's one of Cromwell's methods to remove the queen's support. He tried to prevent me from entering yesterday."

"We should go after them and appeal to the king."

"The authority is that of the king."

"But surely Cromwell did not state plainly how it was to be carried out? Henry cannot have agreed to the arrest of your father?"

They became aware that the rest of the chamber had now fallen silent.

Wolsey rose to his feet. "Please leave or else resume your seats."

Thomasin felt a sweat break out on her forehead. "I cannot stay."

"Come," said More, taking her arm. "I will go with you."

"But the queen…"

"I will remain," promised John, "and report back to her what transpires."

Once outside, Thomasin gulped in the fresh air.

"This cannot be. I must be dreaming."

More led her aside to a spot sheltered by bushes. "I must ask you, Thomasin: does this have anything to do with your strange entrance from the back of the chamber? I could not help noticing."

"It does. I was not going to say, but it is all part of the same. Yesterday, Cromwell sent father a letter, recalling him at once to Suffolk on some legal pretext."

"Designed to prevent him from giving his evidence in court?"

"Exactly as we interpreted it. As it was only a matter of hours, we decided to pretend we did not have the letter, which is now partly true, as it is being kept by Lady Essex. But we did read the contents first. Father was preparing to leave for Suffolk as soon as the court was concluded."

"But not soon enough for Cromwell. The point for him is about his authority. He will say you have ignored his direct order. Or rather, the king's."

"And that is why we came in from the back. We thought the court would offer us some protection."

"He is utterly ruthless. I wonder where he has taken your father."

"To the king, perhaps, or to his own lodgings?"

More looked about. A servant was passing, carrying a pannier of bread. "You, lad, did you see Lord Cromwell pass this way?"

The boy nodded and pointed. "He was getting into a barge on the riverfront."

Thomasin went cold. She knew what this might mean.

"Now, do not panic," said More, sensing her alarm. "It could be Cromwell's own place in the Austin Friars. It does not have to mean the Tower."

She found she could not reply.

"Right, this is what I suggest. Go to the queen and explain. Do not forget to tell her that John Dudley is now her eyes and ears in the courtroom. Then go to your mother at Monk's Place, and calm her for as long as is needed. I am going to the king, and hopefully this matter will be resolved before the day is out."

Thomasin nodded, her limbs numb.

"Take Ellen with you, if the queen permits. You are in shock."

She nodded again, but did not move.

"Go, Thomasin, go now. Do not delay. You will hear from me presently. I shall call at Monk's Place as soon as I can."

More gave her a little push, which seemed to bring her limbs to life at last. Surely this could not be. It must be some mistake. More would solve it; the king would support his old friend Richard Marwood over the upstart snake Cromwell. The air rushed into her lungs again and her legs sped into action.

FIFTEEN

The carriage wheels bumped over the cobbles. All through the brief journey, Thomasin had been trying to think of the best way in which to break the news to her mother.

"There is no best way," Ellen reasoned, "except to be direct and truthful. This is bad news you are delivering, but you are not the cause of it. She will not be angry with you."

"No, but she will be afraid, and heartbroken. Coming on top of her recent illness and Cecilia's disgrace, I don't know if I can bear it."

"Have you considered not telling her? If More is able to secure the king's word, Cromwell might well be overruled, and your father returned home before she need be aware of it."

Thomasin sighed. "I wish it were so, but she will be expecting him back soon, ready to depart for Suffolk, I cannot allow her to wait in suspense."

The carriage rumbled along Thames Street and turned in through the vast stone gates to Monk's Place, the home of her uncle. Thomasin thought of the very first time she had arrived here, not so long ago, full of hopes and excitement for her coming adventures. Usually it was a place of refuge, hospitality and peace.

However, the courtyard before the grey house was not as peaceful as usual. A number of horses stood waiting on the cobbles, held by royal guards, alongside a small carriage bearing Cromwell's arms.

"God in heaven," said Thomasin, scrambling down, "what further trouble is this?"

The front door was standing open, so they hurried inside. The sound was coming from Sir Matthew's private chamber. Thomasin could hear a woman weeping upstairs; it sounded like her sister, Cecilia.

"I do not accept this intrusion," Sir Matthew was saying loudly. "On what authority? For what reason?"

Thomasin hurried into the room, with Ellen following. A number of men were already conducting a search, led by Cromwell's man Ralph Sadler.

"They have arrested Father!" she burst out.

"Yes, we have been informed, although I do not understand on what grounds."

"The refusal to follow orders," stated Sadler baldly. "You will be next if you impede our search. Look, I do not like this any more than you do, but if you cooperate, it will be concluded all the sooner."

"But this is my study and my papers," argued Sir Matthew. "My brother-in-law rarely comes in here, and none of these items are his. They are all my own private affairs."

"I am sorry for it, my lord, but these are our orders," said Sadler.

"From whom?"

"Master Thomas Cromwell, acting on the authority of the king. I recommend that you cease to delay our progress further."

Sir Matthew sunk into a chair, defeated.

"Where is Mother?" Thomasin asked, turning her back on the intruders.

"Upstairs, in her chamber."

Thomasin hurried up the wide, carved wooden staircase that sat at the heart of Monk's Place. The door of her mother's chamber was flung open and the room was in disarray, with clothes and bedlinen strewn across the floor. A heavily pregnant Cecilia had flung herself across the bare mattress and was weeping, while Lady Elizabeth struggled to pack items into a trunk, fighting back her tears. She looked up at Thomasin's approach, but did not pause her task.

"Thomasin, thank goodness, you must help me!"

"What are you doing, Mother?"

"Packing things your father will need. He will catch cold in the Tower, and they will not feed him properly. Then you know what happens…" She broke off with a sob.

"Stop, please," said Thomasin gently. "There will be time enough for this, if it proves necessary. I cannot believe he will remain there. Thomas More is at this moment speaking with the king."

"More is?"

"Yes, he went to him at once. If anyone can make the king see sense, it is him. And good John Dudley will help us too. We are fortunate in our friends, thanks be to God."

"This is Cromwell's evil doing."

"It is indeed, and we must hope that the king's eyes are opened to his wickedness."

"You were there when it happened?"

"Yes, I was in the court. As More said, it was all for show, on the pretext of him failing to follow orders. Everyone could see it was nonsense."

"And how did your father respond?"

Thomasin recalled the shocked look in Sir Richard's eyes. "He was not expecting it. None of us were. But we must take heart. I am sure it will not be for long."

"And the men below? What are they searching for?"

"Nothing, Mother. There is nothing to find — not anything incriminating of ours, nor of our uncle's."

"Not your father's letters to France?"

"What?" Thomasin paused, her blood running cold. "What do you mean, letters to France?"

"Your father sometimes corresponds with an abbot in the Pale of Calais, from a past connection. He shares the letters with your uncle, too. Lately they have been speaking about the king's possible marriage to Renee of France. It is entirely innocent."

"I am sure it is," Thomasin replied, pausing for a moment to think how this might be taken by Cromwell.

At that moment, Cecilia sat up and let out a howl. "We are all going to die! We will all be sent to the Tower and executed, even me, and my child will grow up without a mother. We are done for!"

Thomasin felt the annoyance mount in her chest. "Stop that talk! There is no need to go to extremes. It is hardly the help we need right now."

She had not seen her sister since Christmas. Now, as Cecilia sat up with a struggle, the curve of her stomach was visible beneath her clothes.

"It is her state of mind, due to her condition," said Lady Elizabeth, regaining some of her composure. "It creates certain flights of fancy like this. Do not speak harshly to her."

Thomasin took a deep breath. "For now, we must remain calm and await news from our friends. Then we might decide upon our course of action."

"I am sure the king will not forsake his old friend. Perhaps I should go to him myself and ask for mercy, for the sake of our old connection."

Thomasin had almost forgotten the brief affair her mother had conducted with the king, back when he was a young man. At one point, she had even questioned whether Henry was her own father, but her likeness to Sir Richard had made her disregard that possibility.

"Perhaps it will come to that, but perhaps not. Hopefully not. We must wait and see."

The footsteps of the men downstairs echoed through the hall.

"There is nothing up there, nothing but bedchambers," they heard Sir Matthew saying. "There is no need to disturb the ladies, please!"

But heavy feet were already on the stairs and Rafe Sadler appeared in the doorway. The women turned stiffly to meet him.

Sadler made a small bow. "Forgive me, ladies. I do not wish to trespass upon your peace any further; I only request the surrender of any items or papers relevant to this matter."

"As we are unclear about exactly what the matter might be," replied Thomasin, "it will be difficult to comply. Why don't you tell us what you are looking for? Or better still, what the charges against my father are?"

"Mistress Marwood, I understand your distress. But alas, I cannot give you any more information, only that I seek letters, papers, books…"

"Here," said Lady Elizabeth, holding up a heavy tome. "Here is my Bible. Old-style, in Latin, with all the saints' days. Will this help your cause? It is the only book in this room."

"Thank you, but you may keep your Bible."

"I have books," said Thomasin, seeing a way to distract him. "Come to my chamber."

She led Sadler across the hall, to the little bedroom at the back of the house that overlooked the gardens. "I share this with Ellen, my cousin, when we visit. And here, I keep a few books: poetry, a few romances and legends, the tales of King

Arthur, the movements of the stars. That is all: nothing that might cause offence."

"Are there any letters hereabout, Thomasin?"

"None that I know of. Why has Father been arrested?" She looked Sadler straight in the eye. "You are a good man, I believe. You worked with my Venetian friend Nico once; you helped him. You cannot believe this is right."

"I believe that my master believes it to be right."

"And that is enough for you? You are happy to blindly follow orders, even when they are clearly mistaken?"

"I am happy to follow the king's orders without question. As we all must. My master derives his authority from the king."

"And the king knows that your master has imprisoned one of his oldest friends?"

"The king does not take kindly to being questioned by the servants of his servants. You should be careful, Thomasin. Keep your peace and do not be seen to be questioning his authority, then it will all be resolved sooner. I will leave you in peace."

"And what about my father, and his peace?"

"I cannot untie that knot for you, even though I wish I could."

A man's voice called Sadler from below. He hurried down the stairs and Thomasin followed him, her heart in her mouth.

A guard was holding up a sheaf of letters. "To the Abbot of Guisnes, Pale of Calais," he read aloud.

"What are these?" Sadler snatched the papers.

"Sir Richard's innocent correspondence with an old friend," said Sir Matthew, "nothing more. Read them for yourself. Calais is English — there is no crime in writing to a friend in England, is there?"

"It depends upon the letters' contents. Calais is well placed to entertain rebels and plotters."

"But the king is on friendly terms with Francis. Read them and see. It is merely news, nothing more."

"We shall see." Sadler tucked the letters into a leather packet.

"When shall we hear about Sir Richard?" asked Sir Matthew.

"In due course. I can say nothing more. I recommend you stay at home and remain quiet. That is the best way to help this situation pass."

"He is not…" Sir Matthew shot a glance at Thomasin, but decided to speak despite her presence. "He is not in any danger, is he?"

"I should hope not."

"Is there nothing we can do?" Thomasin asked.

"Nothing more."

They watched the carriage and horses pull away from the courtyard. A servant closed the great gates behind them and finally, peace descended upon Monk's Place. It was only then that Thomasin felt a sob rise up her throat.

"I cannot understand," she said, turning to her uncle, "how God allows this. How the king does. Why must bad things happen to good people?"

"That is the nature of our suffering as human beings," said Sir Matthew, sighing. "The lack of answers is almost worse than the suffering itself."

Thomasin nodded. "I will go back up and check on Mother. She is set to hurry off to the Tower, to ensure Father has all he needs."

"Let us hope it does not come to that."

About an hour later, when they had put Cecilia to bed with a warming spiced caudle, Thomasin and Lady Elizabeth heard the courtyard gates open again. Two horsemen rode up to the front door, dismounting amid the yapping of dogs.

"Wait here," said Thomasin, seeing the nervous look in her mother's eyes. "I will go down and see who it is."

Thomas More and John Dudley were waiting in the hallway, their faces heavy.

"What is the news?" asked Sir Matthew, appearing from his study as Thomasin came down the staircase.

"Nothing good to report, I fear," said More gravely. "I had a brief audience with the king and explained what had happened. I could see he was troubled, but he would only repeat that Cromwell is acting in his name. He would say nothing further. I do not believe he was aware of Cromwell's plan, but now that he knows of it, he will not disturb it. I sense that he believes Cromwell had some purpose in doing so that is in his interests."

"Yes, he does not want Father to speak in favour of his marriage!" said Thomasin. "It is quite clear."

"He would only say that your father had a chance to leave, to return to the country, but did not take it."

Sir Matthew shook his head. "So that is how he calms his conscience. It seems that there is no length he will not go to, in order to achieve his wishes."

"The king believes," added John, "that this court will soon conclude his divorce and he will be free to marry Anne. He sees the end so nearly in sight, I believe he will let nothing stand in his way. Sir Richard's evidence would have attested that his marriage to Catherine was a true one. But hopefully, once the matter is resolved, there will be no need to keep him in the Tower further."

"And if it is not?" asked Thomasin. "If the marriage question is not resolved?"

"What if Sir Richard promised to return at once to Suffolk?" asked Sir Matthew. "To leave at once and remain there for the duration of the court?"

"It has already been suggested," said More, "but the king thinks him safest out of the way, where his voice cannot be heard."

"Surely this is against the law of the court?" Sir Matthew persisted. "The king's authority must give way to that of the Pope. If the cardinals summon Sir Richard, he is bound to attend. If the king prevents him from doing so, he is acting directly against the Pope's command. Surely he will not go that far? He could be excommunicated for less."

There was an awkward silence in the hall.

"I think the king is moving in that direction," said More solemnly. "I fear that if this court does not go his way, he will reject its authority and bring about his own solution. At some point it is inevitable that he will clash with the Pope. This may only bring it forward."

"Then what can be done?" asked Thomasin.

"You saw how Cromwell disregarded the authority of the cardinals by arresting your father in the court. Then, he was a mere observer, seated in the gallery. I think we cannot lose by making the cardinals summon him. It will give the king a chance to step back from this action. We must appeal to the cardinals."

"I suppose there is little that the queen can do? Ellen is speaking with her now."

"The queen can only lend her voice to our appeals."

"Very well."

"We will go at once to Campeggio, and ask him to issue a summons for your father to attend on the morrow. God willing, that will be enough. If the king disregards it, he rejects the very court he has brought to England. It serves him not to question those whom he wishes to grant his request."

"That is sound logic," said Sir Matthew. "Will you take some refreshment before you leave?"

"No, I thank you. We will go straight about our business, to sooner to have it resolved."

"Thank you, good sirs, for your kind efforts on our behalf."

"It is a wrong that I cannot bear to see," stated More.

"Nor I," agreed Dudley. "If this is allowed to pass, which of us will be next?"

SIXTEEN

Thomasin stood and looked at the Thames flowing past the bottom of the garden at Monk's Place. The surface seemed calm, even glassy, but it was possible to see how the waters eddied and swirled in strong currents beneath. It raced past her, carrying along twigs and leaves, and even a pair of swans close to the opposite bank.

She would need to return to court soon. The queen had only granted her a few hours' absence and now that her mother and Cecilia were calmer, Thomasin would need to get back to help prepare the queen for dinner and the night ahead. It was her turn to sleep on the truckle bed in Catherine's chamber, although Thomasin could not imagine she would get any rest, imagining what conditions her father found himself in that night. The only comfort was the presence of Sir William Kingston in the Tower, Sir Richard's old friend, who would do his best to make Sir Richard as comfortable as possible in the circumstances. She drew a deep breath. This situation was terrible, but it would pass. They would all be together again soon.

A figure headed down the path from the house. To her surprise, Thomasin recognised Giles Waterson. A feeling of something like relief flooded through her as she went to meet him. His face was a picture of concern.

"Dear Thomasin, I have just heard your awful news. I would have heard sooner, but I was out riding. I came as soon as I could. Is there anything I can do to help?"

His kindness was almost overwhelming.

"I do not wish to upset you, only to be of service," he went on. "Tell me, what is the news?"

"It happened in the court this morning: Father was arrested by Cromwell's men. He was meant to give evidence today in support of the queen."

"And the king has been informed?"

"He is turning a blind eye to all those whose consciences might prevent him from fulfilling his desires. Even to his oldest friends."

"He is no friend. Remember that. The king is always the king and we are his subjects, never his friends. I am appalled, Thomasin, utterly appalled by the treatment of your father. It is so completely undeserved. If there is anything I can do, everything I own is at your disposal."

"You are so very kind."

"And your mother, your uncle? How are they?"

"Better than before. Some letters belonging to my father were taken by Cromwell's men, but it should come to nothing."

"They have been here? Searching the place?"

"Yes, not so long ago. Ralph Sadler and Cromwell's men."

"I know Sadler. He is not a bad man, but he serves a ruthless master and would be better placed elsewhere. What was in the letters?"

"Only friendly exchanges with an abbot in Guisnes."

"I pray nothing will come of it."

"Oh, and my sister is here — Cecilia. She is expecting a child."

"Then it is imperative that this is resolved as quickly and calmly as possible. Who else is helping your cause?"

"More and Dudley have been here. Their plan is to appeal to the cardinals to summon Father to court. The king cannot ignore a direct summons with papal authority."

Giles went quiet. His face contracted in thought.

"You do not believe so?"

"I wonder," he began, "whether you really want to force the king's hand? He was so determined not to hear your father's testimony that he sent him to the Tower. What would he do if the situation were forced? I understand the reasons for it, but for the sake of your family's peace, you do not want to incur the king's wrath. No Pope in Rome could protect him if the king turns against him. I am sorry to speak bluntly; I do not wish to alarm you."

"But you are right, by God's truth, you are right. I must go back to court at once and warn More and Dudley. The cardinals must not summon Father again."

"I think you are right. Put the king's divorce aside. Nothing matters more than your family's safety."

"I must leave." Thomasin started to hurry towards the house.

"Let me do this for you. I have a horse waiting outside and will go straight to them."

"But ... but I can't let you..."

"We are cousins, remember. Distant cousins, but family nonetheless. Your suffering is also mine."

Thomasin felt tears springing to her eyes and fought them back. "I must return to court anyway."

"Then I will accompany you. If you have a carriage, I will ride alongside."

"Yes, I came by carriage. I can't thank you enough."

"Then let us go. But, Thomasin, I promise this will be resolved. I shall not rest until it is."

She felt a blush rise to her cheeks as she was filled with a mixture of relief and gratitude to have a man like Giles by her side. And then the unpleasant thought arose, unbidden, that it should have been Rafe supporting her through this crisis, speaking the same words that Giles now offered. Where was Rafe at such a time as this? Nursing his grievances?

"Come." Giles offered her his arm. "Let us not wait another minute."

As the carriage trundled through the London streets, Thomasin's anxiety mounted. There always seemed to be something holding them back: a cart blocking the way, a crowd of people, a stray dog which almost went under the wheels. Each time, though, she looked out of her window and could see Giles on his horse, riding alongside, and she felt reassured.

When they finally arrived at court, he opened the carriage door for her, offering his arm.

"I think I should go straight to Wolsey," he said, clearly having thought about a strategy on the journey. "It'll take too long to track down More and Dudley, and Campeggio is more of an unknown quantity, but Wolsey I can appeal to. He has known your father for years and will understand the complexities of this situation."

"Yes, thank you. You are right. But…" Thomasin paused. "I am here now. I will go with you. It will not take long, and then I can return to the queen."

"If you are sure, then let us go."

The afternoon was fading as they hurried through the stable yard and into the main courtyard. Heads of courtiers and servants turned to see them speeding along the paths and through gates and corridors.

"Let us hope he is in his chamber, not with the king," said Giles. "If we find the cardinals together, it would be even better, and save us repeating our reasons."

He hastened towards the block where Wolsey had his apartment. Thomasin was buoyed by his strength of purpose, and a surge of admiration for Giles rushed through her in her haste, so that she did not notice those around her.

"Why the hurry?"

Giles came up short and Thomasin almost crashed into him from behind.

Anne Boleyn stood blocking the way, looking at them with blazing eyes. "You almost caused an accident, running about here like servants. Is there a fire? A flood?"

Behind her, in the shadows, Thomasin caught a glimpse of Mary Boleyn, and beyond her, her heart sank to see Rafe Danvers glowering, no doubt furious to find her in the company of Giles again.

"I beg your pardon, my lady," Giles said with conviction, "but please excuse us."

Anne did not move.

"We are about important business."

"What is so important?"

"My family's private business!" added Thomasin, stepping out from behind Giles. "Please let us pass."

"Ah, Mistress Marwood, what a pleasure," Anne said with a laugh. "Surely you are not behind this chaos?"

"Chaos?" Thomasin replied. "I see no chaos. Only two people about important business whose path is being blocked."

She caught Rafe's eye and read the doubt and annoyance therein, but she had no time for it now. It should have been him beside her, helping her, not her cousin.

"What on earth can be so important?" Anne asked again. "Does it relate to the king's business?"

"It is nothing of your concern," said Giles firmly. "Now please allow us to pass. Time is of the essence."

"Is it?" Anne mused, smiling. "'Time is of the essence' — how poetic!" But she leaned to one side, allowing a space for Giles to push through. He extended his hand to help Thomasin pass too.

As they moved, Thomasin was conscious of Rafe's body close by. She would need to pass him in a second, but there was no time to talk or explain. He deserved little consideration from her right now; her father mattered most.

As she followed Giles past Rafe, there was a sudden jolt. Giles lurched to the left and stumbled. Rafe stepped back, and his furtive movement made her realise that he had deliberately shoved against Giles as he passed.

"Sir," said her cousin, turning and righting himself, "this is no common brawling house. Your conduct is not befitting of a gentlemen. I am about serious and urgent business, but I will be sure to inform your master of your conduct."

Thomasin glanced at the other women, but both Anne and Mary looked coolly on, not raising an eyebrow.

"Nothing to say for yourself?"

"Go to hell," Rafe snarled.

"No, sir, I will not be going to hell," Giles said with firm disappointment. "I have far more important matters to attend to, than dealing with unruly and disgraceful conduct. But your time will come."

He turned and motioned for Thomasin to go ahead of him. Leaving Anne and her followers behind, she suppressed her anger and thought instead of saving her father. Rafe did not deserve to know what was happening. Nor did he deserve her.

Wolsey's chamber door was guarded by two men in his livery. Giles spoke a few quick words and they were admitted at once into his outer chamber.

"He is dining at the moment, but will receive us," Giles explained. "It might be the best way to approach him, as a captive audience."

They were shown into the next room, where a long table was spread with delicacies. Wolsey sat at the head of it, in dark robes, having cast off his papal red, and was flanked on both sides by his household. Thomasin spotted the new arrival Stephen Gardiner tucking into a pie with the delicate manners of a cleric.

"Move along," said the guard. "Make way at the top."

The diners shuffled along the benches to make space for Thomasin and Giles. They sat on Wolsey's left hand, and empty plates were brought for them.

"Forgive me," said the cardinal, "you are welcome to partake of this meal, and tell me your business as you do, although I can guess it."

"You can?" Thomasin had little appetite.

"No doubt it must be your father's arrest. I will tell you now that I had no prior knowledge of it, and did not agree to it. It is all Cromwell's doing."

"Yes, we are aware," said Giles. "But we are here regarding a request that may have been made to you since."

"From More?" Wolsey chewed on a piece of meat. "I am one step ahead of you. You have good friends, Mistress Marwood, I can see that. Yes, More asked me to summon Sir Richard in the name of the Pope, but I have refused."

"You have?"

"I do not think it wise for his cause. There are others who will provide the necessary evidence. Fisher speaks tomorrow, and then the queen herself. I do not wish to put your father in harm's way."

"Oh, thank you," said Thomasin. "That is precisely what we thought, and hoped that we might convince you of."

"No convincing needed, as I told More. We do not need to raise direct conflict between the king and Pope, not before it is needed, and not over this matter. It is best to let it blow over, and then I will urge for your father's release. He is only a small fish in this pond. Cromwell has greater opponents to consider. Now pray, eat something with me, and all will be well."

Giles turned to Thomasin. "There, let that be a comfort to you. I knew Wolsey was the man for us."

"I could not have done it without you. We are in your debt."

"Nonsense. I act in my own interest in this matter too."

Thomasin reached for a glass, uncertain how to interpret his words, and a servant hurried to supply them with wine.

"I feel guilty, eating here, while Father is in…"

"Never fear. He is well provided for. I sent flesh and wine to the Tower kitchens, and paid for a fire to be maintained in his room."

Tears welled in Thomasin's eyes. "You are too good, Giles, too good."

"It is only what I would wish anyone would do for me, were I in the same situation."

"Then I will pray that you never find yourself so."

"Nor you, Thomasin, or any of our friends. Now look, a dish of spiced larks. I recall how much you like them."

SEVENTEEN

The next day was to be an important one in court. Thomasin had almost forgotten that it was Catherine's turn to speak before the cardinals and answer their concerns. She, Ellen, Maria and Mary were to accompany her, as the formalities allowed, and no one, not even Cromwell, could prevent them this time. Thomasin burned with rage as she helped the queen to dress, choosing a formal, sombre gown in black and white to reflect the severity of the moment.

Catherine was quiet while they tied her laces, combed and pinned up her hair and placed her headdress on top. Thomasin knew she had been anticipating this moment for two years. Her future and that of her daughter, even that of England, rested upon the judgement of the court, and her appearance today could make all the difference. As Thomasin pulled on Catherine's sleeves and laced them to her bodice, she could feel the queen trembling under her fingertips, her muscles tense, her shoulders stiff. She felt sorry for Catherine, being put through this ordeal with all the world knowing of the shameful accusations made against her. Thomasin had never doubted Catherine's word that her first marriage had never been consummated, and that she had gone to Henry's bed as a true maid. Reaching for the queen's soft leather shoes, Thomasin shuddered to think of the cruelty that men could inflict upon women regarding the most intimate parts of their lives.

"Are you ready, my lady?" Maria Willoughby appeared in the doorway. "I have your jewels ready if you wish to select some items to wear."

"I am ready," said Catherine, "but I shall not adorn myself today. I will go plain and honest to the court, with no jewels to distract from God's purpose, as he is my only judge."

"Very good, my lady. I will order them to be put away."

Catherine reached for a silver crucifix that sat on the chest beside her and pressed it to her lips. The women waited in silence as she closed her eyes and muttered a few words.

"Now," she said finally, looking at them all, "it is time. We go forth to this as men do to a battlefield: in trepidation and fear, but also with a sense of righteousness and duty, in the knowledge that God is our witness and our eternal father, and that nothing will happen except that which is by his will, and his will alone."

"You speak bravely," said Maria. "He will be at your side always, today and in the days to come."

"Please join me in prayer," said the queen, clasping her hands together.

Thomasin, Ellen and Mary followed her lead, standing in silence while Catherine spoke fervently in Spanish. Her words betrayed the emotion she was suppressing, as her voice occasionally broke, her tone rising and falling. At the end, she drew in a deep breath, straightened her spine and pushed back her shoulders, undergoing the transformation Thomasin had witnessed so many times, from woman to queen.

"Now, let us go and stand before this court. I am ready."

They walked with purpose down the corridor to the flight of stone steps. Here, a number of supporters were awaiting them: other noblewomen who felt for Catherine's cause, and friends from past years, John and Jane Dudley among them, bowing low to show their approval. By the time they had crossed the bridge and entered the Blackfriars site, more had gathered in the yard, including those worshippers at the local church and those at the palace who had been the queen's servants in the cookhouse, gardens and laundry for many years. Thomasin realised they risked much to be there, waving and cheering as the small procession passed. Their presence did much to buoy Catherine's spirits as she saw how much she was supported.

At the great doors, More was waiting. He bowed low. "Fisher, Clerk and the others are within. Everything is ready for you, my lady."

"Is my husband inside the court?"

"Indeed he is, my lady."

This was the first time Thomasin had been aware of Henry attending a session, no doubt in order to hear what his wife had to say, the better to refute her arguments.

"I am ready. Let us proceed."

The court fell silent as the doors swung open and all heads turned towards the back. Catherine ignored them all and walked forward in her best stately manner, her eyes fixed on Henry, who sat on a dais to the right of the two cardinals, opposite the empty chair that awaited her. She did not sit down, but stood in the centre of the space before them, her hands clasped in supplication. The four ladies stood in a line behind her. Thomasin was aware of the faces around them, watching intently, and also of Cromwell at the front, but she could not bring herself to meet his eyes. She was here for Catherine; her hatred of the king's servant could not be allowed to cloud her performance.

"My Lady Catherine, formerly crowned Queen of England, dowager duchess of Wales, you are welcome to court," said Campeggio. "You may be seated."

"I wish to stand."

"As you wish, my lady. You are aware of the questions raised about the validity of your marriage to our right honourable

King Henry, eighth of that name, and the implications of this for the security and future of our realm. You have been summoned to the court to answer in your defence concerning the nature of your marriage, in the sight of God, to the best of your ability. Do you understand?"

"I do."

Clerk stepped towards her, holding out a large, heavy book.

Campeggio continued, "Please place your hand on the Holy Bible and swear that you will speak as true as you can, as God is your witness."

Catherine laid her small, plump right hand upon the book's leather cover. "As God is my eternal witness, in this life and the next, I swear to speak only His truth."

At this, they heard Henry sigh.

"Very well, then let us proceed," said the cardinal. "You may speak, my lady."

Catherine paused for a moment, ensuring that all in the hall were still and quiet. Then, in an unexpected act of drama, she threw herself down upon her knees. Unsure whether to do the same, Thomasin looked to the other women. Maria at once followed the lead of their mistress, so Thomasin, Ellen and Mary also adopted that position.

The queen lifted her head and looked directly at her husband. Henry gestured for her to rise, but she paid him no heed.

"Sir," she began, in a clear, strong voice, "I beseech you, for all the loves that hath been between us, and for the love of God, let me have justice and right, take of me some pity and compassion, for I am a poor woman and a stranger born out of your dominion; I have here no assured friend, and much less indifferent counsel: I flee to you as to the head of justice within this realm."

Henry looked uncomfortable at her words, but he could not stop her. This was her moment.

"Alas! Sir, wherein have I offended you, or what occasion of displeasure have I designed against your will and pleasure? Intending (as I perceive) to put me from you, I take God and all the world to witness, that I have been to you a true and humble wife, ever conformable to your will and pleasure, that never said or did anything to the contrary thereof, being always well pleased and contented with all things wherein ye had any delight or dalliance, whether it were in little or much; I never grudged in word or countenance, or showed a visage or spark of discontent. I loved all those whom ye loved only for your sake, whether I had cause or no; and whether they were my friends or my enemies. This twenty years I have been your true wife or more, and by me ye have had divers children, although it hath pleased God to call them out of this world, which hath been no default in me."

At these words, it was as if the court expelled a collective breath. Here was Catherine stating that they had lost children through no fault of her own. Was she daring to suggest, wondered Thomasin, that the fault might lie in Henry himself? No one else would dare question the king's virility.

The queen kept her eyes fixed on Henry, who could hardly bear to meet them. "And when ye had me at the first, I take God to be my judge, I was a true maid without touch of man; and whether it be true or no, I put it to your conscience."

Everyone turned from her to look at Henry at this point.

"If there be any just cause by the law that ye can allege against me, either of dishonesty or any other impediment to banish and put me from you, I am well content to depart, to my great shame and dishonour; and if there be none, then here I most lowly beseech you let me remain in my former estate, and receive justice at your princely hand. The king your father was in the time of his reign of such estimation through the world for his excellent wisdom, that he was accounted and called of all men the second Solomon; and my father Ferdinand, King of Spain, who was esteemed to be one of the wittiest princes that reigned in Spain many years before, were both wise and excellent kings in wisdom and princely behaviour. It is not therefore to be doubted, but that they were elected and gathered as wise counsellors about them as to their high discretions was thought meet. Also, as me seems there was in those days as wise, as well-learned men, and men of good judgement as be present in both realms, who thought then the marriage between you and me good and lawful."

At the side, Thomasin saw More nodding to himself, and many others joining in, regardless of the king's presence.

Catherine continued, "Therefore is it a wonder to me what new inventions are now invented against me, that never intended but honesty. And cause me to stand to the order and judgment of this new court, wherein ye may do me much wrong, if ye intend any cruelty; for ye may condemn me for lack of sufficient answer, having no indifferent counsel, but such as be assigned me, with whose wisdom and learning I am not acquainted. Ye must consider that they cannot be indifferent counsellors for my part which be your subjects, and taken out of your own council before, wherein they be made privy, and dare not, for your displeasure, disobey your will and intent, being once made privy thereto. Therefore, I most humbly require you, in the way of charity, and for the love of God, who is the just judge, to spare the extremity of this new court, until I may be advertised what way and order my friends in Spain will advise me to take. And if ye will not extend to me so much indifferent favour, your pleasure then be fulfilled, and to God I commit my case!"

For a moment there was silence. Then, applause broke out among her followers, timidly at first, then growing in momentum as more hands and voices joined the chorus.

Catherine rose to her feet, so Thomasin and the others hurriedly followed suit. Campeggio began to speak, but his words were lost amid the din. Turning swiftly on her heel, head held high, the queen walked out of the chamber, despite the clerk calling her back.

"Catherine, Queen of England, come into the court!"

She paused and half-turned. "It makes no difference, for it is no indifferent court to me; therefore, I will not stay."

In her wake, Thomasin felt a rush of exhilaration at having witnessed what had probably been the bravest performance of Catherine's life. They kept walking, without stopping or speaking, all the way back through the courtyards, across the bridge and up the steps until they reached the safety of the queen's apartments.

With the doors closed firmly behind them, Catherine sank exhausted into a chair.

"My lady, that was indeed remarkable," began Maria. "Such a triumph, you had the room at your command."

"I did, didn't I?" The queen smiled weakly.

"Wine," said Mary, gesturing to the guards, "bring wine and sustenance."

"It was all you could have hoped for," Ellen added.

"The best possible advocacy for your case," Thomasin agreed.

Catherine sighed. "The shame of it, that I should have to speak those words before such a crowd. Words that are not fit for the ears of half the people in that chamber. But it is done and I can do no more today. I can only trust in God's will." A smile crept across her face. "Tomorrow, though, I will file my complaint to Rome at such an insult to my queenship."

"It would be very well done, my lady," said Maria, "very well done."

"And the name of that blackguard Cromwell shall be at the very top."

Thomasin thought at once of her father. For a brief while, she had forgotten about Sir Richard languishing in the Tower, and waves of guilt rushed over her. Perhaps, after the queen had rested, she might find a quiet moment to ask permission to visit him.

EIGHTEEN

It was late afternoon by the time Thomasin was able to leave the queen's apartments. Catherine was preparing to travel the short distance downriver to Baynard's Castle, and although there were dresses and jewels and books to be packed away, she insisted that Thomasin take a few hours, with her blessing, to be about her important task.

Thomasin had gathered a few necessaries in a basket to ease her father's suffering: wine, cheese, a venison pie, warming spices, and a jar of preserved oranges from Catherine's own supply. As she crossed the inner garden, anxiety seized her heart: what should she expect from such a place as the Tower of London? In what condition would she find her father? She hurried through the green space, alive with plants and scents, towards the gateway in the wall that led round the side and down to the riverbank. But a figure was waiting there, appearing from behind the bushes, where he had been in conversation with a servant. For a moment, she hoped it was Giles, waiting to accompany her, but the sun glinted in a pair of chestnut eyes and lit up a head of black hair.

The sight of Rafe drew Thomasin up short. He looked weary, with dark circles under his eyes, his skin sallow and dull, far from the sparkling, vibrant figure he had once been. Her annoyance was replaced by concern, which swiftly melted. She had no time to stop and argue with him: her father was waiting in his cell.

"Excuse me, please. I must get to the river."

"No time even to greet me now? Not a single kind word for your betrothed?"

"I am about a matter of the utmost urgency, and I do not think your recent conduct warrants any kind of greeting from me, nor do you merit the title of betrothed. Now please, let me pass."

"So cold, Thomasin. Is this really you? Has that Giles turned your head so far that you see me now as only an inconvenience?"

At once her temper was roused. The words came out like daggers. "I loved you. I would have married you, but your behaviour has repelled me. We will not be married. You will never be happy, nor will any woman in your life, while you remain eaten away by such bitter insecurity and jealousy. Now, let me pass!"

She pushed him to the side and hurried out of the gate. Rafe made no reply, and she did not turn to see how her words had been received. The realisation that he had no idea where she was going or why made her even more certain that she was doing the right thing in breaking with him. He might have moments of insight, times when he could be the man she had hoped for, but these were far outweighed by the darkness in him that could not be repressed.

At the waterside, she hailed one of the small boats that always gathered around the steps of the palace, and directed the rowers downstream. The tide was on the turn, high and full, but it meant that their passage was swift. Soon, the formidable thick walls of the Tower's precincts came into sight, with their huge gates and the keep rising into the sky. She paid her fare and alighted at a slippery flight of steps, guarded at the top by a thick wooden gate and men in royal livery. Catherine had had the foresight to provide her with a letter of recommendation, despite her father's friendship with the constable, Sir William Kingston, and the queen's signature immediately opened the gates and gained her admission. A guard led her across the green towards the main apartments.

Kingston was an old man, but probably not much older than her father, Thomasin realised. He had a sensible, sombre disposition, suitable to his post, and a slight stoop and limp. His chamber was well furnished and comfortable, with a bright fire, a cupboard of silver plate and colourful wall hangings. Thomasin hoped her father was accommodated in a similar fashion.

"Mistress Marwood," he said, rising to greet her. "You are most welcome. I trust you have come to enquire about your father?"

Thomasin was grateful that he had got straight to the point. "I hope I may see him, if that is possible, and bring him this basket."

"Of course. I can tell you that he fares well in spite of his confinement, and his spirits are still strong. He has been most fortunate in his friends; you are not the first visitor he has received today."

"Am I not?"

"A young man came early, with a similar purpose to you. Come this way; you may have an hour with him."

Thomasin followed Kingston gratefully, back outside and across the courtyard towards a solid block containing a central round tower. Passing inside, her eyes took a moment to adjust to the dimness, but it was not as gloomy as she had feared, and torches lit the darkest parts. She followed her guide through a corridor and up a flight of steps, past other locked doors where she imagined more unfortunates to be residing at the pleasure of the king.

Kingston paused outside a chamber door that had an iron grille set at head height, and peered inside.

"Another visitor for you, Sir Richard."

Taking out a heavy iron set of keys from around his waist, he turned one in the large lock and the thick door creaked open.

"I'll have to lock you in, miss, but I'll be back in an hour to let you out. There is no cause for alarm, but I must check inside your basket before I admit you."

"Oh, of course." Thomasin held it out, watching as his hands made a quick search before he nodded in approval.

"People try and smuggle in all sorts; you wouldn't believe it. Here you are."

He stepped aside to reveal a round room with stone walls, a window in the far corner, a desk and chair and a narrow bed. However, she noted that there was no fire. Sir Richard was standing by the window, and came forward when he saw his daughter.

"Thomasin? Is it you? You should not have come to such a place!"

A second figure rose from a stool to her right. Giles had been reading aloud by the light of a lantern.

"Thomasin!" he echoed. "I would have accompanied you, if I had known you were coming."

"I ... I did not know you were here," she said, momentarily overwhelmed.

"Come, come here, let me set eyes on you," said Sir Richard, guiding his daughter into an embrace. "Are you well? And your mother and sister?"

"We are all well, thank you," she replied, "but it was not the object of my visit to come and tell you that! We have been most concerned about you and how you fare in here."

"As you see," said Sir Richard, gesturing around him, "it is not the comfort to which I am accustomed, but I am hardly suffering as others here have."

"He is stoic as ever," said Giles. "He was just speaking of his eyes being weaker. I have told him to refrain from reading and writing letters, and to rest them. The poor light in here strains them."

"It is nothing, just tiredness," said Sir Richard, frowning. "I am well cared for and fortunate in my gaoler."

"Here are a few items," said Thomasin, placing the basket on the table. "And I can act as messenger or scribe, to save your eyes, should you wish to send word to those on the outside."

"I am ably assisted in that already by Giles here, who has written and carried letters for me since my arrival."

Thomasin felt mixed emotions at this news. She was grateful to Giles for his diligence and care of her father; after all, she'd hoped for his company on this visit, but he seemed to be acting a part that should be hers, as if he were Sir Richard's son. It made her a little uneasy.

"I am pleased to hear you have been so well served. I apologise that I was not able to come sooner, but the queen delivered her speech this morning before the court, and I was required to assist her. Now I am here, I may perform any office you require, as well as any man, I hope."

Giles got to his feet and put down the book. "I should leave you to have some time together, as family. I will wait with Sir William until you are ready to depart, Thomasin."

She felt a little churlish as she watched him go, but he was right to allow her time alone with her father. Distant relative he might be, but he should still not come between them at a delicate time like this. As soon as he had gone, she relaxed a little.

"Tell me, Father, how do you really fare? Are you managing to sleep in here? Do they feed you well?"

"I can hardly complain. My nights are troubled, but that is the curse of any unfamiliar place, and I dine as well as Sir William, sometimes in his chamber."

"That is a blessing."

"I am more fortunate than many, but I long for news and the speedy resolution of this matter. Is your sister behaving herself? Does she suffer with the child?"

"She is managing as well as possible. But I must tell you that when I went to Monk's Place, Cromwell's men were there searching every room for books and papers. They removed your correspondence with the Abbot of Guisnes; I hope there was nothing of importance to you in it."

"Those letters? I wonder why. No, they were merely exchanges between old friends, about the harvest and local appointments on his part, and news of court on mine. Goodness, I wonder what I wrote now. Some of it was about the king's business, this marriage trouble and the court, but it was nothing that I would not admit to, nor that the whole of London already whispers."

"I am sure it was nothing." But Thomasin felt a chill at the possibility that her father had been indiscreet.

"I may have written in support of the queen, but that is hardly a crime. We spoke of the old days and the queen's good character. You say Cromwell has these letters?"

"Sadler took them for him."

"Well, I can answer anything he wishes to ask. I do not think that is the main matter, though. I was arrested to silence my support of the queen, in the same way that her lawyers from Flanders were sent back. More and Fisher should be wary of their words, or they might find themselves here as well. I take comfort from the thought that it was not personal. My old friend the king was not angry with me, but acted this way to guard his own interests. I hope I shall be restored to favour in the very near future."

Thomasin was silent, remembering what Giles had recently said about the king having no friends. They were his subjects first and foremost.

Giles was waiting for her, as promised, when she departed. He stood up as Sir William led her back into his chamber.

"Thomasin? All is well?"

"Yes, thank you." She turned to the constable. "How long must he remain here? I thank you heartily for all you are doing for his comfort, but surely you are also of the belief that his imprisonment here is most unjust, most unkind, and occasioned over a trifle!"

Sir William nodded. "My dear girl, the difficulty is that I am a servant of the king. No matter what my private thoughts might be about those sent to me, I am obliged to enact the law in all its particulars, and never to presume to question them. While I can tell you that I feel for your father's plight and do all I can to alleviate his suffering, I can no more comment on his position than I could that of the queen."

Thomasin stared back at him, frustrated. "But what can be done?"

"That is up to you and Sir Giles, and any friends of yours who choose to petition the king for his release. But, given the circumstances, I cannot imagine that his stay here will be too long. It coincides with the trial, whose duration must last the summer out, although the time for the queen's evidence is almost completed, as I understand it."

"You think he may be released as soon as they begin hearing evidence for the king's side?"

"It is possible, so long as there is no other complicating factor."

Thomasin thought of the letters. "He had written to the abbot at Guisnes, a few personal letters, the contents of which he can scarcely recall, but they touched upon the queen's suffering. I hope those will not count against him."

"From what I have observed," said Giles, "the matter rests more with Cromwell, acting on the king's behalf. It will be his decision as to whether or not to use the letters, I am afraid."

"And he is no friend to my family," Thomasin said with a sigh.

"But surely the king will not let him ruin you all," Giles assured her. "Take heart, I believe all will be resolved with the Papal Court. Come, let us depart. I shall accompany you back to Bridewell."

"For the last time, as the queen removes to Baynard's Castle on the morrow."

"Then let us go at once, so you might be back in time for dinner."

"In truth, I have little appetite."

"But you do your father no assistance in starving yourself. Come, let us go and take a boat."

They took their leave of Sir William and found a vessel awaiting them at the bottom of the steps, summoned by the guards. Thomasin watched the squat grey shape of the Tower complex receding with a shiver. She resolved to ask Catherine for permission to visit Monk's Place and inform her mother about her father's keeping as soon as possible.

"You are quiet," said Giles as they sat side by side, with the oarsmen behind them.

"I have much on my mind."

"I am sure that you do. If there is anything I can do to assist you or your family, please let me know at once. I will do all I can for you."

Thomasin was silent. His words went beyond what was required, what was expected, and made her feel uncomfortable. She had welcomed his help, but something about his promises struck a strange chord with her.

Soon they approached Bridewell, with the boat drawing close to the steps. Giles jumped out and offered her his hand.

"Thank you, I can walk by myself."

His blue-green eyes were baffled for a moment. "Have I somehow offended you, Thomasin?"

At once she felt guilty. "No, no, I just wish to walk unaided."

They passed along the landing stage and in through the side gate where she had seen Rafe earlier. As afternoon became evening, the light was beginning to deepen in its warmth, with hints of the night ahead.

"Forgive me, whatever it is," he continued, following her. "I would not have upset you for the world. But only tell me what is wrong, so I may correct it."

"Please, stop! It's too much."

"Too much?"

"All of this. I am grateful for your help, and I know we are family, but sometimes it feels … I don't know, too much."

His face changed as he grasped her meaning. "Surely you know why, Thomasin. Surely you must have guessed?"

But a wall rose up within her. The memory of Rafe's bad behaviour lingered.

"I must get to the queen."

"You must know, Thomasin?"

"No! Stop! I am expected back!"

She hurried away from him towards the doors and out of sight, her heart pounding.

NINETEEN

Thomasin smoothed down her dress and approached the main court doors. Catherine and the rest of her ladies were removing to Baynard's that morning, but she was to remain and listen to the evidence given by the king. It was not a task she relished, given that Cromwell would be present, and the matter distasteful, but she had faithfully promised the queen that she would report back all the details. If she was to join her father in the Tower for supporting Catherine, then so be it.

Bishop Fisher was waiting for Thomasin inside. "Come and sit with me, today."

He led her to the seats at the side, where Clerk was also seated. She noticed a number of new faces in the chamber that morning, no doubt the legal experts the king had consulted on the final details of his divorce. Henry himself was sitting at the front, in the same place he had occupied the day before, looking out at the arrivals with an air of expectation. At his side, Cromwell was gathering his papers, preoccupied for a moment. Thomasin allowed herself to shoot him a look of pure venom while his head was bowed.

"I saw Father yesterday," she told Fisher. "He is in fairly good spirits still, and Sir William is taking good care of him, but his eyes are strained."

"I am sorry to hear that. He has a good keeper in Sir William, although it should never have come to this."

"He hopes to be released once the court has reached its decision, but there is the question of his letters."

"Letters?"

"To the Abbot of Guisnes, an old friend."

"John? I know him well. We have also corresponded. What is the problem with these letters?"

"Cromwell has them; they were taken from my uncle's house. Father may have written in favour of the queen's cause — he has copies — and the abbot has replied in a similar tone. I've not seen them myself."

Fisher looked at Cromwell, who was taking a paper forward to show the king. "He will use anything he can to punish your father for not following his instruction."

The clerk to the court had risen and people began to take their seats in readiness. He announced the opening of the session and proceeded to welcome the first expert witnesses, men from the universities and Inns of Court, whose judgement was in favour of the king.

A sound behind them drew Thomasin's attention. She turned to see Thomas More, white-faced, appear at her shoulder.

"What is it?" she whispered, shocked at his appearance.

"I am being sent to Cambrai. I depart at once for the summit between France and the Emperor, taking Wolsey's place."

"A summit?"

"Peace talks, supposedly, but filled with so much animosity. I am to support the French in their military action against Milan."

"You're leaving at once?"

"I should be on the road already, but I had to come and tell you. I couldn't just disappear. It is another ploy on Cromwell's part to suggest me. Wolsey asked for the talks to be delayed so he could attend. Now I am to be sent away!"

"I can't believe it," said Fisher. "Are we all to be dismissed, one by one, until the king gets his wish?"

"I must away. I can stay no more, but all my prayers and wishes remain behind with you."

Thomasin sat stunned as her dear friend hurried out of the chamber. When would she see him again, and hear the comfort of his words? How many more turns would this unpleasant matter take before the king achieved his aim?

Henry had risen to his feet, ready to address the cardinals, but Thomasin could hardly bear to look at him. She listened while he spoke about his reasons for requesting an investigation into his marriage, quoting a passage from Leviticus as justification for why it had been wrong to marry his brother's wife. He announced twenty-one articles that justified his position and called upon those present to witness his true intentions and desire to serve England before God. It was nothing that Thomasin had not heard before. In turn, the experts were called to support his view, with other references, precedents and arguments. Listening to them turned Thomasin's stomach. She thought of Queen Catherine, her head bent in prayer, her tears at night, her fears for her daughter and the future. The whole matter seemed cruel. There was nothing new here. Nothing to keep her.

"I can't stay here," she whispered to Fisher. "I must go."

Rising to her feet, she ignored the heads turning in her direction, walking swiftly through the doors and into the sunny courtyard.

Catherine would already have left. An army of servants were probably in her apartments, sweeping out the hearth, washing down the walls and floor, and removing the waste for burning. All that remained for Thomasin was to follow them to Baynard's.

She sat down on one of the stone benches in a bower planted with roses. The sunshine played across her skirts, picking out the silver threads in the fabric, making them seem gaudy in the daylight. She looked up at the beautiful palace, with its long windows, stone carvings, and twisted chimneys, and the gardens with their colours and scents, the early summer clouds overhead. All seemed idyllic. How many people would never experience a paradise like this? Never wear cloth of gold or silver, or dine on venison, or dance to a lute? And yet, all the court brought was unkindness and suffering. Rafe's eyes flashed before her again, full of anger. Thomasin's head dropped and tears welled in her eyes. Embarrassed, she attempted to stem the flow, but was powerless to stop them falling.

"My Lady Thomasin? What distresses you?"

Harry Letchmere had approached her along the path, but she had been too absorbed to notice. She did not know him well enough to confess all, but she believed him to be a good man, from the little she had observed.

"Forgive me, it is nothing. You have just caught me in an unguarded moment."

"They come to us all. I try not to have mine in the palace gardens, though, when strange eyes might interrupt."

"Very true," said Thomasin, wiping her eyes and wondering what Sir Henry's unguarded moments might look like.

"Might I be of assistance in any way?"

"Thank you, but no. I should really be on my way to join the queen."

"She has departed for Baynard's Castle, I believe?"

"Yes, not so far, but far enough from here. How did you know?"

"Your fair cousin confided in me before the departure. I hope to call on the queen before long and see you all well settled there."

"It is a mere moment's walk from here, so do not delay in paying your visit. We shall live quietly enough there, now that our business at court is concluded."

"I heard the queen spoke most bravely, like a true warrior queen of England."

"Yes, she spoke well. She spoke her truth."

"And I hope it shall bring her the peace she deserves."

"Thank you. She needs all the friends she can muster at this time."

Thomasin looked at him again. He was not a young man, with his greying temples, but his face was kindly and his eyes were warm. She recalled that she had first met him when he accompanied Giles to the queen's apartments, and wondered how close the pair of them were.

"You are an acquaintance of my cousin Giles, I believe."

"Oh, more than acquaintance. I am proud to call him my friend, such a noble and blessed gentleman as him."

Thomasin was surprised; was this merely the exalted praise of a friend?

"You have known him long, then?"

"Since we were boys. He is, in truth, the kindest, most sincere man I have ever met. When we lost my father, and my mother was ailing in her grief, he rode over to visit us every day for a month, devising means to cheer her spirits. He had a hand in my sister's marriage too, adding to her dowry from his own purse. I have never heard another fellow speak a bad word about him, save from jealousy."

Thomasin thought of Rafe at once. "He must indeed be a saint, if all you say is true."

"He is your cousin; you should know the mettle of the man."

It was true, Thomasin realised. Despite not having known him for as long as Sir Henry had, she instinctively felt that Giles was the best of men, everything that was good and true in a gentleman. She felt her cheeks blushing.

"Do come and visit us soon," she insisted. "My other cousin, Ellen, will be pleased to see you."

"It will be my pleasure. I will take my leave of you, Mistress Thomasin." He gave a short bow and strode off towards the river. Watching him depart, with his long stride and fine calves, Thomasin had to admit he was not an unattractive man.

She decided she would take this opportunity to go to Monk's Place and tell her mother about her visit to the Tower. It would be a short ride by carriage, and she need stay only an hour. She turned towards the northern court, which gave out onto the church and London streets, where the palace's horses were stabled. She knew some of the young men who worked here; they often carried the queen's messages, and one of them would surely find her a carriage to travel into Thames Street.

As she headed through the gateway, a distant figure came into her line of her sight. It was a woman with a hood pulled down over her face, moving slowly, laboriously, in a long tan and cream dress, open-laced about her swollen belly. Even across the courtyard, Thomasin recognised Cecilia as she disappeared into one of the corridors. A jolt of surprise moved her forward in pursuit. What on earth was Cecilia doing at court? Had something happened at home? Did she bring news?

"Cecilia?"

Thomasin caught up with her as she reached the dark point of the corridor, by the turning towards the cellars. Cecilia turned, wide-eyed with surprise.

"What are you doing here? Has something happened?"

"Hush! No! All is well."

"Were you seeking me?"

Cecilia shook her head. "Leave me be, Thomasin. Pretend you have not seen me; go about your business."

"But why? What is your business here?"

"Mother believes I have gone to the tailor in search of new linen for my lying-in. Do not reveal this to her."

"I was about to visit her myself. Might I take you home with me, in a carriage? You should not be walking about here, not in your condition."

"I still have three months before the child arrives. I do not need your concern."

"I disagree. Come, tell me, why are you here? Otherwise you will have to explain to the guards at the gate. You can't just wander into the palace." She paused and frowned. "Is Mother faring well?"

"She is still upset, as you can imagine."

"And you left her?"

"Well, Thomasin, it's not as if you are there with her either."

The rebuke stung but was true. Thomasin's role at court had kept her from Lady Elizabeth's side in a time of need. But she had been able to stay away in the belief that Cecilia and Sir Matthew were with her mother.

"That is hardly fair. And I have visited Father in the Tower today. That was the news I was to take her."

"You went to the Tower?"

"Yes, Cecilia. I saw Father and took him some supplies. He is in fairly good spirits, considering, and he is fortunate in his guardian. With any luck, he will be released when this matter of the royal marriage is concluded."

Thomasin did not mention her father's weak eyes. There was no need to trouble her mother and sister just yet on that front.

"Well, that is good news. I shall tell Mother upon my return."

"But you still have not told me why you are here. Come now, I am your sister. What has brought you here? It must be important."

Cecilia's hands wound around her stomach. "I am due to bear his child soon, Thomasin, and he does not know. He should know that his child is coming, do you not think?"

"William Hatton? You are here to see him?"

Thomasin thought of the awful moment last Christmas at Greenwich, when she and her parents had discovered Cecilia and Hatton in bed together.

"Not to see him. It is not an assignation. A man has a right to know he is about to become a father, Thomasin. Surely even you must see that?"

Even you? Thought Thomasin. Their childhood animosity clearly still lingered. "I must dissuade you in the strongest possible terms, and insist that you return to Monk's Place at once."

"I will not do that, Thomasin. I am here now. I will not leave." Cecilia's stubbornness was legendary in the family: if she refused to do something, she would never do it.

"Hatton does not know you are here?"

"I do not even know that he is."

"And yet you have come all this way?"

"I had to, Thomasin, I had to take the chance." She cradled her belly again. "You cannot understand what it is like."

"No," Thomasin replied quietly. "I cannot. He is here, or he was a few days ago, in the company of the king."

"Thank you. Where should I find him?"

"I came from the court not long ago, and he was not there. He is likely to be in the king's chambers, I imagine, awaiting Henry's return."

"Would you take me there?" Her pale blue eyes pleaded with a sincerity that was rare for Cecilia.

Thomasin sighed. "I suppose I must, although I fear we are heading for the lion's den."

TWENTY

There was music coming from Henry's rooms. Thomasin frowned at the jaunty tune that was being played on a lute and recorder, with the rhythm struck up on a tabor. The king himself was not there, of course; he remained where Thomasin had left him, still seated before the Papal Court, listening to the advice of his legal experts. But then ealization dawned: there was only one other person who might command music to be played in his chamber, just like she commanded every other aspect of his life, laughing at every sorrow that her behaviour had caused.

Thomasin paused outside the doors and turned to Cecilia, mindful of the last unpleasant encounter they had had with Anne, who had been jealous over Henry's divided attention.

"You really want Anne Boleyn to see you like this?"

Her sister did not care for the shame of it. "I am a married woman. It might make her realise there are other women more than capable of providing the king with the heir he desires."

"Very well, then." Thomasin took a deep breath and went to knock on the door.

"Wait. Perhaps it is best to draw him out. If I wait somewhere nearby, then the shock for him will be less."

"I think that is wise."

"I will return to the courtyard, by the rose bower. Bring him to me there."

"If he is within, I will do so."

Thomasin waited for her sister to disappear, then knocked on the door. A guard answered and let her in.

All Anne's favourites were gathered. Anne Gainsford and Bess Holland, with George Boleyn and Henry Norris, made up the closest group to her. Thomasin could see the swish of skirts as they danced, laughing and moving in rhythm, as if the queen's future had already been decided in their favour. Anne's distinctive tones rose above the music as she conducted her friends: "More swiftly now, quicker of foot. Be ready to turn, less like a dullard, please!"

Thomasin would have turned away had she not committed herself to helping her sister.

"Who is it?" called Anne, above the heads of the guards. She came to a halt behind them. She wore a startling gown of tawny and gold, her face flushed and her eyes glittering. "Thomasin Marwood, I can scarcely believe it. This day gets better and better. It must be a sign." She threw back her head and roared with laughter.

Thomasin wanted to pull her hair, but she gritted her teeth and remained calm. "I have no wish to intrude on your frivolities. I am here to enquire whether William Hatton is within."

"Hatton?" Anne smiled. "What, is he to have a turn with you, too? Now the elder sister is married, the younger one comes begging."

Anne had gone too far. Thomasin's rage began to boil at the insult, but she stood her ground. "I am here on business. Is Hatton within?" She tried to see past Anne into the room.

"Do you hear this, Rafe?" Anne called back, presumably to where Rafe was enjoying himself in the dance. "Your beloved is here seeking Will Hatton. What do you think of that? Replaced so soon."

Thomasin turned, fuming with rage. She knew that Anne had deliberately said the most provocative things she could think of, but she could not bear to stand and be insulted.

"Wait, wait," Anne called in conciliatory tones. "No need for that. Hatton is here."

Hatton appeared in the doorway, his fair hair tousled, his face full of questions.

"I will leave you to your … business," said Anne. "Thomasin, what a delicious pleasure it was to see you. Sadly so brief."

The door closed sharply behind them.

"How can I help you?" said Hatton.

"I am here about your own business, as you will discover shortly. Come with me."

Thomasin started walking and Hatton hurried behind. She felt no inclination to speak to him or make the situation less awkward, and he was not prepared to make the effort either. Soon they emerged from the corridor into the courtyard. Thomasin caught a flash of her sister's dress among the roses.

"Your business lies over there, among the roses. If you speak so much as a single unkind word, you will have me to deal with!"

Giving him a little shove in the right direction, Thomasin was satisfied to see him walk towards Cecilia, then turned away to find herself a spot for repose. She felt tired now, with all the strains of the past weeks creeping up on her, and settled down on one of the benches on the far side, out of sight and earshot of the lovers.

The sun fell heavy and warm upon her skirts and she settled back, hoping for a decent stretch of rest while Cecilia's predicament was resolved. Soon, the judgement of the court would be pronounced and there would be a path laid out before her, either with Catherine victorious as queen or, Heaven forbid, discarded and banished somewhere. Would the queen need her ladies in a nunnery or a remote house of retirement?

Once Sir Richard was freed and Cecilia's baby born, Thomasin imagined her parents would wish to retire to Suffolk. There would always be a place for her there, but what a life it would be in comparison to that which she enjoyed now. What kind of marriage would she make there — the son of some local landowner, perhaps? And Cecilia? What would become of her, now that Hugh wished to have no more to do with her? She might return to Suffolk too, unless a different future was being decided for her right now.

Thomasin closed her eyes. It was warm for May. Maria had told her how this used to be Catherine and Henry's favourite month, dressing up in Lincoln green and riding out into the fields for feasts and hunting. There had been such happiness between them, which had lasted for so long.

Thomasin woke with a start. John Dudley was shaking her arm.

"Thomasin? Are you well?"

She rubbed her eyes and looked around, dazed. The sun had shifted position behind the chimney pots. "I … yes. Oh, John, I think I fell asleep. What hour is it?"

"Close upon dinner. How long have you slept?"

"Longer than I should."

She got to her feet, looking over towards the rose bower. There was no sign of either Cecilia or Hatton.

"God's blood! You've not seen my sister, have you?"

"I just came in through that door. I saw no one."

Thomasin sighed. "Very well, forgive me."

"I have come from the court. It has concluded for the day, with no resolution to speak of. Henry is sour enough about it. Look out, he comes this way!"

They both sprang back as the royal guards appeared, at the head of a procession snaking its way towards the royal apartments. Thomasin wondered if Anne was still dancing there, and whether the king would be in the mood to join her. And where had Cecilia disappeared to?

When Henry appeared, resplendent in his furs and gold chains, she decided at once that there would be no music and dancing, given the severity of his frown.

"And so another day is required," said John, as the line faded from sight. "They have been at loggerheads for so many years, I do not suppose a few days will matter, although it is more likely to be weeks at this rate."

"That long?"

"I fear so. Campeggio is so determined to draw the proceedings out, I am starting to believe he has secret instructions to delay. Will you dine in the hall here tonight?"

"No, I must make my way to the queen. She has repaired to Baynard's Castle and is expecting me."

"Then it would be my pleasure to escort you. It is but a moment's walk, but I should not wish to see you go unaccompanied."

"That is most kind of you, if you can spare the time."

"I can, and the pleasure of your company is fair recompense. You can tell me if you prefer rose water or lavender to perfume gloves with, because I wish to buy some for Jane, but I am sure she had both!"

Thomasin laughed. "I am sure she would like either."

"She is with child again, we have just discovered. We are blessed by it, but it comes round again so soon."

"You are fortunate indeed. My congratulations to you both."

They crossed the bridge to Blackfriars and passed through the palace, along a short street of tall houses and out into St Andrew's Hill, which led down to the river. John pointed out the site of the old mill from years past, and talked about the ownership of the buildings on each side, along with their histories and former residents. On the left was a gate, giving into the precincts of Baynard's Castle.

"Here I will leave you and take a boat home to Jane," said John, with a short bow.

"Thank you. I appreciate the escort."

"It is always a pleasure. I intend to visit your father tomorrow, if you have any message for him."

"Only my love and prayers, as ever. I saw him earlier and he was in fair spirits, but I do not know how he fares when I am not present."

John nodded, understanding her request. "I will report back his true state, if he will show it to me. I will join my prayers with yours for a speedy resolution to his situation."

"Thank you, dear John."

Now that her dear Thomas More had been sent to Cambrai, she appreciated having John's friendship.

Baynard's Castle was solid, grey and unforgiving, even in the late afternoon sunshine. It felt more like a fort than a palace or townhouse such as the great lords occupied. Thomasin entered with trepidation, shown by the guards to the rooms that Catherine occupied. It was dark, with few torches, but the lingering smell of food that had passed along this corridor recently offered a little comfort.

She was shown into a high-ceilinged room, still chilly despite the fires being lit. Ellen rose from a window seat, where she had been darning with Mary. Thomasin noticed that the windows were small and deep-set, letting in very little light.

"Here you are, at last! We were getting worried about you."

"I am here now. John Dudley escorted me."

"Did you remain in court all this time?"

"Not quite all. I had some business of my own to attend to as well."

"The queen asked after you. She is at prayer now, but she wishes to hear about all the proceedings."

"I will do all I can, but Bishop Fisher promised to pay a visit, and he understands the legal matters far better than I."

"Have you eaten?"

Thomasin realised she had not done so since the morning, and her stomach was growling with hunger.

"There, some of our meal remains. You are lucky to have arrived before the servants could remove it." Ellen pointed to a round table where dishes remained uncleared: a venison pasty, wings of chicken, a game pie, spices and pancakes with cream. Thomasin quickly sated her appetite.

"Is the queen well?" she asked.

"She has spent most of the time since our arrival in prayer, so I cannot really tell you. This morning she was in a state of anxiety, expecting the court's verdict at any time," Ellen replied.

Thomasin recalled what John had told her. "It will not be yet, certainly. There is far more to come. She should expect nothing for a good few days yet."

"Perhaps you can tell her that," said Mary, "as she has us all on edge."

"I will, as soon as she emerges. I hope her spirits are not too affected by being in this place. Must we stay here long?"

Ellen shook her head. "Only until our chambers at Bridewell have been cleaned, then we may return, although she speaks of going to Windsor for the summer with Princess Mary. She is lifted by hope at the moment, although it is depressing enough for the rest of us."

"Oh, I do hope we'll go to Windsor and have a merry summer."

After an hour, when the candles were burning low, there came a knock upon the door. Catherine had still not emerged from her private prayers, so Thomasin went to enquire who was there. She found Bishop Fisher upon the threshold, looking tired.

"My dear, I have come to make full report to the queen, as I promised I would. Is she receiving visitors?"

"I am sure she would like to hear from you. Please step inside and come close to the fire."

"Goodness," he said, looking around as he entered. "It is gloomy in here, is it not?"

The women nodded their agreement.

"This must be a stop of convenience, nothing more," he continued. "This place will be no good for your health, any of you. It is so dark and damp that you might as well be..." He paused, suddenly realising where his words were leading.

"In the Tower?" asked Thomasin, grasping his meaning.

"Forgive me, it was a careless comment."

"And fortunately not reflective of my father's treatment, as his room is dry and light enough, and his meals are solid."

Fisher looked uneasy. "I am pleased to hear that is the case. I had feared otherwise, given its history. No doubt the king will come to his senses soon."

The women were silent, wondering what was meant by the Tower's history, but none wished to ask.

At that moment, Catherine emerged from her inner chamber, dressed in sombre black.

"Ah, Thomasin and Bishop Fisher, I am glad to see you both. Tell me, what tidings of the day?"

"Little of comfort, my lady," offered the bishop. "All legal knots and loops and biblical verses; it was most tedious."

"And no resolution?"

"None yet, but I am to address the court myself in a few days and will leave them in no doubt about my convictions on the matter."

"That is good to hear. And More, will he speak?"

"My lady, I regret to inform you that our friend More has been dispatched to Cambrai for the summit between the French and the Emperor. He came into the court especially to tell us, for he had just received instructions himself, much against his inclination."

"Another friend lost. My husband is determined to reduce my support in whatever way he can."

"I am sorry for it, my lady. I will give my speech the equivalent force of three men."

"I believe you will, dear John. I believe you will." The queen turned to Thomasin. "This afternoon, I have dispatched more supplies and books to your father, God preserve and keep him. I have also written a letter to the king, asking for his release, although it may be upon the condition that he is to return to Suffolk at once."

"He will go gladly, my lady. Thank you for your kindness."

"We must keep our old friends close in these difficult times. Whatever the outcome of the court, I will never forget those who have stood beside me throughout it. Never."

TWENTY-ONE

Bishop Mendoza leaned in towards the queen, the rings upon his fingers sparkling in the candlelight.

"I shall pray for you every day, asking God to show his mercy upon your situation and advancing years."

Catherine's face did not betray a flicker at the mention of her age: she was then halfway through her forty-third year. She placed her own hand lightly on top of the bishop's furred cap.

"I give you my blessing for your voyage. May your final years be easy among your family and friends."

"We shall correspond," he said. "I shall not forget my English friends and their suffering. Many have been good to me here, amid my own travails."

"I have more salve for your legs." Catherine gestured to Maria, who brought forward a pot of the ointment that Thomasin had once applied to the old bishop's painful limbs.

"You are too gracious, my lady."

"You have been a good friend to me, Inigo, at a time when I have learned who my real friends are."

"I only wish I could have done more, and I regret that I must leave before the court has made its final decision."

"Is there any news of your replacement?"

"A Savoyard by the name of Eustace Chapuys has been appointed. I know little of him, but his recommendations are good. I understand he will be a great friend to your cause."

"I shall anticipate his arrival. What time do you depart?"

"I am taking ship at Dartford and will alight on the coast north of Canterbury, for the ride down to Dover. The progress on water is far better for my legs than on the land."

"God go with you, my friend." Catherine handed over a letter, folded and sealed in her distinctive gold wax. "Keep this for the eyes of the Emperor, my nephew, only. Let no other man read its contents."

Mendoza tucked the letter into his sleeve. "I shall guard it with my life and pass it to him in person on my journey through Italy. I hope to see him crowned there before I return to Spain."

The bishop bowed again and then slowly straightened up his aged frame. He ran his eyes over the line of the queen's ladies, where Thomasin and Ellen waited.

"You are well attended. Ladies, I commend you for your diligence and loyalty."

Taking out a purse, he placed a gold coin in the hands of each woman in the line, adding his own personal blessing. Reaching Thomasin last, he folded his hands over hers.

"I have not forgotten your kindnesses to me, Mistress Marwood. May God bless you and grant you many long, peaceful years ahead."

"Thank you, your Grace. I wish you a safe and speedy journey."

"Look out for this Chapuys when he comes. He may need you to show him the ropes."

Thomasin nodded.

"Well." Mendoza stood back and surveyed them all. "This is my farewell to England — a nasty, wet country it is, lacking in good wine and overrun by meat-eaters. I wish you all joy of it!"

Thomasin smiled as the old man waved his farewell and disappeared through the doors. Just as he left, though, a servant appeared, carrying a letter. He knelt before the queen.

"For Mistress Marwood, my lady, just brought to the castle by a boy."

Catherine looked up. "Thomasin? Are you expecting a letter?"

"I am not, my lady."

"Better discover its news swiftly, then."

She took the letter from the servant, recognising the seal of her uncle, Sir Matthew, and tore it open. A few lines were contained within, summoning her back to Monk's Place as soon as possible. She flushed and frowned at the necessity to ask the queen for release again, but was concerned about what had occasioned the request.

"Not good news, I think," said Catherine, studying her face. "Not your father, I hope?"

"No, I don't think so." Thomasin walked towards the queen's chair and placed the letter in her hands.

Catherine scanned it quickly. "You may take two hours this afternoon and return in time for dinner, as I have guests. Tomorrow, I want you back in court for Fisher's speech."

"You are most kind, my lady. I apologise again for the disruption."

"I will send some more cloves for your mother, and some warming spices, as she must be suffering."

"She will receive them with gratitude, I am sure."

Anxiety knotted Thomasin's stomach as she left Baynard's Castle. A carriage was waiting to take her the short distance along Thames Street. The letter had been written by Sir Matthew, who had simply stated that her mother was distressed and wished to see her on an urgent matter. Thomasin had no doubt that the matter was, indeed, of a most urgent nature, as her uncle was not prone to hyperbole.

A faint drizzle had begun to fall over the city as the carriage moved down the busy street. Their progress was slow, as horses, carts and children weaved in and out before them. Thomasin had little choice but to sit back and wait, although it would have been swifter to get out and walk the final distance. Finally, the driver turned in through the gates and the horses' hooves clattered over the cobbles. Inside the house, Sir Matthew's dogs started barking their welcome as he came out to greet her. His face looked aged and full of frowns.

"Thank you for coming. I know it cannot have been easy."

"Luckily the queen is understanding. Is it Father?"

"Nothing like that. Your mother expects you in the front chamber."

Thomasin picked up her skirts and hurried inside, through the corridor that smelled of beeswax and herbs, then left into the room where a fire was burning. Lady Elizabeth was seated on a carved wooden chair; the long trestle table where they usually dined had been pushed to the side. Her pale face looked taut and angry.

"Mother." Thomasin dropped a curtsey.

"Up, up, enough of that. I'm not the queen!"

"What is the matter? I came as soon as I could."

Sir Matthew was hovering in the doorway behind them.

"What is this assignation you set up between Cecilia and that wretched Hatton man?"

"Assignation? There was no assignation."

"But you took him to meet her, did you not? Remember, I have had your sister's own side of this, so do not think to deceive me."

"Mother, it is not my intention to deceive you. You make it sound as if I planned it all, when it is quite the opposite. I take it Cecilia is home, then? She evaded me in the palace gardens."

"She came home late last night, giving us great cause for alarm."

"At least she came home. She has not always done that."

"Enough! Tell me what occurred. Do you not think I have enough to worry me, with your father locked in the Tower for goodness knows how long?"

"Yes, Mother, I am aware, and I have done nothing to add to your distress. Yesterday, I saw Cecilia at court. She had come there of her own volition, seeking Hatton, because she said he had a right to know about his child. I did my best to persuade her to return home, telling her it was not the proper thing to do and that she would be thrown out by the guards, but she was adamant. She was going to stay whether I helped her or not, so I thought it best to make things as quick as possible, so as to not cause a scene. The Papal Court were sitting that day, so it was quiet, fortunately, but I did not wish to risk the king seeing her."

"Hmm. You should have sent her straight back to me."

"I tried, believe me, but you know what she is like. She absolutely refused, so I sought to minimise the damage. I took Hatton to meet her in the garden and sat a little way off, to keep an eye on them, but I had the misfortune to fall asleep in the sun. When I woke, both of them had gone. Neither thought to wake me. I have not heard from either since."

"You fell asleep?"

"It was not of my choosing! I was tired and it was warm. Cecilia should have woken me after their meeting."

"And what transpired during this meeting?"

"I cannot answer that as I was asleep. It was my intention that she be allowed to inform him of his fatherhood, and I arranged for them to meet in the garden, in plain sight, so there could be no privacy."

"And they both disappeared. When was this?"

"Late afternoon, I think. I woke shortly before the king's dinner hour."

"And she came back here at night." Lady Elizabeth frowned. "What has she said on the matter?"

"Only that Hatton is prepared to make an honest woman of her for the sake of the child, but no divorced woman is an honest woman. It will take Parliament to separate her from Hugh. God's wounds, that such troubles should come to our door!"

Thomasin had not heard her mother curse that way before, not even upon the occasion of Cecilia's first elopement.

"She says he is to call here, today, to make his case. I know not what to do in your father's absence. I thank God that we have the protection of my dear brother."

"All will be well," said Sir Matthew, stepping further into the room. "I will meet with him and resolve this matter."

"She is three months away from giving birth," Thomasin calculated. "How can it be effected so quickly?"

"It is possible," Sir Matthew continued. "I shall draw up a special bill to submit to Parliament, and Hatton will need to speak with the king, but it is possible."

"So she will become his wife?"

"It appears so," said Lady Elizabeth, "although Hugh will cast her off without a penny."

"Mother, she does not really deserve a single penny of his, does she?"

"No, I suppose she does not."

"Is she upstairs?"

Lady Elizabeth nodded.

"Then I will go up and speak a few words with her."

"I pray you, do not upset her. We have had enough tears in this house already."

Thomasin found her sister in the chamber she had once slept in, embroidering a baby's bonnet.

Cecilia looked up at her approach. "I thought it would be you."

"Really? You didn't think I might still be waiting in the garden?"

"I'm sorry for that. We had to speak in private. We had important matters to discuss, Thomasin. We had to resolve our lives for the sake of the child — surely you understand?"

Thomasin sat on the wooden window seat, taking in the view across the garden, down to the river. A soft breeze blew in from outside. "Yes, I do understand."

"He is going to marry me," Cecilia went on. "He promised, for the sake of the child, but also my own sake. I know we have caused trouble and gone about this the wrong way, but we have been drawn to each other from the first moment we met. It really feels right, Thomasin."

"Your other marriage will be dissolved by Parliament, then?"

"We hope so. Will has gone to speak to Henry, and then he comes here. It is what we all want. I am sorry for the distress to Hugh, but he can marry again once it has passed, with no shame attached."

Thomasin was quiet. There was always shame attached to a divorce, regardless of who was to blame. At least Hugh's vast wealth would lessen the stigma.

"I hope it will be resolved quickly, and you will both be very happy."

"Thank you, Thomasin. I am gladdened to hear that." She rested her free hand on her belly. "Sometimes Mother treats me as if I am a mere nuisance, not a person with feelings. I never meant to cause her distress, nor Father, but I could not be the person they wanted me to be. Yes, I know how frivolous and ungrateful that sounds, but I could not go through life as an obedient servant if it was making me unhappy. They had the good fortune of making a love match, and I want that for myself."

Thomasin had never thought of it that way before. She had seen her sister's shame write large in her parents' faces; Cecilia had been decried her for her selfishness and reckless behaviour in the pursuit of love. But she was only striving for what they all desired, although she had been more brazen about it.

"Can you picture me as a quiet, country wife with a brood of children?"

Thomasin laughed. "I can't, but I am sure you will do it with your own style."

"That is what I intend. And you must come and stay with me, when the baby is due. Say you will!"

This request came as a surprise. "If the queen is willing to spare me."

"It will be September. All will be resolved in the court by then, I hope. And you must attend my wedding, of course. We plan to marry here, in London, as soon as we can."

"It seems that you resolved much yesterday."

"We did. I must thank you for your part in it, although it brought you trouble."

"No great trouble. It sounds as if you have all this planned out now, so long as the divorce is approved. But are you certain that Hatton is the man to make you happy, for the rest of your life? He will not deceive you or prove untrustworthy?"

Cecilia shook her head. "If you had heard him yesterday, you would not ask. He is the only man I could spend my life with, and he feels the same way about me."

"Well, that is fortunate indeed."

"He has inherited a new estate in Surrey, so we shall live there, not too far from court. It is quite near Hampton, actually, so when the court is there, we may ride over and see you."

Thomasin sat and listened to her sister talk, planning out her future, with the clothes she would wear, the guests she would invite to her new home, the horses and dogs she would own, and the names she might give her children. She couldn't help feeling a little twinge of jealousy at Cecilia's certainty of being loved, and the way her life would unfold, but a sliver of doubt crept into her mind. All this depended upon William Hatton being as good as his word, and the king's rapid agreement to grant a divorce when he was being denied one himself.

The sisters had been sitting together for a while when horse hooves were heard in the front courtyard, followed by a knock upon the door. Cecilia rose as swiftly as she could for a woman in her condition.

"It must be him."

Thomasin followed her down the staircase to find William Hatton standing in the hallway, with Lady Elizabeth beside him. Thomasin tried to shake off her former distaste, telling herself that this was the man she must now call brother.

"All is well?" Cecilia asked anxiously, before she reached the bottom.

"Come, sweetheart." Hatton offered her his hand. "Let us talk."

"What is amiss?"

"Nothing, but come and be seated while we plan."

Cecilia let herself be guided to the chair her mother had vacated. Lady Elizabeth stood to the side, clearly apprised of Hatton's news already.

"You are worrying me. What is it?"

"Merely a short delay. The king will not act at once; he needs time to consider the matter."

"My baby will not wait for his consideration! He is aware of the child?"

Hatton nodded. "It seems Sir Hugh has already made a petition to him, so he is aware of our difficulties."

"And he will not grant the divorce?"

"It's not that he won't. His mind is so occupied at the moment with his own situation, he does not care to hear about other divorces, let alone grant them."

"So we are stuck? What shall we do?"

Hatton took her hands. "For now, you will concentrate wholly upon your health and that of the child. I will continue to petition the king, but the time matters not. We will be wed, even if the child arrives first. It is what everyone wishes for; there can be no benefit in delay. I will make the king see as much."

"In the meantime," said Lady Elizabeth, placing her hand upon her daughter's shoulder, "we will stay here with Matthew, and after your father's release, we will all repair to Suffolk. You can lie in there, in your old chamber."

"And I will come to you in Suffolk, never fear. This will be resolved, even if Hugh and I have to work together!"

"A strange sight that would be." Cecilia gave a weak smile.

"It is only a temporary pause, nothing more. Do not let it trouble you. Stay serene and calm, for the sake of the child. No more worries."

"You promise that all will work out as we hoped?"

Thomasin was the only one who saw Hatton flinch. It was only the slightest twitch about his eyes, but she caught it.

"I promise," he said.

TWENTY-TWO

The Papal Court was in session again. Thomasin dressed herself carefully in sombre dark grey, alleviated only by the whiteness of her cuffs, headdress and trimmings. John Dudley called at Baynard's Castle to walk her back into Blackfriars, ready to hear Fisher's speech.

"I saw your father yesterday," he began at once. "He is well and in good spirits, as we had hoped."

"Oh, that is good to hear."

"Sir William keeps him well, although he says he cannot spare more candles for his chamber than the quota allows. I think it is this which is affecting his eyes, as he tries to read and write in the gloom."

"Oh, such a small thing. I will send some at once."

"No need. I have ordered a crate, to be delivered today."

"Thank you, John."

"I also sent him your love, which he was pleased to receive, and he sends his in return."

Thomasin smiled in relief. As they walked past the tightly packed houses, she thought about her father, sitting alone in that dim cell. The little London street between the palaces was quiet enough, but the sounds of voices and chickens reached them, along with the sound of horse hooves on the cobbles ahead. John noticed her silence.

"You are well this morning, Thomasin?"

"Well enough for the day ahead."

"Something ails you? Apart from your father's situation and the unfairness of the court?"

"Those are bad enough, adding to the queen's suffering, but we have troubles at home, too. I should not let them cloud my mind, but it is my sister again."

"Ah." John already knew all about Cecilia and her history. "She is with child, is she not?"

"Yes, it will be born in the early autumn, God willing. But the matter is complicated."

"I am not one to gossip, Thomasin, but you must know she is spoken of at court. I cannot say from which quarter, but I suspect the rumours come from a source very close to the king."

"That does not surprise me. She has made an enemy of Anne Boleyn, who will do all she can to besmirch her name. Not that she needs much help in doing so; Cecilia has been her own worst enemy in that."

"What is the new difficulty?"

"She wishes to be married to the father of her child, William Hatton."

If Dudley was surprised or scandalised, he concealed it well. "I see. But she is already married, to…"

"Sir Hugh Truegood, a worthy enough gentleman who wed her willingly, but he has since discovered her secret and cast her out. He has been petitioning the king for a divorce to be sped through Parliament before the child arrives."

"Hatton," mused Dudley. "Isn't he the fellow with very fair hair?"

"Yes, that's him."

"I hate to say this, and I may be speaking out of turn, but I have my doubts about this."

"Why? Do tell me. I have doubted him from the start."

"Well, I may be wrong, but I had thought him to be betrothed to a lady on the south coast. I only know this because my stepfather, Lord Lisle, has a residence near Portsmouth and knows the woman's family. Some distant relative on his mother's side, I think. But it may have been one of those childhood betrothals, as I have not heard it spoken of at court, and after all, many a betrothal has been broken in favour of a marriage."

Thomasin digested this information. "It is a question Hatton must answer."

They paused outside the gate that led into the Blackfriars complex. "You have far too much to think about at the moment," said Dudley. "Let me look into it. If there is any truth in the matter, I shall hold Hatton to account."

"You are so kind. I do not know how we would manage without friends like you."

"Think nothing of it. We cannot have your sister taking the name of a scoundrel. Now, let us go and hear what the good bishop has to say."

A crowd had already gathered outside the courtroom doors as they arrived. Cromwell stood on the threshold, watching as they filed inside, keen to hear this crucial day's evidence. News of Fisher's speech had spread, and Catherine's supporters had left their chambers and offices to be present in the name of their queen. A buzz of anticipation ran through them, just as it had on the trial's first day.

As Thomasin and Dudley were entering, Cromwell turned his head away, unwilling to look at them. Thomasin almost dared to wish him a good morning, to force him to acknowledge her, but she decided she was grateful to not have to interact with the odious man. They took their seats towards the back, among friends, as Fisher was already seated at the front, ready to be examined. Wolsey and Campeggio occupied the dais as usual, but Thomasin noted that the king himself was not present. However, she was surprised to see that Sir Thomas Boleyn was seated on the right, attentive to the proceedings, no doubt intending to report back to Henry and Anne.

The court opened with the usual official statements read by the clerk. Thomasin was used to the legal formalities by now, and switched off as they were read. Fisher was to speak first, but it still took a good length of time before he was called to the stand.

The bishop looked out across the assembled heads, then turned to address the cardinals.

"Your Graces, lords and ladies, I come to address this court having spent the past two years studying the intricacies of this difficult case. My belief in the justness of the queen's cause has been questioned, dissected and put to the test many times, but it has weathered every storm. I stand before you after appealing to my conscience according to God's law, urging you to attend the word of an honest, devout and Christian man, driven by nothing but what I sincerely believe to be the truth of this matter."

At the side, Thomasin saw Cromwell roll his eyes.

"I am present here today as a true, honest and loyal subject of the king. After much deliberation I have concluded that I must speak the truth in order to not procure the damnation of my soul, nor to fail in the duty I owe those present, in such a matter of great importance. Though my words may seem unfaithful to my king, they are faithful indeed to the truth, and to God. I stand here before your reverend lordships to declare, affirm and with forcible reasons, demonstrate that this marriage of the king and queen can be dissolved by no power, human or Divine, and for this opinion, I would even lay down my life. To this end, I have written a book upon this very subject, which I present to the court, and ask every man here present to uphold the Sacraments and fulfil his duty as a true Christian. None of us have the power to dissolve the bonds between those whom God has joined."

A muted ripple of applause ran through the court. Thomasin sighed deeply. Fisher could not have been clearer in his support of the queen, but as she watched Thomas Boleyn frowning, she wondered what it might cost him.

Fisher spoke again, at length, detailing his arguments and quoting his sources, but he had made his main points. Campeggio sat very still throughout, but Wolsey was perched on his chair like a hawk, absorbing Fisher's message. When he had finished, Wolsey thanked him for his evidence, then called a brief adjournment to allow the cardinals to confer.

"They are unlikely to convene again today," said John. "The bishop's speech has given them much to discuss. They need to adjust their case accordingly."

"Do you think it will have made a difference?"

"Very much so. I cannot see how any devout Catholic can argue against Fisher's logic."

"This is good news. I will repair to the queen at once. This surely will cheer her."

Thomasin found the queen reminiscing about happier times at Baynard's Castle. She was seated at a game of chess with Maria, before a roaring fire, while a boy played gentle tunes on the lute. Thomasin paused, unwilling to interrupt.

"I recall the visit of my dear sister-in-law, Margaret, the former queen of the Scots. We danced here, in this very chamber, maybe ten or twelve years ago."

"It was thirteen summers ago, my lady," said Maria, "and she wore a dress of dark red, and caught a thread upon the leg of a chair."

"Now you mention that, I remember it well! What a good memory you have, Maria. Was it not about this time of year?"

"It was May, I think, as the roses were the same as they are now."

"Ah, the roses. We had brought an armful inside, and the scent filled the room. We should do the same now." Catherine turned and gestured to Ellen, who had been embroidering.

"Ellen and Mary, go outside and gather roses. Bring them inside. Let us have the chamber filled with roses again, as it was then."

Ellen dropped a curtsey and went to fetch Mary. She widened her eyes at Thomasin, standing in the door, just as the queen spotted her.

"Thomasin, you have come from court? Do tell us how the bishop fared."

Thomasin approached the chess table and curtseyed. "My lady, he could not have done better. His speech was full of passion and conviction, his arguments and motives most sound. Surely no Christian man can now deny that to dissolve the marriage would be to go against the Sacraments."

Catherine nodded. "That is excellent."

"The cardinals have dismissed the court for today, in order to discuss his arguments."

"With my happy memories, I almost feel hopeful. The court must find in my favour, and very soon!"

"I hope so, my lady. I cannot see otherwise, now."

"Where is Fisher? I wish to thank him in person."

"He remained, but I am sure he will come and visit you in person soon."

"More wine. Wine and roses! We will not celebrate just yet, but by God's grace, we might allow ourselves a little pleasure, I think."

*

It was midafternoon when visitors arrived. The chamber was heady with the scent of roses and ringing with laughter when Giles Waterson and Harry Letchmere were shown in. Both were dressed splendidly, in rich doublets, caps and gold chains, as befitted a visit to a queen, and they carried gifts of wafers, jars of honey, wine and candied suckets. Thomasin felt a twinge of guilt at the sight of Giles, recalling their last awkward encounter. She had forbidden him from speaking then, surprised by the realisation that he had feelings for her. Until then, she had not considered Giles in a romantic light, more as an attractive, helpful cousin, while all her affection had been for Rafe. But how did she feel now? She watched the men bow low before the queen.

"Gentlemen," said Catherine, "how very welcome you are. What wonderful gifts you bring to lighten our afternoon."

"It seems we already find you very merry, which gladdens my heart," said Giles, looking around at the roses. "What is the occasion of this celebration?"

"Hope," replied the queen, "hope for the future. Come, will you drink with us?"

The men accepted a glass of wine each, and raised them along with the queen. As they drank, Giles met Thomasin's eyes with a mixture of curiosity and warmth. She looked away quickly. Whatever this was between them, she did not want it to play out in public.

It was Harry Letchmere who approached Thomasin and Ellen, as if Giles had somehow understood her thoughts.

"Ladies, it is a pleasure to see you again, both looking radiant as ever."

It was a platitude, but Thomasin noticed how Ellen smiled.

"The queen is keeping you busy, no doubt?"

"Oh, we live fairly quietly here," said Ellen, smiling, "save for Thomasin's visits to the court, but we hope those will soon cease."

"Ah yes, the Papal Court. Surely that is everyone's dearest wish?"

"So long as it brings the desired outcome," said Thomasin, more guarded.

"I heard that Fisher's speech was excellent. It must influence the outcome."

"Thomasin was in the courtroom," said Ellen. "She heard it all."

"It was a good speech," Thomasin agreed, "but let us wait and see."

Harry looked across the chamber to where Catherine was laughing at something Giles had said. "The queen seems in good cheer. That alone is a blessing."

"It is," said Thomasin, suddenly tiring. "Would you excuse me? I just need to sit down for a moment."

"Are you well?" asked Ellen, concerned. "Shall I come too?"

"I am quite well. It has just been a long day and I wish to rest. Please, don't let me stop you."

Leaving them in silence, Thomasin poured herself a glass of wine and headed into the anteroom where she might find a moment's rest. Her head felt a little foggy and the wave of fatigue had caught her unawares. She hoped she hadn't caught a chill when she'd slept in the garden the other day.

"Thomasin?"

Of course Giles had followed her. He must have been watching her from across the room, but she did not wish him to think she had deliberately removed herself in order to allow him a chance to seek her out.

"I am just a little tired, nothing more. I wanted to rest a moment."

"I understand. Is there anything I can bring you?"

"Nothing more, thank you."

"Shall I tell the queen you are indisposed?"

"No, I'm sure I will be well in a moment. I will just rest here for a moment to regather my strength."

"Very well, but call for me if you require anything."

He stood in the doorway, looking down at her, reluctant to leave. Thomasin could see she would need to dismiss him.

"All is well. You may leave me now."

He gave a brief nod and disappeared. She sat back in the chair and closed her eyes.

"Thomasin?"

She woke with a start. Ellen was standing over her.

"You were asleep? It is the dinner hour."

Thomasin sat up, rubbing her eyes. "I am sorry. I hope the queen was not upset at my absence."

"Not at all. She is quite content and already dressed for dinner. But you must rouse yourself now."

"I will. I don't know how it happened. I just felt a little tired, that is all."

"Well, you have been busy lately, and had many concerns regarding your family."

Thomasin nodded. "I feel well otherwise. I hope I have not caught a cold."

"Take some warming spices and hot wine at dinner, and hopefully those will sort you out."

"Yes, I will, thank you. Are the guests still here?"

"They're waiting in the hall to dine, along with Fisher and a few others."

Thomasin jumped up at once and started tweaking her bonnet. "I must tidy myself up! You go ahead. I will be along to join you in a moment."

By the time Thomasin joined them in the main hall at Baynard's Castle, the first dinner plates had already been served. Catherine was seated at the head of the table, with Fisher to her right and John Clerk on her left, along with a few other bishops and supporters. Giles and Letchmere sat in the middle, with Ellen opposite, who was clearly saving a space beside her on the bench.

Thomasin nodded to the queen in apology and hurried over, sitting down just as a dish of steaming ox cheeks was placed before her. Immediately her gorge rose and she turned away, unable to look at food, let alone eat it. The room began to swim around her.

"Thomasin, you are still unwell," Ellen said softly.

"Yes, not well," she managed to say. "The food!"

"Come, let us get you somewhere quiet."

Gently, Ellen helped Thomasin back to her feet and led her through to the antechamber again, where she pulled out a trestle and blanket. "Here, you must lie down. The queen will send for Dr Butts." She held her hand to Thomasin's forehead. "You are developing a fever. I will instruct the kitchens to bring you something cooling. Never fear; rest and the right medicine will fix you."

"Thank you." Thomasin climbed into bed. "I do not wish to be a nuisance."

"Not at all. Do you want me to sit with you?"

"I think I will try and sleep. Please, return to the meal."

"Very well, but take this." Ellen handed her the small hand bell they sometimes used. "Ring this if you need anything. Try to sleep."

"I will," said Thomasin, her eyes already closing.

TWENTY-THREE

When Thomasin woke, there were soft voices in the room. It was dark and cool, with one figure outlined in the doorway while another leaned over her. She recognised the familiar outline of Dr Butts, who had once treated her mother for her chest complaint.

"Ah, you are awake," he said softly, looking at her closely. "And how are you feeling today, Thomasin?"

She blinked up at him, trying to work out exactly how she was feeling. "I was tired, very tired. And dizzy, and then I couldn't bear the smell of the food."

He nodded. "I have seen a few cases like this at court in the past day. It is an infection that is spreading when people come together, which preys on young women. A kind of green sickness. When did it start?"

"Just before dinner."

"You mean yesterday?"

Had she slept that long, all through the night?"

"I suppose so, but the other day I feel asleep in the garden at court."

"And I understand you have been facing family difficulties, as well as being very busy yourself?"

"I suppose. Yes, my family has troubles."

"There is nothing to worry about. I am making you up a revitalising elixir. That and more rest will restore you in a few days."

"I am sorry for the trouble I have caused."

"It is no trouble. I am glad that I was summoned so soon. Are you otherwise well? No other complaints, no aches and pains or dullness of spirits?"

"Not at all."

"You are young and strong; I am confident you will recover. However, it is not desirable that you remain near to the queen's ladies while you are unwell."

"Oh no, of course not. I would not wish to make them ill."

Butts looked to the figure in the doorway, which resolved itself into Ellen.

"Your mother is sending her carriage to take you back to Monk's Place for a few days. By then, the queen will have returned to Bridewell and you may join us there."

"But am I not needed? What about the court?"

"Thomasin, you can do no one any good like this. You must rest and recover, then you can be useful again."

"Here are the herbs," said Mary, Lady Essex, appearing behind her, "and the spices from the queen."

Thomasin felt tears springing to her eyes. "I did not wish to be a burden to anyone."

"You are not," said Dr Butts. "Everyone gets ill from time to time, even royalty! You will be well again very soon."

"But my sister is there, at Monk's Place," she went on. "I cannot risk infecting her."

"Never fear," Dr Butts replied. "As I said, it is a green sickness, arising from the condition of maidenhood. Your sister will not be in danger from it, I assure you."

Thomasin felt her cheeks redden furiously. She was ill because she was still a maid?

"But how?"

"Well, to put it delicately, there is a build-up of the humours in the womb which only the act of a male can reverse. It is a common illness among the unmarried. The simplest remedy is obvious, but until you are wedded, rest and medicine will assist you."

Thomasin turned her head away in shame.

"Come now," said Ellen, "the carriage will be here soon. We should get you ready."

After Dr Butts had retired with the queen, Thomasin stuck her feet indignantly into her shoes, with Ellen guiding them into place.

"I can't believe this. I cannot be ill because I have not had contact with a man! Does that not sound ridiculous to you?"

"I don't know. Dr Butts is a reputable physician with years of experience. I would not presume to question him."

"But the idea is preposterous — that I should need intimacy with a man in order to be well!"

"Perhaps it is time to think of a husband, Thomasin. After all, you are of an age now."

"I am not yet twenty."

"Many women, including myself, were already wed by that age."

"I will rest, drink this elixir and take spices and herbs, and I shall be quite well again. How about nuns in the convent? How do they manage?"

"I don't know anything about nuns, Thomasin," Ellen said, smiling, "but there is no point making yourself angry about it. Your course is fixed now. You must rest and recover, as there is no doubt you are ill."

Thomasin was about to object, but as she rose to her feet another wave of nausea overtook her. She leaned against the wall to steady herself.

"Very well, but I refuse to believe that the cure lies in a man!"

"Well, there are some who might hope that you would jump at the chance of such a cure."

"What do you mean?"

"Giles. He was most concerned for you last night. He did not wish to leave without being reassured that you were well; we had to tell him you were sleeping and insist that he depart. Honestly, I am surprised he has not returned this morning."

At that moment, Maria entered, with her arms full of flowers. "Just delivered," she said, "for the patient, along with cordials and marmalade. From Mr Waterson."

Ellen laughed. "Now, what did I tell you? There is someone eager to cure you himself."

"Oh, stop it!"

"I shall load these into the carriage to go with you," suggested Maria. "The flowers will cheer your chamber."

Thomasin took the arm Ellen offered and walked carefully towards the door. Perhaps a rest was exactly what she needed after all.

The carriage took her straight to Monk's Place, where Lady Elizabeth and Sir Matthew came out to meet her. Thomasin climbed out in a fever, with the heady scents of Giles's flowers still in her nostrils. Leaning on her uncle, she walked slowly through the hallway and up the stairs. Her chamber had been prepared with fresh white linen sheets and bunches of lavender hanging from the ceiling to ward off bad vapours. A fire burned in the grate with a scented pastille, intended to cleanse the air, but it made the atmosphere heavy.

Thomasin's hand flew to her nose. "The window, please?"

"But cold air is not good for you!" said her mother.

"Please, the smell."

Sir Matthew strode over and threw the window open. Thomasin crawled into bed and drew the covers up to her chin.

"Now I will prepare one of Dr Butts' special drinks for you, and then I shall sit and read to you, if you like," said Lady Elizabeth.

"Cecilia?"

"She is in the other room, never fear. She is quite content. We have not yet heard from Sir William, but we expect him daily."

Thomasin sighed and closed her eyes.

When she woke again, the light had changed. There were voices coming from the garden, underneath her open window, but the air had turned a little chilly.

Carefully swinging her legs out from beneath the covers, she crept shakily over to the window seat and reached to secure the latch.

"But what will Mother say?" Cecilia was saying. "And Father, when he is released. Neither of them will like it one bit, and they will ask questions."

Thomasin's ears pricked up at once. The second voice was definitely Hatton's.

"What other choice do we have, if the divorce will not be granted? You will be considered a whore at court, confined to live in the country, your name blackened forever."

"Many there already consider me that. I do not care for people's opinions of me; I just want to live quietly with you and our child. How can that be so difficult?"

"But that is my plan, don't you see? In Italy, we can pass as man and wife without judgement."

"But it is so far, and so hot, and I can't speak a word of Italian."

"We will hire English servants. The house is on a hill and designed to be cool in the summer months."

"But I do not want to make the journey in this condition. What if it causes trouble for the child? A sea crossing, and all that way by road?"

"Many women have travelled before in your condition."

"But I have not, Will. I have not. I do not want the discomfort and strain and fear of it, not for my first child. I want to be at home, with Mother, in familiar surroundings."

"Then we wait and go after the child is born? Is that what you want?"

"No, none of this is what I want."

"Or perhaps it is me that you don't want."

"How can you say that? Look at my condition! I think we should confide in Mother."

"You can't. You know she will do all she can to prevent it, and then we will never be together."

"That is not her purpose. Mother just wants me to be safe. Why can't you petition the king again?"

"He was adamant. No divorce for him, so none for us."

"That seems very unfair."

"Try telling him that!"

They moved away from the window and down the path towards the river. Thomasin saw their shapes outlined against the bushes. She was troubled by what she had heard. She should speak with Cecilia, before the pair made any rash decisions.

The night air was cool on her face. The temperature in the chamber had dropped and the overpowering smell of burning pastilles had dissipated. Thomasin pulled the window shut and crept back into bed. By the time Lady Elizabeth came in to check on her, Thomasin was asleep again.

TWENTY-FOUR

Thomasin woke to find a figure sitting beside her bed.

"Ellen?"

Her cousin looked up. "Ah, you are awake. How are you feeling?"

"Tired and strange. How come you are here?"

"Well, you know how quiet things are at Baynard's Castle, so the queen gave me leave to visit. I've brought some books, if you are up to reading, and a few treats from the queen's table."

Thomasin propped herself up on her elbows. "Oh, that is very kind. How are things with the queen?"

"She is doing well, full of hope. She dined with Bishop Fisher and has gone out riding this morning, on account of it being such a fine day."

"That is unusual. She must be feeling better."

"She has gone up to the fields above the city walls, taking the Scottish ambassador and his wife with her; she seemed quite her old self again. I can only pray that the court's verdict merits this confidence."

"Who is in court today?"

"No one is needed now. The main arguments have been made and the cardinals are consulting the legal documentation provided by the universities. So fear not; you are not missing out on your duty."

Thomasin sighed. "Is Mother about? Has there been any news of Father?"

"When I arrived, she and Cecilia said they would take the opportunity of me being here to visit him, so they have ridden out in the carriage with Sir Matthew, bound for the Tower."

"I must speak with Cecilia upon her return."

"I am sure you will, but until their return, there is little more that you can do but rest."

"I suppose so."

"Or you can pass the time by gossiping with me, should you have the strength." Ellen had a mischievous look upon her face that Thomasin knew well.

"What is it? What gossip is there?"

"Very little, save that one of the queen's ladies, who you know very well, might be about to become betrothed in the next day or so."

Thomasin's addled brain struggled to grasp this. "What, who? Not you, Ellen? Tell me, is it you?"

A shy smile crept across her face. "None other than me."

"Betrothed? But I cannot… Sir Henry Letchmere? I can think of no other."

"And I can think of no other either, Thomasin. Yes, it is Harry Letchmere. He is on the verge of proposing; he hinted as much to me last night and only awaits the queen's permission. But tell me: what do you think of my choice?"

"I am stunned, honestly. I had no idea things had progressed so far. You have kept this secret to yourself."

"It's not so much a secret. You have seen us together. It has been fast, I admit, and I did not wish to get my hopes up, but I am minded to accept him when he asks."

"Goodness. I feel I hardly know him."

"Well," said Ellen, frowning a little, "it is not you who he is asking. I hope you can be a little happy for me."

"Yes, of course I am. Dear Ellen, of course I am. You have taken me by surprise, that is all. Tell me all about him."

"I hardly know where to start. It is not the same as with Hugh; he is a very different character, quiet and gentle."

"Yes, I have seen that myself."

"He has also been married before and is a widower with no children, so it is ideal for us to start again. I am not too old yet; I might have the family I always hoped for."

"Yes! I am delighted for you, truly I am. And he is all you would wish for?"

"I believe he is. Kind and thoughtful and generous. He has a house in the north of Essex, near the forest of Epping, not too far from court, so I will remain in the queen's household until such time as I may bring forth children."

Thomasin could see the happiness radiating from her cousin's face. "I had not expected it, but this is the best news I could have hoped for. You deserve it, Ellen, after all you have been through."

"And we'll have my inheritance, along with his, so we might have no concerns about providing for ourselves. We have not yet ironed out the details, but he wishes for me to keep a generous portion of it under my own control. I could not ask for more."

"How about love?" Thomasin mused. "This is all very well, but do you think you love him, Ellen?"

Her smile answered the question. "If it is not love yet, it very soon will be. I have twice been burned by the infatuation of love, but this is a slow-burning affection based on respect and companionship. He is simply the best man I know, and a friend of Giles, of course, which speaks volumes."

"It does?"

"Of course. Anyone who Giles considers a friend must be a trustworthy and honourable man, like himself."

"You have a high opinion of Sir Giles."

"Yes, he merits it. Don't you?"

"Indeed, I do, for the kind help he has given my family in our hour of need."

"There is more to him than that, is there not? After Harry, I will admit he is a true paragon of a gentleman, unequalled at court."

"Yes, well." Thomasin shifted in bed, uneasy at this talk. "I wonder if I might be strong enough to get up today."

"Dr Butts said you should stay in bed. I do not want you collapsing while I am here with the sole charge of you."

"All right, I will wait until my mother returns and collapse then. Is there wine?"

Ellen poured some from the flask on the table. Thomasin drank gratefully, her throat parched after her long sleep and their talk. She wondered what her cousin would say about the conversation she had overheard the previous evening.

"I am concerned about Cecilia," she began. "I think William Hatton visited the house yesterday evening. I woke in the darkness and heard them in the garden. Their plan was to ask the king for a quick divorce so they could marry before the child arrives, but it seems that Henry is reluctant to grant them what he longs for himself. So, they are making plans to run away together and live abroad as man and wife, in Italy, I think. Hatton is a lot more certain, while Cecilia is afraid to travel in her condition."

"I cannot blame her for that. I would not wish for the discomfort, or to be away from home and family at such a time."

"That is what I thought. Mother had hoped she would lie in at Eastwell Hall, where she can be on hand. I cannot think of Cecilia undergoing such an ordeal among strangers, in a foreign land, unable to speak the language."

"No, it does not bear thinking about. It cannot be."

"This is why I wish to speak with her, but it must be soon."

"They will be back soon, I am sure."

"There is also another matter. I do not trust Hatton at all. No matter what she feels for him, I have always had my doubts, but I was prepared to see them happily married until John Dudley mentioned something. He has heard reports of Hatton having a betrothed down on the south coast, near the residence of his stepfather. Hatton must refute this himself. We can't have Cecilia being lied to again."

"No, all must be clear and above board if they are to be together."

"But the matter of the child is pressing. It is due in September, although it may come early, as first children often do, or so Mother says."

Ellen sat up. "Wait, what was that?"

Thomasin strained to follow the sound, and soon she was also aware of hooves on the cobbles outside, followed by footsteps in the downstairs hallway.

"They are back! I will not get up, as you advise, but please ask my mother to come up as soon as she is able to."

Ellen nodded and left the room, her steps receding down the staircase.

Thomasin lay back on her pillows. She knew she was right to speak up about Italy, but should she have mentioned the reputed betrothed? The last thing she wanted to do was stand in the way of her sister's happiness, but what if she might be protecting her from further heartbreak?

The voices from the hallway were rising in pitch and energy. Thomasin turned her ear to the door, trying to discern her mother and uncle's words, as the former seemed almost beside herself with excitement. It was all Thomasin could do not to shuffle out of bed and across the floor towards the door, although she feared she would stumble on the stairs.

Soon, the sounds grew louder, mounting the staircase, turning the bend and heading up to the rooms above. Thomasin could barely contain her anticipation.

"Hello?" she called out. "What is it?"

Ellen entered the room first. "You will not believe it, Thomasin, but your mother has brought home a surprise."

Two figures followed her into the room, more slowly. Lady Elizabeth was leading a man by the arm, whom Thomasin suddenly recognised with a shock of delight.

"Father!"

She sat up in bed and reached out her arms.

"He has finally been released," said Lady Elizabeth, her face a mixture of relief and concern. "Just as we were visiting, a letter arrived from the king giving permission for him to leave."

Sir Richard stepped into the light, revealing just how tired he looked. The ordeal had drawn the colour from his face, and he was clearly in need of rest. He leaned over the bed and wrapped his daughter in an embrace.

"And you are unwell in bed?" he asked, before letting her go.

"Oh, it is nothing. Dr Butts calls it the green sickness, but I am resting and already feel better."

"It is good to see that. And thank you for your visit, and all those of your friends."

"My friends?"

"More and Fisher and Dudley have been keeping me company, but none more regularly than your cousin Giles."

Thomasin knew this, but hearing it again struck her anew.

"Every day he came, bringing gifts, reading to me, composing letters on my behalf. I cannot thank him enough."

"Such a treasure he is," said Lady Elizabeth. "He has done us so much good. I am sure his hand is behind this release; he must have been petitioning the king."

Behind her, Ellen raised her eyebrows at Thomasin.

Thomasin refused to be drawn. "But how are you feeling, Father?"

"If truth be told, I am a little weary of it all. For all the companionship I had during the day, the nights were long and my bed was not comfortable. I had a lot of time to think, and I have come to the conclusion that my time at court is at an end. I am done with the nonsense of men and their vanity and cruelty to each other. I intend to rest for a few days and recover my strength, and then we are returning to Suffolk. There is no place I would rather be than among the trees and birds and wide skies of my own peaceful home, where I am king and master, and there is no divorce or decree or incarceration."

Lady Elizabeth flinched a little at the mention of divorce. Thomasin realised she had not yet told Sir Richard of Cecilia and Hatton's plans, but this was not the time to raise them.

"Where is Cecilia?" asked Thomasin. "Could she not make the stairs?"

"She is with Dr Butts," said Lady Elizabeth, "consulting him about her condition. I am to send the carriage for her again in an hour."

A sudden wave of concern struck Thomasin. There was every chance that her sister was meeting the doctor, but after the conversation she had overheard the previous night, there was a possibility that she was with Hatton, making plans, or even embarking upon their escape.

Ellen had the same idea. "We should not tire you, dear Uncle Richard, nor Thomasin either. Let us leave her to her rest and take you to yours. Shall I send to the kitchen for wine and spices, or would you rather have a caudle made from honey and almond milk?"

"A caudle would be most beneficial," he said, leaning on the arm she offered, just as Thomasin gestured for Lady Elizabeth to remain with her.

When their voices had receded down the stairs, Thomasin took a deep breath.

"Mother, close the chamber door. I would not disturb Father with this."

"What is it? Are you unwell?"

"No more than before."

"Such good news! I can't express how grateful we are for your father's release. It was all Sir Giles, you know, all down to his good offices. Sir William Kingston said as much."

"Yes, it is wonderful news. But, Mother, are you certain that Cecilia is with Dr Butts?"

"We dropped her outside his house."

"Did you see her go inside?"

"Into the courtyard, but not inside the house itself. Why do you ask?"

"Hopefully it is only my caution that makes me doubt her."

Lady Elizabeth frowned. "She has done much to cause doubt. What else do you fear?"

"Last night, I woke and heard voices outside my open window. I do not know what time, but it was Cecilia and William Hatton."

"Yes, he was here last night. He called before supper to speak with her about their plans."

"Their plans to wed after her divorce from Hugh?"

"That's right."

"Well, they are planning more than that. It seems that the king is reluctant to grant their wish and Hatton is all for whisking her away to some other country. He spoke of going to Italy."

"Italy? In her condition? He must be mad."

"That is what I thought. So he has said nothing of the sort to you?"

"No, I would have nipped that nonsense in the bud had he dared to do so. Your sister will come to Suffolk with us and spend her lying-in at Eastwell Hall."

"Unless she has already flown."

"No, surely not. She has no necessaries with her. She has been rash in the past, impulsive for the sake of love, but she is not stupid. She would not risk the life of her unborn child for a whim of Hatton's, would she?"

"I hope not, Mother. There is more. John Dudley spoke to me of a woman on the south coast who may be betrothed to Hatton. I do not know the truth of it, but I do not like it."

Lady Elizabeth rose to her full, diminutive height. "I will send the carriage for her at once. There is no need to trouble your father with this. You must rest and recover now, Thomasin. I thank you for your vigilance."

"I pray it is unnecessary."

"I think your sister is past prayer, now."

TWENTY-FIVE

Presently, Thomasin heard the carriage arrive in the courtyard again. This time, she could not bear to remain in bed and wait for the news, so she wrapped a shawl about her shoulders and shuffled gingerly to the staircase. To her relief, she heard Cecilia loudly complaining about her back as Lady Elizabeth ushered her into a chair. However, another voice came after hers, its male tones rather familiar.

Thomasin retreated back into her chamber and scrambled into bed. Giles was here, downstairs in the hallway, speaking with her mother. She felt ashamed at the thought that he might come up and see her lying in bed, her hair unbrushed and loose, her nightgown untidy. She lay still, silent, planning to feign sleep should she hear his footsteps, but the front door clicked shut and silence fell again within the house. Her frustration ate away at her, teasing out all sorts of questions in her mind, until she heard Ellen's soft tread. Her cousin entered the chamber carrying a tray of food.

"Well, I hope you are hungry."

She placed the tray across Thomasin's lap, with its array of invalid foods: a sweet almond custard, boiled chicken in spinach, a slice of beef pie and wafers with honey. The smell of it awakened Thomasin's tastebuds, and she realised she'd not eaten properly for days.

"Cecilia is back?"

"Oh yes, she is back. She was not planning to run away at all; if anything, she has seen sense."

"What a relief. Was that Giles downstairs?"

"It was." Ellen took a seat in the carved chair. "Now, don't hold back. You enjoy this spread and I will tell you everything."

"He is still here?"

"No, he has gone, but he sends his best wishes. The pie and wafers came from him."

Was that disappointment Thomasin felt? Something stirred in her as she wondered why Giles had not come up to see her, although she knew she would have felt awkward if he had.

"Come, tell me," Thomasin said, having sated her appetite. "How came Giles to be here?"

"He brought Cecilia home. It seems that she went first to Dr Butts, as she intended, and asked his advice about travelling abroad in her condition. He advised her in the strongest terms against such an action, explaining the danger to herself and her child. This caused her to travel to court in another attempt to find Hatton. Apparently, they quarrelled, which was when Giles found her. Now she is adamant she will deliver the child at Eastwell Hall, which has greatly pleased your parents. She will depart with them."

Thomasin sighed. "It is the best outcome for her. Any marriage to Hatton, if it takes place, will have to wait."

"I believe Giles spoke to her in the carriage on the way home. He explained the foolishness of her actions."

"And she knows nothing yet about Hatton's reputed betrothal?"

"No, she does not. It's probably better that way."

"I do not doubt it. But why did Giles go so soon? He did not come up to see how I was."

"I think he did not want to intrude at a difficult time."

"Yes, that would be like him."

"And now what will you do, Thomasin? Are you stronger? Will you remain here after your parents leave, or return to the queen?"

"I am already feeling much better. I will see them depart, and then join you at Bridewell."

"The queen makes the move tomorrow, so we shall look forward to your return, although do not rush back before you are fully well."

"I will not. Is there no other court news?"

"Only that Norfolk's mistress Bess Holland has quarrelled with Anne, the cardinals are still in deliberation and Wolsey looks like a walking ghost, and Henry is out hunting today, trying to hurry away the days until the court pronounces its verdict."

"And how are things with you?"

"I am quite content with Harry, and we plan to be wed in the late summer."

They heard feet upon the staircase and Lady Elizabeth appeared, red-faced and puffing from exertion, but triumphantly holding out a letter. She handed it to Thomasin, who did not recognise the seal.

"A boy delivered it to the house just now," she explained. "It looks to be of some importance, so I thought you should have it at once."

Thomasin broke the seal and unfolded the sheet to reveal neat, upright handwriting. She scanned the few lines quickly, down to the signature.

"Oh, how lovely, it is a wedding invitation. John Dudley spoke to me before about his step-uncle, Arthur, Lord Lisle. He is getting married at court in three days' time and John has invited me to attend, as he said he would."

"Lord Lisle?" asked her mother. "Is he not uncle to the king himself? A bastard son of Edward the Fourth, I believe?"

"He is of royal blood, yes."

"An invitation to a royal wedding! Thomasin, you are honoured! What will you wear? Who is the bride?"

"Lady Honor Basset, a widow from the West Country, reputed to be very beautiful."

"A summer wedding too! Alas, I have my best cream silk in the countryside still, and it would not arrive in time if I sent for it. How about the pale blue gown, the one with the pearl bodice?"

"I always like you in the dusky pink dress for summer," suggested Ellen. "It suits your colouring better."

"Or my dark red," mused Thomasin, "although it is heavy fabric if the weather should prove warm."

"How very exciting," said Lady Elizabeth. "You must choose carefully. I am glad that you have been singled out in this way; the Dudleys are good friends to us, with John visiting your father too. I will send them a side of venison."

"Jane is with child again," said Thomasin.

"Good news. Then I shall send some of my herbs and ointments to her, as well. Now, I must go back and try to calm Cecilia, who is unsettled and angry about Hatton. By the stars, I wish she had never laid eyes upon that man!"

When her mother had left, Thomasin took a pinch of the warming spices and let them crackle on her tongue. In truth, she was feeling a lot better. Her nausea had gone, leaving a ravenous appetite.

"All this nonsense about green sickness," she said to Ellen. "Rest and a good, wholesome diet have cured my malaise, not any man."

Ellen smiled. "You are a doctor now?"

"No, but that's the truth. I was probably tired, perhaps with a little chill. I do not believe this notion that women's bodies suffer without connection with a man. We can manage quite well without one."

"Well, Thomasin, remember that you are speaking to someone who is making plans for her wedding."

"Yes, but you are marrying Letchmere because you want to, not because you will sicken and die without him."

Ellen smiled. "Sicken, maybe."

"Oh, this is just romantic foolishness. I thought the same about Rafe not so long ago, and now look at us."

"Yes, here you are, ill in bed."

"But not because of him, although his behaviour has sickened me at times. I could live quite happily without him."

"So it is quite over between you and Rafe."

"Quite over, finally. I told him the last time I saw him. I can't live with his jealousy and bad temper. I had thought him quite over it, and glimpsed the man he could become, but I was mistaken. It would always be hanging over our lives like a shadow, every time he drank or perceived a rival. I could not live like that."

"Then it is fortunate that you did not announce your engagement. Hugh turning up at the house that evening actually saved you from that fate."

"It did indeed. No, I am quite over Rafe. I rarely ever think of him now, and when I do, it is with regret, and a little sadness for him, because he might have been so much more."

"Do you think it is the influence of the Boleyns? Living so closely with Sir Thomas, who we know is a schemer?"

"Perhaps, but that is not my problem anymore. I wash my hands of him." Thomasin picked up a slice of spiced pear and bit into it.

Ellen watched her eat. "So, there is a vacancy in your heart? I wonder who might fill it. Someone beside whom Rafe pales in comparison."

"Oh, stop that. It is too soon. Let me be."

Ellen raised her eyebrows. "Unless that person has already found their way into your favours?"

"Nothing like that has happened. I have been about the queen's business, nothing more. I should get up and dressed soon. When must you return to court?"

Ellen got reluctantly to her feet. "I have been overlong here. The queen wants me to help pack up her items in readiness for the move, and then to attend her this afternoon when she is in church. I fear Mary and Maria will frown at me for my lateness."

"But it has been so pleasant to have your company. You did me such good by being here, and helping me forget my illness."

"Then it has not been wasted. I will see you soon, upon your return to Bridewell, and I hope to reintroduce you to Harry as my future husband." Ellen could barely keep the smile from her face.

"It is good to see you so happy at last, after everything that you have been through."

Ellen pressed her hand. "If only we could say the same for you, Thomasin."

TWENTY-SIX

It was a glorious day at the height of summer. Thomasin breathed in the morning air, with its scents of chimney smoke and fresh flowers masking the ever-present undertone of the river. On the dock, a vessel decked in ribbons and pennants awaited the guests, bobbing gently against the Bridewell steps. From there, it would sail upriver, around the bends and turns, to Westminster Abbey, where the wedding of Arthur, Lord Lisle, and Honor Basset, née Grenville, was due to take place.

Thomasin had settled on the dusky pink gown that Ellen favoured. Her cousin had helped dress her that morning, in the queen's new chambers, lacing and pinning her into the bodice and smoothing out the long folds of the skirts with their embroidered hem, and placing her pearled hood carefully on her long, dark hair. Ellen had been right: the colour perfectly complimented Thomasin's skin, which had picked up a light hue of gold from the time she had slept in the gardens. Her paleness from the illness had quite faded and her usual colour had returned, highlighted by pearls in her ears and at her throat. The queen had lent her a pair of her old gold slippers, worn out by days of dancing that were behind her now, but they shimmered softly when Thomasin walked. She could not conceal her glee to be wearing royal slippers, even if they were cast-offs.

A few other courtiers were waiting on the bank, including some of Anne's ladies. Thomasin recognised Nan Gainsford and Bess Holland, decked out in bright dresses, accompanied by George Zouche, Francis Bryan and George Boleyn, but she kept her distance, chatting with friends of the bride. John and

Jane Dudley were already at Westminster, while others were travelling on horseback or by coach.

As they began to climb into the boat, a second vessel drew up behind them to the sound of trumpets blown on the bow. This was a wide barge, comfortably decked out with carpets and cushions under a canopy, flying the royal flag, with silver bells tinkling. Thomasin realised that this was the means by which Henry and Anne were travelling to Westminster, and they were no doubt waiting nearby, as guests of honour at the wedding. Looking around, she saw no one from Catherine's circle, only those who were guests of the bride and groom or favoured the Boleyns. As Thomasin took her seat, slightly queasy at the way the waves hit the side, she hoped her presence would not be seen as endorsing one side over another, at the expense of the queen. It was so difficult to navigate the subtle loyalties at court, but she should have realised that Henry's uncle would align with the king over his Spanish wife.

The tide was behind them, so fortunately the journey was quick. The oarsmen pulled them along, past the great mansions of courtiers and lords, giving a glimpse of their splendid grounds that ran down to the water's edge, past the Savoy Palace on the bend, and past Durham House, where Catherine had once lived, but which now housed the Boleyns. Next to it, Wolsey's home at York Place sat in darkness while the cardinal deliberated over the finer matters of law, as the whole court awaited the Papal Court's verdict. They passed the building works at Whitehall, which was to be transformed into a palace to rival those Anne had seen in Europe, and then the spires of Westminster loomed above them. Thomasin was grateful to be dismounting on the wide stone steps, where John Dudley was waiting to greet the guests. He extended his hand to help her up onto the quay.

"Thomasin, you look radiant. I am so glad you overcame your illness and are able to attend."

"So am I. I was honoured to receive the invitation, especially as I am not known personally to the bride and groom."

"As my guest, they welcome you. But come inside, have some wine. The ceremony will be taking place shortly."

Thomasin eyed the Boleyn party entering ahead of her through the carved stone gate, already conversing in excited tones.

"The king's barge follows shortly after us," she told John. "It was awaiting him at Bridewell as we left."

John led her along a corridor hung with tapestries into a chamber with painted walls. Here, guests were already partaking of spiced cakes, gingerbread and marzipan covered in gold leaf. Jane Dudley, dressed in maroon velvet and a headdress shimmering with bright stones, came to greet her. Her voluminous skirts concealed her early pregnancy, but her eyes and cheeks were glowing.

"I am so delighted to see you again, Thomasin, especially since you have been indisposed. Are you quite well now?"

"Quite well, thank you, and glad to see you, Jane."

"Why don't you two ladies eat some cake?" John suggested. "I must return to greet the king."

"That sounds like a good idea to me," said Jane. "The cinnamon and apple ones come highly recommended, but the saffron buns look delicious too. Shall we, Thomasin?"

Thomasin didn't need asking twice. The wedding fare looked far more elaborate and expensive than her usual fare, even that served at the queen's table. There was no doubt that money was being directed to certain quarters rather than others. She wondered whether she might smuggle a few items out for Ellen.

Before long, the sound of trumpets came from outside, declaring the arrival of the royal barge. Thomasin grabbed a last cake and reluctantly joined the line of guests ready to greet the king and Anne. This was not a part of the ceremony that she had anticipated, although she had known that Henry would attend; his presence eclipsed that of the couple getting married.

She dropped a curtsey as the party approached, hearing the tones of Henry's booming voice before he came through the doors. He was dressed in white and gold, with heavy chains about his throat, his shoulders draped with furs despite the season. At his side, Anne's outfit send a ripple of surprise among those gathered. Thomasin risked a look to see her dressed in a gown to match the king's, white and gold, with embroidery and pearls, topped by a chain. They were already behaving like a married couple, coordinating their clothing in the way that Henry and Catherine used to do. Thomasin had a sudden glimpse of the future at court: everyone bowing down before the king with his new queen, while his old, abandoned spouse sat quietly in her darkened room.

Henry and Anne passed through the chamber, heading for the abbey. This was the sign that the ceremony would be commencing soon, and the guests were to follow. With John joining them, Thomasin and Jane headed out through the main hall, a vast space with the roof so high overhead that Thomasin had to squint to see it. She had never seen such a large chamber before, not even at Windsor. Trestle tables with white cloths and wooden benches were already laid out ahead of the feast that would be served after the ceremony. The double doors led them out into a yard which had been sanded for jousting, with wooden stands erected at the sides and colourful tents at each end. The abbey lay beyond, inviting them to follow down the vast nave and take their places on the seats just before the central crossing. Henry and Anne, with several lords and ladies, were already seated ahead. Thomasin spotted the heads of Thomas and George Boleyn, and then, to her discomfort, Rafe Danvers sitting beside them. She kept her eyes averted, hoping that the bride and groom would soon appear to distract her from his presence.

Arthur, Lord Lisle, came first, a tall, lean ascetic man with greying hair, dressed in silver and black. He paused to greet the king, bowing low, so that Thomasin caught a glimpse of his handsome features. People claimed that he looked just like his father, Edward IV, with his strong jaw and striking eyes, although he was past the flush of youth and well into middle age now, older than his father had ever been.

After a while, the bride followed, with a train of her ladies behind her. Honor Basset wore a dress of emerald green trimmed with gold and a headdress with a long, cloth of gold train hanging low to her trim waist. She was a tiny woman, well-formed and elegant, with great charm in her little, piquant face. As she stood beside Arthur, her husband-to-be towering over her, the pair exchanged a smile that revealed the deep affection between them. Soon, this would be Ellen, Thomasin thought, walking to meet her bridegroom, excited by the future that stretched out before them. In that moment, she could not resist looking at the back of Rafe's head, several rows in front. It might so easily have been the two of them taking their vows, making promises to honour and love each other, but that could never be, now. Rafe did not turn round. At the moment when the bishop pronounced them man and wife, Thomasin saw him lift a hand to stifle a yawn.

When it was over, Thomasin took her seat beside Jane Dudley in the great hall. John was to be a server, carving the meat for the newly wedded couple who sat together at the dais with Henry and Anne. Brightly coloured hangings had been unfurled from the walls, below a line of austere-looking stone statues of past kings. The Boleyn family and their friends sat on a different table, so Thomasin at least felt safe until Rafe entered with Jane Boleyn on his arm, and headed for a place beside Anne's sister, Mary, who was casting her eyes around the room, letting them briefly rest on Thomasin. The spite in her eyes was palpable before she turned away. She had never forgiven Thomasin for the affection her husband William Carey had developed for her, in the weeks before his early death from the sweating sickness. Out of the corner of her eye, Thomasin saw Mary lean in to whisper a few words in Rafe's ear as he sat down. Thomasin turned her attention back to the food being laid in front of her, but was certain that Rafe turned to see where she sat. She could almost feel his eyes boring into her skin, a most unpleasant sensation.

"What a wonderful spread," she said to Jane Dudley, trying to appear oblivious to the attention she was receiving. "Would you pass me that dish of goose in green sauce, please?"

After the meal, the guests made their way back to the pier in order to board the barges. Thomasin had placed herself as far away as possible from the royal party, behind the large group of Dudleys, Bassets and Grenvilles who now found themselves related.

"Thomasin Marwood," said a familiar voice behind her, causing Thomasin to turn round.

Rafe was standing between Mary Boleyn and Anne Gainsford, his face spoiled by a dark sneer. Thomasin knew at once that she had made the right choice. She would have turned away without acknowledging him, but he spoke again.

"Did you enjoy the ceremony?"

It was impossible not to answer, with so many wedding guests around, but she kept it as brief as possible. "Thank you, yes."

"As did we," he said, indicating the women around him, as if attempting to demonstrate his popularity with them, "but we were surprised to find you here and not tending to your dear cousin."

Thomasin thought at once of Ellen. Had something happened? "What do you mean?"

"After the accident?" He looked at his friends again for confirmation, then back to her. "You mean you do not know?"

"Know what? Do not play with me."

"It was your cousin, Giles," said Anne, the most sympathetic character of the three. "He had a fall while out riding this morning. We saw him carried into the palace on a stretcher as we were leaving."

Thomasin went cold. For a moment she was unable to speak.

"No," said Rafe, his voice strangely strained. "It appears she did not know."

Then, suddenly, she found her feet. Pushing past them, Thomasin hurried straight to the water's edge. A boat was loading up with passengers.

"Bridewell?" she asked one of the rowers, impatient.

"No, Southbank. Try the next," he offered.

Her mind racing, Thomasin looked around wildly for the next barge in line, only to see that it was the royal vessel, with its flags and pennants flapping in the breeze. There was no way she would find a seat there. Henry and Anne were already making their way down to the waterfront, with the guests parting to create a pathway, bowing and curtseying. She was forced to do the same as they passed her. She hurried round the back of the crowd to the further spot where the third barge was waiting to dock. It seemed to take forever for the boats to fill, and she noticed Rafe taking his place ahead of her, alongside the king and Anne. All she could think of was getting to Giles. What if he lay injured and in pain, or dying?

Thomasin was the first on the steps as the barge finally pulled close. She jumped in without waiting to be asked, seating herself close to the front, as if that could somehow make a difference. The other guests took forever to embark, wobbling and laughing, while she sat there in turmoil. Eventually, they set sail to the sound of trumpets and pipes, battling against the current. The day would soon fade; the dinner hour was approaching, and Thomasin was due back at the queen's side.

At last, the bulk of Bridewell became visible after the long stretch of mansion gardens, and they were within reach of the steps. Thomasin had to wait again as others disembarked, willing herself to remain calm, resisting the urge to call out and barge past them. She had left the Dudleys behind and would have to find them and apologise another time. But when she finally set foot on dry land again, she realised she had no idea where she might find Giles. Which rooms were his? Or perhaps he was being nursed elsewhere?

She ran into the courtyard, causing those around her to look at her strangely, wondering what the emergency was. By a twist of fate, the first face she recognised was that of William Hatton, who was exercising a pair of lively spaniels.

"Mr Hatton!" She hurried towards him, panting. "Please do me a kindness. Where would I find my cousin, Giles Waterson?"

"Goodness, Mistress Marwood, what is the matter?"

"I just need to find Giles. Please."

"Come this way." He turned round and passed through an archway, Thomasin in close pursuit, before pointing to a distant staircase. "Up there, third floor, the final door on the corridor. The men's quarters."

"Thank you, thank you."

Thomasin hurried, panting, up three flights of steps to the top, where a narrow corridor was lit with torches. It was cool and quiet, with no guards, but not a place a lady such as her should be unaccompanied. She could not help herself, but ran the length of it, before hammering on the final door, hoping that Hatton's instructions had been correct.

"Enter."

The room was small, with merely a bed, a chest, a small table, a single window and a chair by the fire, in which Giles sat. He looked startled at the sight of Thomasin, as she took in his loose gown and the bound foot, which rested upon a stool.

"Thomasin?"

"Giles! You are … I mean … you aren't…?"

A smile crept over his face. "I take it you have heard about my fall. Yes, I am alive, if that is what you feared."

"I had no idea. What happened?"

"My horse was startled in the street and threw me upon the cobbles. I have a few bruises and a twisted ankle, but it could have been far worse."

Relief flooded through her.

"But you have been at the wedding?"

"Yes, I was. I did not know about this, or I would have come sooner. I thought… I feared…"

He held out his hand to her. "Come closer. All is well."

She went and took his hand without thinking.

"You were worried."

"I didn't know what to think. I was only told that you had an accident and were carried back on a stretcher."

"Yes, I was advised not to put weight on my foot, but Dr Butts has been, and all it requires is poultices and rest."

"Well, I am relieved to hear it. I imagined all kinds of things."

"Did you, Thomasin?" He was looking at her very intently with his blue-green eyes. She felt her emotions conflicting, with part of her screaming to run away. "Why do you think that was?"

Suddenly her words would not come.

"It is almost as if you care for me, Thomasin, as more than a cousin?"

She could only stare back at him, open-mouthed as the truth of his words seeped through her.

Holding the back of his seat, Giles pushed himself up to a standing position, so his face was level with hers. "I could almost believe that you care for me the same way that I do for you. I love you, Thomasin. I think I have for a long while, only I did not realise it until lately."

He leaned forward and kissed her, gently at first, but when she did not pull away, his lips became more urgent. The kiss had taken Thomasin by surprise, but it seemed to wake her from sleep, shaking her into a realisation she had been denying. It felt right — different from Rafe's kisses, but exactly what should happen.

Giles pulled back briefly and looked at her. "You do feel the same?"

The admission sprang to her lips at once. "Yes, I do. I know that I do!"

"I think I felt it the first time we met, two years ago, but I thought it a passing fancy, and we were cousins, although your mother had hopes for us. While I was away in the north, I found myself thinking of you often, as I went about my business, and since my return, every occasion that I have seen you has filled me with a conviction that there is no other woman I would choose. You must have guessed, Thomasin? Everything I have done for your family, I have done for your sake, as a mark of my devotion to you. I looked for signs in you, Thomasin, that you might return my feelings, but sometimes I thought you shied away from me, until today, that is."

"I did not realise my feelings until today. I knew your worth at once. I saw, long ago, that you were the truest and best of men, quite deserving of my love, but I feared getting close to you. I must tell you, I have trusted men before, and been betrayed by them, and I've seen the same happen to my sister and cousin, and to the queen. I feared giving my heart away, only for it to be broken."

"I would never hurt you, Thomasin. I have only the most honourable of intentions."

"Of course you do, but I still doubted … whether a man and woman might be happily married for their lifetimes, in such an atmosphere as this."

"Then let us prove it. I mean it, Thomasin; let us be the example. We will live quietly, away from court, among those we love, enjoying the simple pleasures of everyday life, raising a family, tending our estates, doing what good we can in the world. All you need to do is say yes."

"You are asking me to marry you?"

"Yes, Thomasin," he said, laughing. "Marry me. Be my wife. What do you say?"

She did not need a minute to think. "Yes, a thousand times yes!"

He laughed, his eyes shining, and pressed his lips against hers. "I never thought I could be as happy as in this moment. But when does your father depart for Suffolk? I must ask his permission."

"On the morrow, so you had better be quick."

"Ah." He pointed down at his foot. "Quick is one thing I cannot be. I will take a carriage first thing, if you will be available to assist me?"

"Of course."

"You do not mind marrying an invalid?"

"Oh, you will be quite well enough when the time comes to walk down the aisle, I am sure."

"Nothing on earth will stop me!"

"You are…" she began, faltering, "not afraid to marry into a family that has suffered such misfortunes as mine?"

"My darling Thomasin, there is nothing so shameful in your family that could deter me. I have made your family struggles my own, but it is nothing more than that your sister has fallen in love with an unsuitable man, and that is something that might befall even the wisest of people."

She thought briefly of Rafe, with his cruelty, jealousy and arrogance. She had felt intoxicating passion for him, but his behaviour had destroyed all her finer emotions. How little Rafe had anticipated this outcome when he had taunted her with Giles's accident.

"Such feeling is infatuation, not love. Love comes from respect, kindness and understanding."

"And impatience! Let us be married as soon as we can. I can't wait until you are Mrs Waterson." He pressed his lips to hers again.

TWENTY-SEVEN

Thomasin curtseyed low before the queen. Catherine sat back in her chair, beside the roaring fire, trying to digest what her lady-in-waiting was asking her.

"You need a carriage, to take yourself and Sir Giles Waterson to Thames Street?"

"Yes, my lady."

"So that he might ask your father's permission to wed you?"

"Yes, my lady."

Thomasin kept her head low, unable to read the expression on Catherine's face, but the queen sounded amused.

"But if I grant you leave, then you will return as a betrothed woman."

"I very much hope so, my lady, with your blessing."

"And I shall be losing two members of my household, as you and your cousin are both deserting me to become wives."

"It is not a desertion, my lady," said Ellen, who was standing at the side. "Our hearts will always be with you, along with our warmest wishes."

"You plan to be wed soon?"

"In the early autumn, I think," said Thomasin.

"Then I will keep you with me but a few weeks more, until the end of July, when the Papal Court will adjourn for the summer. We shall go to Windsor and pass our time quietly in the countryside, and then you shall be free."

Thomasin could not suppress her smile. "Thank you, my lady. It has been the honour of my life to serve you."

"But you wish for happier times. It is only natural."

"I only wish for my husband, my lady."

The queen sighed. "As all maids do. Marriage is not what maids think it to be. It is a trial for women, a source of both joy and sorrow. Look at me, Thomasin — you too, Ellen. The pair of you have served me well, with loyalty and honour. I cannot deny you the happiness that you deserve, but my blessings come with a warning. You are fortunate in being matched for love. Do not give the whole of your heart; keep a small part of it back for yourself, in case you might need it one day."

Outside, Giles was waiting at the gate, leaning on a wooden crutch for support. Harry Letchmere had assisted him with his dress, and with getting down the stairs and out into the early morning sunlight. His face lit up when he saw Thomasin hurrying along the path in her rich, dark blue gown, dressed with pearls and silver embroidery. It was the finest gown she had ever owned, adapted from an old one of the queen's that no longer fitted her, but it made Thomasin feel like a princess.

Giles leaned forward and kissed her on the cheek. "I have a carriage waiting. You have not changed your mind overnight?"

Thomasin laughed. "Do you think me so changeable that the wind might blow my affections away?"

"No, I do not think that of you." He looked up at the blue sky above them. "But still I am grateful for fine weather today, to better complement our news."

"I spoke with the queen. She is sorry to lose me, but she is prepared to let me go. Ellen too."

Letchmere bowed his head in appreciation.

"What could be better than a joint wedding?" Giles smiled. "Cousins and friends together?"

"Oh!" Thomasin gasped. "Ellen and I married together? What a wonderful idea. I had not thought of it myself, but if she and this good lord agree, it would be the best day we could imagine."

"Now, come into the carriage. We must catch your parents before they leave."

They passed along the city streets, busy despite the hour, jolting on the cobbles, pausing to let a flock of geese pass. Giles had taken her hand when they were seated and held it in his until the gates of Monk's Place came into view. Sir Matthew's dogs began their welcoming bark at once, and they drew to a halt before the familiar doorway. The door already stood open and a second carriage, laden with chests, was waiting for its occupants.

Sir Matthew Russell came striding out, then paused upon seeing the new arrivals.

"Here she is!" he called back into the house. "Thomasin, we knew you would not let them depart without bidding farewell. And Giles Waterson too, you are most welcome."

"I am glad not to have missed them," said Thomasin. "I knew of their intention to leave early, but had to ask permission from the queen."

"Of course. But they would not have left without seeing you! Won't you step inside?"

The greyhounds came rushing out, pressing their noses into Thomasin's palm eagerly. She did not make it into the hall before her father appeared, dressed in his brown cloak, his eyes tired.

"You have come to take your leave, then!" He embraced his daughter, kissing her cheek.

"Of course. Is all in readiness?"

"All the chests are packed. It only remains for your mother and sister to be ready, and you know how long it takes them! It is good of you, Sir Giles, to come over so early to see us on our way."

"I have a particular reason, sir, for coming, apart from sending you my best wishes for your health and the journey ahead."

"A particular reason? What can that be? No more court business, I pray. I am done with it."

"Nothing of the sort, I promise you. Something far more pleasant."

"Good, we could do with a bit of good news. Speak up then, man."

Giles laughed nervously. "It is more of a request, actually, sir. I hope, with your good wishes and blessing, to make an offer of marriage to your daughter."

Sir Richard looked briefly stunned. "Cecilia? To help her out of her predicament?"

"No, Father, not Cecilia!" cried Thomasin.

"I wish to ask your permission to marry Thomasin," Giles continued, "whom I have long been convinced is the best, most radiant, honourable and true woman I have ever had the pleasure to meet."

"Well," said Sir Richard, "I might have told you that myself. So you have become aware of her worth?"

"I have, my lord, and I would like nothing more than to make her my wife. I have estates in Surrey and Essex, an income sufficient for all her needs and wants and a heart ready to do service to her for the duration of my lifetime."

"What do you say to this, Thomasin?" Sir Richard looked at her. "Do you wish to become Sir Giles's wife? He argues his case most persuasively."

"I can say yes without hesitation. I love Giles as much as he loves me."

"Well then, who am I to stand in your way?" Sir Richard shook Giles by the hand. "Congratulations, and welcome to the family. I could not have chosen better myself."

"You will not be disappointed in me, sir, I promise you."

"No, young man, from what I have observed of you, I do not think that I will."

Lady Elizabeth was coming down the stairs in a rustle of cream-coloured silk, with Cecilia following behind, taking care with each step. Her dresses were open-laced now, showing the extent of her advancing pregnancy, but now that the birth was planned, she had a calmer expression than Thomasin had seen her wear lately.

"What is all this commotion?" asked Lady Elizabeth. "Has Thomasin come to bid us goodbye?"

"Much more than that," said Sir Richard, turning to greet his wife. "She has brought her betrothed with her."

"Her what?" Lady Elizabeth paused mid-step.

"Sir Giles has just asked me for permission to marry Thomasin and I have given it."

The two women looked from Thomasin to Giles and back again.

"How can it be?" asked Lady Elizabeth. "I was only on the landing. You could not have waited for a moment?"

"My apologies," said Giles at once, "I hope also to secure your gracious permission."

"Yes!" cried Lady Elizabeth. "As soon as possible! A wedding! And what a bridegroom. We could not have asked for better."

"Exactly what I said, my dear," said Sir Richard.

Lady Elizabeth came forward and threw her arms about Thomasin. "How proud I am of you. A splendid match."

Reaching the bottom of the steps, even Cecilia managed a smile. Thomasin was pleased to see it, given her sister's own recent marital disappointments. "This is truly good news. Where will you marry?"

"We have not thought yet," said Thomasin, turning to Giles. "But we would like a quiet life in the country, at least at first."

"A country wedding suits us well," said Lady Elizabeth.

"And perhaps a joint one, with dear Ellen and Sir Henry Letchmere."

"A double wedding! I must start thinking of what to wear, and all the people you can invite."

"Slow down, Mother. There is no rush. All that will come in time."

"But a double wedding — I never thought to see it!"

"Congratulations," added Sir Matthew, coming forward to shake Giles's hand and kiss Thomasin. "Such good news. I am pleased to hear about Ellen too; she deserves this happiness."

"And now, we must be on the road," said Sir Richard, "otherwise we will be kissing and shaking hands all day long. Come, ladies." He held out his hand to Cecilia first, helping her to climb slowly inside and settle herself upon the seat. Then, he assisted his wife.

"We will see you again soon, very soon," said Lady Elizabeth, beaming as she took her place alongside her elder daughter.

"You do know this journey is going to be nothing but wedding talk now!" Sir Richard smiled, rolling his eyes at the same time. "But it will give your mother a lift. She will feed off this for months to come, so do not leave it too long."

"Safe journey, sir," said Giles, securing the carriage door after he had got in. "And you take with you my profuse gratitude."

"Take care of Thomasin. I know you will."

"All ready?" asked Sir Matthew, nodding at the driver.

The carriage rolled slowly across the cobbles and out through the gates, away from Monk's Place, the bustling city and the treacherous court forever.

TWENTY-EIGHT

The sound of approaching laughter wafted through the roses. Thomasin paused under the archway, looking around the Bridewell garden one last time, taking in its beauty and colour, its rich scents, the warm sun on the red bricks. She had spent many happy times here, and some challenging ones, but now she was moving on, and she could not be happier.

She waited for the party to appear. King Henry came first, dressed in scarlet and crimson, a feathered cap upon his head, sparkling with jewels. On his arm, Anne wore a deep saffron yellow dress, her skirts swishing as she kept pace beside him. After them came a train of their followers: Thomas Boleyn in conversation with George; Jane and Mary Boleyn, reluctantly thrown together; Norris; Bryan; Zouche and an array of women in bright clothes, after which came Rafe — the very person Thomasin was waiting to see.

They had come from somewhere full of merriment and music, and were clearly headed somewhere equally enthralling, confident that the world was theirs and that a new royal marriage was imminent. The Papal Court had been adjourned for the summer, with the promise of a return in October, although Campeggio had privately visited Catherine in her chambers and informed her that he had no intention of reconvening. The court would not pronounce one way or another, but would instead refer the case back to Rome, where it would be kicked around the corridors of the Vatican indefinitely. In effect, Catherine had won this round, although it was only one battle in a whole war, and Henry was as determined as ever to make Anne his queen. The failure had been placed firmly on Thomas Wolsey's shoulders: he had been removed from his position as Lord Chancellor and frequently found the doors to the king's chamber closed to him these days.

As they approached the spot where Thomasin waited, she dropped a curtsey, her eyes on the toes of their shoes.

"Mistress Marwood?" said Henry.

"My lord."

"Please, rise. You were waiting to see me?"

She squinted at the group behind him, all peering around to see what it was that she wanted.

"Yes, my lord. If it please you, I have come to beg my leave. I am to be married and will retire to the country."

"Is that so?" Henry looked her up and down. "Well, it is about time, given your age. You are a comely enough woman for any man to take to wife. Who is the lucky man?"

"Sir Giles Waterson, my lord." She kept her eyes off Rafe as she spoke.

"Well, you have my blessing. A fine gentleman. I suppose your mistress has also given her approval?"

"She has, my lord."

"Sir Giles," said Anne, her smile hovering on a sneer. "So you are to become a country wife. How on earth will you manage all that peace and quiet?"

"With gratitude and humility, my lady," Thomasin said, looking Anne straight in the eye.

"Oh, ha!" Anne laughed. "Those are blessings indeed, once a woman reaches three score and ten."

"Good day, mistress," said Henry. "My best wishes to your mother."

Thomasin noticed that he did not include her father in the blessing, but paid it no attention. She dropped a quick curtsey as the king and Anne moved past her, followed by their train. Mary Boleyn shot her a particularly waspish look. Her father Thomas nodded to her with a look of curiosity, but Jane Boleyn paused for a moment and pressed Thomasin's hand.

"I do hope your marriage is a happy one. I never forgot the kindness you showed me once."

"Thank you, Jane."

Rafe was approaching, his expression sour, his eyes fixed ahead, as if he did not intend to acknowledge Thomasin at all.

"Rafe? May we speak?"

He stopped dead. "I will be late."

"For a moment, please. You can give me that much."

He ran a hand through his dark hair.

"I am to marry and leave court. I wanted to tell you myself."

"So I heard." He would not look at her. "So Sir Giles is the lucky man?"

"Yes, it is Giles, but I consider myself the lucky one. My betrothed is kind, gentle, honourable and reliable: everything I could have wished for."

"How very exciting," he replied, rolling his eyes. "But does your pulse beat for him? Does he excite you?"

Thomasin smiled. "He does. Is that all you think a marriage should be? A case of physical attraction that may fade over time?"

"I wouldn't know."

"No, you have proved that to me many times."

"Have you finished?"

"Were you always this rude? Yes, looking back, I believe that you were, only I did not wish to see it then. My eyes are truly open now, Rafe. I did love you. I truly did. I saw something in you that could have been noble, something good and strong and true that I hoped to connect with. There were times when

I thought that was possible. I would have married you, against all odds and the company you keep, but I came to realise that was not possible, because of your behaviour."

He shook his head. "You know nothing of me, of my struggles."

"No, you never opened up to me. Instead, you reacted with jealousy, fear and anger at times when we could have grown closer. You never trusted me."

"Oh, I suppose you have seen the light now: I'm the poor villain on your stage, while you look for your fairy-tale ending, Thomasin, behaving like a princess instead of living in the real world."

"Not at all. I have found my happy ending. I have found a man who shows me how good life can be."

"Well, how pleased I am for you. Why have you come here to rub my nose in it?"

"I had to come and say goodbye. After all we have been through together, it did not feel right to leave without drawing this to a close. I have learned much these past two years, but the biggest lesson of all, I think, is about the pursuit of my own happiness. The ability to make my own decisions, to exercise my free will and choose what suits me, not what appeals to my vanity or my fears or my base desires."

"Is that what I was, a base desire?"

"No, Rafe. You were far more than that. But I have learned and grown, and am moving towards the future that I will live as a woman, not a giddy girl whose head can be turned by a few fine words and sparkling costumes. I am happy to be leaving court."

"You are imprisoning yourself in a backwater to prove a point. Stubborn as ever, Thomasin."

His words rankled. "Not at all. You are lashing out. I have merely come to say goodbye and to wish you good health and happiness."

"So you are deserting the queen?"

"Not deserting. She has given me her blessing. She understands my desires: they were once her own."

"You know her days are numbered. The court has stagnated; the cardinals have failed."

"Yes, there is a stalemate."

"Only briefly. This will force the king's hand to some desperate act. And where will you be? Luxuriating in some country house. Do you not care?"

Thomasin refused to be drawn. "As you once told me, Rafe, we cannot bind our lives to the great ones we serve. We can offer them our devotion, but our lives must be our own. I will always love and serve the queen, no matter where I am."

"So you really are going?" He looked her in the eye for the first time, and she recalled the tenderness she had once seen there.

"I am. The queen has me until the end of the month, then I will depart for Suffolk."

"Oh, you will be back. I know you, Thomasin. You have something within you that craves this place: you want the attention, the excitement, the passion. You will not find that anywhere else, certainly not with the sedate Sir Giles, and the years will hang heavy upon you until you come to resent him. Then you will come running back here, your looks gone, your body grown stout with childbearing, too slow for the new dances, only to find that life has passed you by. What a tragedy that will be."

Thomasin was stunned at his words. She turned to leave.

"Goodbye, Thomasin. For now," Rafe called after her, as she hurried towards the queen's steps.

His prediction burned inside her, threatening to eat away at her happiness. How dare he make such assumptions about her. It was his bitterness, nothing more. He had lost her, and he needed to make her suffer, to cast doubt upon her bright future because she would not share it with him. She had been right about him all along. What an escape she had had!

Hurrying up the steps to help the queen dress, she pictured herself casting the dark shadow of Rafe clean off her shoulders like a cloak, and stepped into the bright warmth of Catherine's chamber.

TWENTY-NINE

The October skies hung white and mottled above the twisted chimneys of Eastwell Hall. Luckily the day was dry, with a chance of sunshine, so there was no need to alter the carefully laid plans that Lady Elizabeth had been so proud of. The grounds were looking splendid, having been raked clear of leaves. All the bushes had been trimmed, the grass flattened under huge rollers, and the late-blooming autumn roses were putting on a heartwarming display of pink and yellow. The last vestiges of summer still clung about the place, reluctant to give way to the harsh winter months ahead.

The joint wedding had been delayed long enough for Cecilia to recover from her ordeal. Six weeks before, she had delivered her daughter in the old blue chamber at Eastwell, with heavy curtains hanging across the windows and the fire built up to a suffocating warmth. Lady Elizabeth, Thomasin, and her eldest sibling Lettice had spent hours with her, waiting, praying, reading, sewing and playing games to while away the hours until the child put in its appearance. They had been fortunate to have the assistance of Margery Gaines from the village, a well-known midwife who had assisted in the delivery of the Marwoods' two younger children, Alice and Susanna.

When the pains had started to take hold one evening, a carriage had brought the sage old woman up to the Hall, and the baby had been delivered at dawn. It had been a difficult labour, progressing slowly, with Cecilia's spirits flagging as she slipped in and out of consciousness. Still, a tiny girl had arrived, red-faced and angry, balling up her little fists. She had a shock of fair hair, white-blond like her father's, and her mother's clear, glassy eyes. She was christened two days later in the local church, carried to the stone font by Sir Richard, and given the name Rose. Cecilia had recovered slowly, experiencing a little fever and a lot of restlessness, which were treated with herbs and remedies that her mother made.

She emerged from the blue chamber three weeks later, refusing to remain there a moment longer, heading to her churching with the determined face Thomasin recognised from their childhood. However, as the days passed, it was clear that this was a different Cecilia. She was quiet, more reflective, with a fierce love for her little daughter.

Thomasin stood looking out of the window across the back lawns. This room had been hers as a girl, and her favourite locations spread out before her: the nut walk, the rose garden, the fishpond with its central statue. Perhaps this was the last day she would stand here, like this, the last morning she would wake up at Eastwell, definitely her last day as a Marwood. She looked down at the dress that had been specially made in London for her: the gown of pale violet, worn over a white kirtle shot through with silver. Her headdress lay on the bed, ready to be pinned into position at the last moment: a confection of pearls and tiny diamonds with a long white veil, thin and gauzy. About her throat, she was wearing the Marwood diamonds, a string of priceless stones that her own mother had worn on her wedding day more than twenty years earlier, along with matching heavy earrings and a sparkling ring.

There came a knock upon the door. Sir Richard Marwood entered, dressed in his new coat of tawny and gold, another masterpiece from the same tailor. He beamed with pride as he took in his daughter's appearance.

"Well, I had never thought to see this day come."

"Never, Father?"

"I feared I would not live to see it. But God, in his wisdom, has spared me for this moment. The proudest moment of my life."

Thomasin felt tears well in her eyes at once. "Oh stop, do stop, or else you will be walking a weeping bride down the aisle."

"Are you ready?"

"As ready as I will ever be. Is it time?"

"Not quite yet. We still have a half hour, but there are guests downstairs I think you would wish to see."

"Guests? Here?"

"They stopped ahead of the church to speak with you in person. Will you come down?"

Thomasin picked up her skirts and hurried after her father, wondering who might be waiting downstairs in her childhood home.

As she rounded the top of the staircase, the group waiting at the bottom ceased their chatter and looked up at her. Her mother was in the centre, dressed in a tawny gown to match Sir Richard's, while Cecilia had opted for a pale watered green. Their little brother Digby stood smartly in front, now a lively, sharp boy of thirteen. Seven-year-old Alice and her younger sister, Susanna, almost four, were waiting with armfuls of flowers. To their right, Thomasin was delighted to see a familiar group waiting.

Her dear friend Thomas More, back from Cambrai, had travelled up to Suffolk for the occasion. With him was his daughter Margaret, Thomasin's great friend, and her husband, the stoic William Roper. Also of the party were John and Jane Dudley, her bodice loose to accommodate her advancing pregnancy. The sight of them almost took Thomasin's breath away, and she paused at the top of the steps to fix this moment in her mind forever. Her friends below applauded at the sight of her, their dear, beloved Thomasin, soon to be heading to the church.

"Do not keep your admirers waiting," said her father gently.

Thomasin descended slowly, going first to her mother's arms. Lady Elizabeth smelled of rosewater and citrus, the softness of her silk sleeves wrapping about her daughter's waist.

"You are beautiful. Such a picture, Thomasin. I knew that gown was the perfect one."

"You do look well," added Cecilia, who was keeping one ear out for the baby with her nurse. "I wish you every happiness, as you deserve. We have not always been close, but I hope that will change."

"I am sure it will," Thomasin replied, smiling. "And I also hope that one day you will be as happy as I am. You deserve that, too."

"Thomasin!" More came forward to kiss her cheek. "We had to come and see you for the last time as a Marwood. Forgive us the intrusion, but it comes with our love and best wishes."

"You are so very welcome," said Thomasin, looking at the More and Dudley group. "I am so happy that you have come, for it is a distance from London."

"Not so far as Cambrai, although that matter is all sorted now."

"We would not have missed this for the world," said Margaret, hugging her friend. "Although Father has other news he will not raise, because this is your day. But the king has appointed him Lord Chancellor, as Wolsey's replacement. And Wolsey is charged with…"

More raised his hand to silence her. Thomasin looked at him in wonder at this news, but read a mixture of emotions on his face. "We will not discuss this matter now," he said. "This is a day for festivities. Let no clouds dim its brilliance."

Thomasin smiled, grateful for his kindness, although she could not help wondering about Wolsey's fate.

"Welcome, Will," she said to Margaret's husband. "John, Jane, thank you for coming. I hope your journey was not too arduous."

"We stopped overnight at Hatfield and Hedingham," Jane told her, "so it was quite endurable. This is a beautiful part of the country and I am inclined to visit more often."

"Here!" said little Susanna, rushing up to her sister with armfuls of late roses. "Here is your bouquet. You must take it now before it prickles me!"

There was laughter all round at this.

"Now," said Lady Elizabeth, "we must away to the church. Allow a short while before you follow. The time has come."

"Is Ellen there already?" asked Thomasin.

"She went ahead, with Sir Henry's sister. She will be wondering where we all are!"

St Luke's Church sat a little beyond the Marwood land, surrounded by fields of sheep. Around lay a tumble of gravestones, weathered by the ages, bearing the names of those who had lived and died in this landscape long before them. Thomasin knew well the impressive stone box tombs in the south shadow of the tower, where the name of Marwood was carved with pride by the junior members of her family, although her grandparents and their parents had been buried inside, under the choir. As she alighted outside, with her father at her side, Thomasin saw that the porch had been decorated with flowers, hanging low to shower her with their rich blooms. Her heart raced as she realised that all the people she loved best in the world were gathered under that roof.

"Thomasin?"

Ellen came forward into the light, her apricot gown a perfect contrast to Thomasin's violet, her brown eyes sparkling as much as the diamonds at her throat. She looked the happiest her cousin had ever seen her.

"Ellen, you look the picture of a perfect bride."

"As do you, Thomasin. That soft violet is the perfect colour for you, restrained but warm."

"Thank you. It took an age to choose and I rejected a green one, a white one, and a grey."

"And the gold thread, and the cream," added her father. "At one point, I feared that she would be walking down the aisle in her old shift! Which would, of course, have been much easier on my purse."

"I cannot believe this day has come," said Thomasin, taking her cousin's hands. In many ways, Ellen had been the sister she had always wanted, close in temperament, gentle, kind and forgiving, but fiercely loyal. Since their earliest days at court, the pair had supported each other through the trials of the royal marriage, through heartbreak and sorrow, and were now to be united in happiness.

"It feels like we have been waiting a long time for it," said Ellen. "But I do not think there are two women who are more ready for it than you and I. Not now that we have the right men waiting for us at the end."

"I can honestly say," said Thomasin, "that I do not regret any of it. All the difficult times, all the heartbreak we have endured has brought us here, today, side by side, to embark upon this future together."

"You with Sir Giles."

"And you with Sir Henry."

"How lucky they both are!" added Sir Richard. "I hope they know it."

"Oh yes," Ellen laughed, "I am sure they do. And one last thing! I almost forgot." She reached into her sleeve and pulled out a small package, wrapped in cloth. "Before we left, Queen Catherine gave me these, to open on the morning of our wedding."

Unwrapping the layers, she revealed two small heart-shaped brooches, one ruby and one sapphire, set in gold. She held them up for Thomasin to see.

"Which would you prefer?"

"Oh, the sapphire must be yours. It is your colour."

"And the ruby is yours. I wonder if the queen chose them that way."

Thomasin pinned the brooch to her chest, where the red sat rich and warm against the white panel of her bodice. Likewise, Ellen pinned hers close to her heart.

"Reminders of the queen, our generous mistress, as if she were here with us."

Above them, the church bells began to peal. The long, sonorous notes drowned out their voices.

"Come," said Sir Richard, offering each of them an arm. "It is time. No going back now. No doubts, Ellen?"

"Absolutely none."

"Thomasin?"

"None whatsoever."

Thomasin looped her arm through his right, while Ellen linked up on the left. Slowly, they turned towards the darkness of the church interior, where more flowers brightened the gloom and the scent of cool stone surrounded them.

"Let's go and get married," said Thomasin.

Inside, the church was full. More guests had travelled up from London, while local families who had known the Marwoods for generations filled the pews. Everyone rose at the sight of the two brides, but Thomasin's eyes were fixed firmly on the altar ahead. Candles burned brightly and the stained glass depiction of the virgin and child filtered gentle light down upon them. It seemed to take forever to walk slowly towards them.

Thomasin saw Sir Henry Letchmere first, standing on the left-hand side of the priest, a little nervous in his blue coat as he came forward to take Ellen's hand. And then, while she was searching for him, Giles appeared, his eyes dancing, his smile welcoming and broad. Her heart leapt at the sight of him, knowing she had never been as perfectly happy as she was at that moment.

"You look so beautiful," he whispered, as she took her place beside him.

The bells overhead stopped their pealing as the priest began to speak the first words of the ceremony. By the time those ancient bells sounded again, they had been pronounced man and wife.

Above the church, a flock of birds circled the spire on their way towards the nearby oak tree, drawn by the activity below. The white clouds briefly parted and bathed the tower in golden light, picking out the colours of the flowers on the porch. To the left and right, green fields rolled away, and light reflected off the surface of ponds and rivers. It penetrated the denseness of the woods, picking out a hare in the middle of a clearing and the flash of a fox's tail.

Beyond that lay the distant red and greyness of a town, then a large estate, a group of horses grazing, a team of men digging the brown earth, and even further still, a few miles to the east, lay the wide, clean expanse of the sea.

A NOTE TO THE READER

Dear Reader,

Reviews do matter to writers and I would appreciate a review on **Amazon** or **Goodreads**. Often, we're writing in isolation, working in something of a vacuum, living most intensely in our heads and sending manuscripts into the ether. It's lovely to receive feedback from readers, to know our work is being enjoyed and to see the ways we can improve when planning our next part of the story. You can contact me **on Twitter** (@PrufrocksPeach; I am a T. S. Eliot fan) via **my author page on Facebook** (Amy Licence Author), or **via my website**.

Kind regards,

Amy Licence

www.amylicence.weebly.com

Sapere Books is an exciting new publisher of brilliant fiction and popular history.

To find out more about our latest releases and our monthly bargain books visit our website:
saperebooks.com